Wakefield Libraries
& Information Services

ST 5|22

This book should be returned by the last date stamped
above. You may renew the loan personally, by post or
telephone for a further period if the book is not required by
another reader.

intelligent Josie, as she navigates her way through the dark years of WW2. It has all the elements of a thriller that I look for.
– **Novelist Colin Hollis**, author of *No Second Thoughts* and *Herbmaster of Tarodash.*

Michael Yates writes with an ear for the everyday magic of speech, and an eye for the telling image that will hold an idea or nudge a story along. His prose does heavy lifting effortlessly, and the reader feels in safe and experienced hands.
– **Ian McMillan**, Poet and broadcaster.

During WWII everyone in England had the bulldog spirit. Or did they? I found the detail in this story about a bright Catholic girl who gets entangled with duplicitous Yorkshire gangsters utterly fascinating. Michael Yates successfully conveys what life must have been like for ordinary folk who had to live fast and loose when death was only an air raid away.
– **Ivor Tymchak**, author of *Sex & Death and Other Stories.*

About the Author

Michael Yates was a reporter and later film critic with the *Sheffield Star.* He taught playwriting at Harrogate Theatre and creative writing for the WEA. He has had a dozen plays performed by various companies in the north of England, including Leeds, Bradford, Sheffield, Liverpool and Manchester. He has also been Poet in Residence in Whitby and Wakefield Cathedral and in 2021 became Poet in Residence in Mid-Yorkshire Hospitals, writing a set of poems about the struggle against Covid.

Dying
is the Last Thing You Ever Want to Do

Michael Yates

Published by Armley Press Ltd, 2022
ISBN: 978-1-9160165-4-5
©Michael Yates

Cover photograph of the Sheffield blitz used by kind
permission of Sheffield Newspapers
Cover by Mick Lake
Typesetting by Ian Dobson
Print on demand by Lightning Source

Acknowledgements

In researching this book, I have used a large number of sources. But I would like to thank in particular *Sheffield at War*, edited by Clive Hardy and published by Archive Publications; also the *Sheffield Star* and *Yorkshire Post*, whose back numbers I plundered on microfilm; and a big cheer for Matthew Thomas of Wakefield Libraries, Janet Ring of Sheffield Libraries and Sally Hughes of Leeds Libraries for digging out some hideously obscure facts on my behalf. Any subsequent errors are down to me.

This book is dedicated to my lovely daughter-in-law Keira and my two splendid grandsons, Rufus and Otis.

Stave I: The Father in the Box

When Christ's faithful strive to confess all the sins that they can remember, they undoubtedly place all of them before the divine mercy for pardon. But those who fail to do so and knowingly withhold some, place nothing before the divine goodness for remission through the mediation of the priest – for if the sick person is too ashamed to show his wound to the doctor, the medicine cannot heal what it does not know.

......Catechism of the Catholic Church

Chapter One

FATHER ALBERT CARMODY was smoking when he heard the Penitents' Door open again. The Confessional Box was designed so the Priest's Door opened into the Presbytery of St Cuthbert's church while the Penitents' Door opened from the nave.

Father Albert was, naturally, sitting on his own side, with his own door open. ("Minding my own business – if I can call God's business my own," was what he liked to say to Fr Trimble.) So the smoke from his Woodbine wouldn't be detected by incoming penitents. As soon as he heard the opening of the other door, he stubbed out his cigarette between thumb and forefinger, where the habitual action had resulted in calluses that meant it no longer caused him pain. And he threw the stub hurriedly into the waste paper bin he kept just outside the Priest's Door. ("One day," Fr Trimble had told him, "you'll do that once too often and start a blaze and bring the whole bloody church down.") And he waved both arms to dissipate the remaining fumes before closing his door. Then he coughed and bowed his head and raised his eyes and moved the slide across the partition and stared as best he could through the grille.

Ah. It was a woman. The heady smell of her (he didn't know the names of such things as perfumes but it was certainly something more than lavender water) would happily counteract the Woodbine. And he could just make out she was blonde. Perhaps unnaturally so. The glimpse of artificial hair colouring, much used (he believed) by film stars and barmaids, persuaded him she might even be pretty. But, of course, he couldn't see for sure. And that was definitely *not* his business.

The woman knelt down. She said: "Bless me, Father, for I have sinned." She had a young voice. Her accent was definitely local, at least *some kind* of local. Fr Carmody was a Shropshire lad but he had been in Yorkshire now for nine years and in Sheffield for four. He knew there were as many variations of the accent as there were of the local vocabulary, but he was still not confident of distinguishing one from another.

He said: "Tell me, my child, how you have sinned." And yes, he felt a *frisson* of excitement.

"Firstly, Father, I have missed Mass." She spoke slowly and firmly. He noted she had said *firstly*, not *first*. He placed her now as working class, but educated. He assumed a convent school. You could always count on nuns for turning out well-spoken pupils.

He thought to make a joke with the possibly pretty young woman. He said: "Ah, that's something new to me then, because if you didn't come along, I'd never know about it, would I?"

The woman said: "This isn't *actually* my parish church." Then: "But I don't go along to the church that *is* my parish church, if you see what I mean."

He said: "Yes, I do." He felt his joke had fallen flat. He said: "Anyway, how many times have you missed Mass?"

She said: "Approximately, Father? Will approximately do?"

He said: "I guess approximately will *have* to do."

"I've not been now for five years. Five times 52 is..." She paused. "I've never been good at mental arithmetic."

"Two hundred and sixty," said Fr Carmody. *He* had always been good at it. But now he feared she was teasing him. The nuns would surely have been strong on mental arithmetic.

"Two hundred and sixty," she repeated. Then: "And I have been guilty of Avarice."

Fr Carmody was unused to people using the word. His parishioners usually said *greed* or occasionally *covetousness*. The last penitent who used the word had pronounced it ava-*rice* as in (he had joked to Fr Trimble) "Ave a rice pudding after dinner."

"And," she said, "of Anger and of Pride. And..." she took a deep breath, "also of Fornication."

He almost repeated "How many times?" but thankfully

stopped himself. He didn't want to be dealing with approximations again.

Another deep breath. "And I've stolen money. But from people who deserved to lose it. *I* think so anyway."

Fr Carmody was now perfectly *sure* he was being teased. He occasionally encountered female penitents who enjoyed trying to shock him, but he'd been warned about such things in his seminary. And part of him, as he once admitted to Fr Trimble, was amused by this sort of silliness. He and Fr Trimble agreed that a priest had to be a Man of the World as well as a Man of the Cloth. Fr Trimble, a burly man with thick red hair, was much into such worldly things as boxing and playing rugby; whereas Fr Carmody, small and balding, lacked the confidence of his friend.

Before he could speak again, the woman said: "Also I have been responsible for someone's death. May the Father in the Sky forgive me."

He was baffled by her mention of the sky. But the rest seemed straightforward. Now he was on safer ground. He had heard a lot of this in the past few years. He had heard the soldiers and sailors on leave, the workers from the local armaments factories – Vickers, Hadfields, Brown Bayley – of which she must certainly be one. It was, after all, only a month since Victory over Japan had been celebrated. And he had always emphasised to his penitents that the Catholic Church was *not* a pacifist organisation; that it recognised the concept of a just war; that monsters like Hitler and Hirohito had to be defeated if the Christian message were to survive; that the Holy Father in Rome had himself emphasised this stance on many occasions. Though not so much (he kept this last bit to himself) while Mussolini had been alive.

Fr Carmody said: "God expects we obey His Commandments. But God will surely look mercifully on those who have broken them and have genuine regret." He was thinking: *What penance should I give?* There was still the Fornication. Normally, he would prescribe a Decade of the Rosary. But, if she'd really stolen money as well, maybe a Full Rosary was called for. It wasn't something he normally considered, lest inflation creep in. Recently he had started to think of it, from a phrase he picked up in the newspapers, as his "nuclear option". He said: "And are you *sorry* for your sins?"

"Sorry?" she shouted. She stood up abruptly and burst into tears. "No, I'm not sorry. I'm the first murderer in our family, but I'm not sorry." He could just about see through the grille that she was wiping her eyes on a small white handkerchief. She blew her nose. "I killed a man called Alonzo McIntyre and he deserved it. And I'm going to have to kill again."

Fr Carmody sat back abruptly, tipping his chair and almost falling.

Clearly, the woman had sensed his shock. "No, no," she said more calmly, "I don't mean *you*, Father. You have nothing to fear." And she put away the handkerchief and she turned, and she opened her door, and she was outside again and walking away.

Fr Carmody controlled himself with effort. Walking out in the middle of Confession! He'd never known such a thing! Whatever would Fr Trimble say? He sighed and reached for his Woodbines.

Stave II: The Father in the Sky

If happy little bluebirds fly beyond the rainbow, why, oh, why can't I?

......YP 'Yip' Harburg,
as sung by Judy Garland, *The Wizard of Oz*, 1939

In peace there's nothing so becomes a man as modest stillness and humility. But when the blast of war blows in our ears, then imitate the action of the tiger; stiffen the sinews, summon up the blood, disguise fair nature with hard-favour'd rage.

......William Shakespeare, *Henry V*, circa 1599

Chapter Two

AUNT MAY USED TO SAY: "It's not the Father in the Box you have to worry about, Josie." (Josie was my name in those days.) "The Father in the Sky is the one you have to heed."

What she meant was this: Priests are just people like you and me. They do their best. Well, *sometimes* they do their best. But they don't always get it right. So you have to have a bit of *nous*, you have to second-guess them. You have to ask what the Father in the Sky thinks about it. He's the only one Who's never wrong.

And I reckon the Father in the Sky would have been very happy when he saw me kill Lonzo Mack. God would have very much enjoyed it. Like He enjoyed it when He struck down the Firstborn of Egypt. He'd've clapped. If He'd got hands.

I know I'm wandering a bit now, getting into serious debate about what God looks like. The question of whether God does have hands is one of those things that scholars are probably still debating when they go down the pub. But God made us in His Image, didn't He? So it makes sense to think He's got hands. And Michelangelo gave Him hands, so it's not beyond imagining. And a beard, Michelangelo gave Him a beard. We used to discuss this at St Elfreda's – I mean us girls, I don't mean the teachers – and I'd always say: "If God made us in His image, why should God have a beard? *We've* not got beards because we're girls, so why should God have a beard?" Then some smart knickers like Ester Petheridge would say: "Us girls grow beards when we're older, don't we? Only we grow them in a different place." And I'd give her a push because I don't like smutty talk, not when we're talking something serious like God. I think it brings down the tone.

So. Anyway. I never wanted to upset the priest. He seemed like a decent sort. I didn't want to act like a big kid. I should've thought it through before I went in. I should've known I wasn't going to say sorry. I should have known I wasn't going to get Absolution, from this priest or any other priest. And I should've remembered Aunt May. I should've realised it didn't matter. It's only the Father in the Sky that matters.

May was my mother's sister but they weren't anything like. My mum was a lovely person, she really was, small and dark and delicate. But she was soft. She had to be as soft as a month-old pear to get married to my dad. He was a miner and I can see why she did it. He was big and strong with arms like tree trunks and a Joe Stalin moustache.

"Not the sharpest knife in the box," was how May spoke about Dad when we were out shopping one time while Mum was in bed with a headache. I asked Mum afterwards what it meant and she was really mad with May. But only for a couple of days. Then they were pals again.

Another thing May said to me: "Your mum was a real looker in them days. She could've had any man laid eyes on her. She could've had Arthur for one. I know that for a fact." She said this one day when we were sitting in the front room of her two-up-two-down which was only two streets away from ours, and she was smoking a Park Drive and she offered me one, which I took, though I was really too young. "Don't tell your mum," said May.

Arthur was my Uncle Arthur, the man May married. So that seemed to me a funny thing for May to say. Now I think it was something she had to get out of her system.

It's true my mum was a looker with her black lustrous hair and gentle eyes – even after marriage and me coming along and the medical problems that meant I was always going to be an only child. And it was true that May *wasn't* – she had a square jaw and thick eyebrows like a man; and a way of talking, deep and persistent, that helped her win arguments.

Why did May have a downer on my dad? Main reason was his job, fettling about on his belly in some two-foot seam and filling a paper bag (as she put it) *every time he scoffed his snap.* By the time she said *this* to me, I had better sense than to ask Mum what it meant. But Ester said that's what the men had to do when they *did their business*. No lavs down the pit, so they brought back their souvenirs in a bag to the pithead. I was shocked. Then I laughed. I could suddenly picture Dad doing it.

Dad worked down Algrave Colliery between Sheffield and Nether Fields. May said they named the pit because they expected a disaster any day soon and everybody would get buried no matter what. You can see she had a wry sense of humour.

But it wasn't just the job May hated about my dad. It was everything. Dad was the sort of man who'd come back after work and his bath had to be ready in front of the fire and his tea had to be ready on the table and then he'd be dressed up and Brylcreemed and out to the Miners' Club and we wouldn't see him till midnight. And then – as May used to say, though I didn't understand till I was older – his comfort had to be ready for him between the sheets.

The only time I ever really saw Dad much was on a Sunday morning, though he didn't talk a lot even then. After breakfast, after sausage and egg, he'd get ready to go out with his mates. He'd shave round his moustache in the kitchen in front of a little mirror he'd prop up by the window. He'd clean his false teeth and leave them to dry on the side of the sink. He'd read the sports section of the *Sunday Despatch*, lay it down on the kitchen floor, polish his Sunday shoes and put them on top of it. Then he'd put on his Sunday suit – the blue chalk stripe – and take another look in the mirror, pull out the hairs in his nose. That always made him sneeze, and I'd laugh, and he'd look round at me and he'd laugh too. So that was nice. Then he'd go off to the Temple Bar and Mum would say: "It's dinner at half past one," and he'd nod. And when he'd gone, she'd say to me: "It's beef and Yorkshire, and God knows the piece of beef is small enough, but it's always spoilt by the time he comes back." And I'd nod and we'd both laugh. So that was nice too.

Then Mum would pick up the bits of the *Despatch* and go in the front room and smoke her Park Drive and read the news. She never talked about what she was reading; I think she thought news wasn't meant for young girls. Every so often, she'd glance at the clock on the mantelpiece, go into the kitchen and see to the meat or the veg or the knives and forks. Then she'd say: "Come on, our Josie, I'll wash and you can dry," and we'd do the dishes that were already lying around, mainly from breakfast. And she'd say: "Sundays are nice, aren't they?" And I'd always say "Yes". And we'd listen to the wireless, though it was mainly people talking. Music and jokes – like Gracie Fields and George Formby – weren't considered serious enough for Sundays, not even on the Light Programme. And Mum would say: "I'm glad your dad's on days again next week. It's good when he's not sleeping the livelong day."

So Mum could find some good. But May hated the Pits altogether. When I was round her house, she used to say to me: "You go to school. You do history. What's a pit town like, eh? I'll tell you what it's like. The Coal Owners are Lords of the Manor. They own the job, they own the houses we live in, they own the people. Serfs, that's what we are."

"Well," I replied, thinking well of myself for thinking it, "they don't own the Church."

"Church!" she said. It was a snort. "Wherever there's Lords and wherever there's serfs, there's the Church."

I was shocked. I said: "Are you a Protestant?"

"No," she said, "not yet, I'm not. But I *am* a Socialist, and one day – you'll see if I'm not right – even the Pope will have to be a Socialist." And she pressed my hand.

Uncle Arthur went down the Pit, like every man else. But Uncle Arthur was a Deputy. He was the sort of man who only went down to tell people like my dad what to do. Also he was a regional official in NACODS. "That's the National Association of Colliery Overmen, Deputies and Shotfirers," said May, though I was never interested enough to ask. And he had political ambition. "One day he'll be a Labour MP," she said, "maybe even a Minister."

But it never happened. A heart attack finished him and dashed May's hopes the year I left school. The funeral was on a sunny August day, a month after my 17th birthday and the day after I got my School Certificate. I still remember two Distinctions for English and French, two Credits for History and Religious Instruction, and three Passes – Mathematics, Latin and Sewing.

May drew me aside at the Wake, pressing my hand again. She said: "Your mother had the looks and I had the brains. Now look where we've both ended up. But I could always see you were going to turn out looking like your mum and now I hear you've got the brains as well. You'll have to make up for us, Josie. You're the one that's going to show the men what she can do."

There was a good-looking boy at the funeral called Alan Grantley who was Arthur's nephew. He had a fresh face and brown curly hair in a parting on the left, and I didn't mind it that he wore glasses. He seemed to like me and I was sorry I'd worn my school uniform instead of dressing up – it was a skirt and blazer and Mum said it would do because the blazer was black, and it didn't matter that the skirt was grey. Alan persuaded me to share a glass of whisky with him. I drank it too fast and it made me cough. But I decided it was something I would probably enjoy doing, given time. And I decided to use some of my mum's lipstick in future – make-up was generally frowned upon in my family, but Aunt May had persuaded my mum to use a little.

Still, there was already a war on. The men had got back from Dunkirk alright, thanks to all those boats we were still reading about. But Hitler had done for the French and was thinking what fun he might try next. The Kimberworth Arms was already sandbagged and had pieces of sticky tape across the windows. The bombers came over Sheffield and we had to shelter in the pub cellar. For the first time ever, I had to put on my gasmask without it being an exercise. I can't remember how many people I read they killed in the streets round about, but it was nothing compared with how many they killed later on.

Chapter Three

WE BOTH KNOW WHAT I'M DOING, Father. I'm trying to work out how it was I was different. How it turned out I'm the only person in my family who's ever murdered anybody. But I'm not taking the easy way, I'm not saying it was somebody else's fault. I'm not saying it was having a soft mum or a dull dad that did it for me. Or the Lords of Capitalism who owned the pits and the pit houses, which is what May would think. No; we weren't badly off at all, compared with some, what with my dad in regular work. And it was *necessary* work, reserved occupation, so he didn't get called up. Though he *was* forty anyway.

And I'm not going to say it was loved ones killed in the Blitz. Everybody has people close to them that die. That's something you have to cope with.

At first, if I'm honest, the bombing was mainly OK. There were lots of barrage balloons by now, standing guard over the city, and that made us feel almost safe. Once the sirens went, we'd go down the Wicker, to the railway arches. The outer arches on both sides had been bricked up to form air raid shelters. It was a crush alright. I'd be sandwiched in between Mum and May and everybody was singing. It was "Underneath the Arches", of course it was. There were about a hundred people there most nights and you could hear the thunder of the bombs, see the flashes light up the buildings, smell the smoke. People used to joke: "It's German smoke you can smell. They don't allow us locals to smoke down here."

But I could read, at least a bit of the time. As long as I took my torch. When people got exhausted from the singing, they'd be stretching out their legs, nodding off, lolling on the pillows and cushions they'd brought in. Snoring. Snoring with all that stuff going on! And that's when I'd read.

Of course, I'd done a lot of reading at school – I'd got that Distinction in English, remember! My English Literature teacher, Sister Margaret Mary, made a point of taking me to one side after the results came out, and telling me what a good pupil I'd been. Sister Margaret Mary was my favourite – she was a small pretty woman and she seemed to know an awful lot about everything. She even knew popular songs, which was something I never thought nuns listened to. But one day I was singing "Begin the Beguine", or mostly humming it.

When they begin the beguine
Hum-hum-hum music so tender,
It brings back a night of tropical splendour...

And Sister Margaret Mary interrupted me – I didn't even know she was in hearing distance. And she said: "Josie, do you know what a beguine is?"

And I said: "No, sister."

And she said: "The beguine is a dance from the French West Indies. And also," she hesitated here and smiled, "it has another meaning. There are *some* nuns who are permitted to return to the outside world if things don't work out."

And I said: "But you're not one of those, are you, Sister?" I had a sudden fear she might be about to tell me she wouldn't be my teacher anymore.

But she said: "Oh no, oh no. I've taken my final vows and I regard them very seriously."

So I could breathe a sigh of relief. But I have to say we girls always thought of her as the *funny* nun – there's always one – who doesn't seem to belong in a convent and you wonder how she ever got there.

Anyway, this day the results came out, after she'd congratulated me on my exams, we chatted for a bit and agreed the English set books were a bit old-fashioned. Shakespeare, you had to have, of course. But we both reckoned Charles Dickens was overrated and *David Copperfield* was not his best book. We decided we much preferred *A Christmas Carol*.

"Yes," she said, "and one of the things I like about it is that it's divided into *staves*, not *chapters*. That's very musical, isn't it? I think life is much more musical than literary. It has slow passages and fast ones, mournful and merry... There. I'm getting pretentious."

"No," I said, "I agree with you. If *I* ever did anything autobiographical, I'd do it in staves."

And then Sister Margaret Mary did a funny thing – she kissed me on the cheek and wished me luck.

Talking about Sister Margaret Mary reminds me of another problem about my talking things over with You, Father. She always said there were four things wrong with the way I wrote essays. First, I repeated myself a lot. *Yes! Repeated myself!* (Hey, that's a joke.) Second I often contradicted myself, which showed I'd not really thought things through the first time. And third, I often wrote long, wordy sentences, which she always referred to as "boneless wonders", and that may very well be true, I believe. (Another joke!)

And finally, *I couldn't stop myself making jokes*, as you can see. "The examiners," she said, "are serious. They do not take kindly to people making jokes."

English Literature! Well, May was the great reader in our family. So, after school, she was the one who pointed me: *The Citadel, Howard's End* and *The Ragged Trousered Philanthropists.* I loved the bit in *Philanthropists* when Frank organises his mates to cut up bread and swap coins back and forth to show that the employer, who never works, gets rich while the workers are no better off. But then a bit of me thought: Well, why not? If someone's got the brains to be an employer, why shouldn't he make something out of it?

Mum didn't mind the reading but she couldn't understand it. "You don't want to turn out a brain box," she'd say. "Men don't want a brain box."

We were getting ready for Christmas – the tree was up in the front room – and I knew I was getting a book as a present, and I made Mum promise she'd ask May's advice before she bought it. She couldn't ask me, obviously, else it wouldn't be a surprise! And I didn't want to get Jane Austen again because I'd read everything she'd written. She's alright is Jane Austen, but *her* war is too far away. It only gets in the picture when the girls are fancying the soldiers. What I wanted was something that told me how to be *in* a war, not standing round on the terraces like men at a football match.

As I said, the bombing so far didn't seem so bad. After a while there'd be the lull with people growing expectant and the odd voice proclaiming: "That's it then. Must be over." The singing had petered out altogether by then and they would wait, quiet and alert, for the all-clear. After that, it was *T'ra, Goo'bye, Alsithee, Same time, same place. Oh, that's a good 'un. That's a deaf 'un.*

Afterwards it was back to our house in the pitch dark of the blackout and Mum would say: "I'll get us a sherry to strengthen us nerves. You light the gas for us, Josie, and I'll get you a lemonade." And Mum and May would get to reminiscing and I'd go on reading. Except after a while I needed my sleep because I was working at Balfours by then.

One particular night, when the raid hadn't lasted more than half an hour and we'd got back early after the all-clear, Mum put the wireless on and it was Jack Payne and his Orchestra playing "As Time Goes By". May said to Mum: "Give our Josie a sherry, why don't you? She's old enough by now." And Mum said: "Right you are." It wasn't that she'd ever refused me a sherry, just that maybe she still thought of me as a kid and it didn't cross my mind to tell her different.

And while she was in the kitchen, May said: "Look at you. All grown up now. A job of your own. Though I don't suppose it's what you wanted. I had you pegged to go on to Higher School Certificate. Are you disappointed?"

I said: "We'd've needed the extra money, even without the war. Staying on at school wasn't going to happen."

May said: "Maybe I could've found you the money. Maybe. Arthur had a bit of insurance."

"Well, anyway," I said and left it at that.

But May wouldn't leave it. "You're in the office, I understand."

"Well, I'm not in the smelting works. I'm a filing clerk."

"Interesting, is it?"

"No." I didn't know where the conversation was going

and I was wary.

"I should think it's pretty boring for a bright girl like you."

"Helps the war effort."

"Oh yes, helps the war effort alright."

"It'll do."

"Oh yes, I'm sure it'll do." Then she looked at me hard. "That's where our Alan works. Arthur's Alan."

"He helped me get the job," I said.

"I bet he did," she said. Then: "Do you know what a rubber johnnie is?"

I think I blushed. I think I actually dropped *Howard's End*. I said: "Well…"

She said: "Well *nothing*! You do or you don't. And if you don't, you better be finding out fast."

Just then Mum came back with the drinks on a tray. She handed me one. She said: "May's right." I nearly dropped the sherry. She said: "May's right that you're old enough to drink sherry now."

"Of course I'm right," said May and raised her glass. "Family," she said, and we clinked them and drank to it.

*

So that was it. So I went round to May's just after work the very next day and she showed me a rubber and she told me how it worked, as much as a woman can tell you something like that without a man around to model it. She said: "I've no idea how far you've gone with Alan, and he's a nice lad to be sure. But I wouldn't want you not taking precautions. That way, bright girls like you end up in the soup, just as much as *silly* girls like Jennie Holdsworth."

Jennie Holdsworth lived a couple of streets away and she was about my age and I knew her to say "hello" to. And I knew there was something about Jennie lately. I'd overheard bits of conversation in the street from women a bit older than me and they'd shut up sharp when they saw I was earwigging.

"It's all a bit late for rubbers as far as Jennie was concerned," said May, "but we've took care of it. She should be alright now."

And I was shocked. And I said: "Isn't that illegal?"

"Yes," said May, "and if it got out, I'd be in prison."

I said: "Isn't it against our religion?"

"Well," she said, "Jennie's a Protestant, poor girl, and I don't know how it stands with some of them. But yes, it's against our religion. And so are the johnnies."

"May," I said, "you're a wicked woman." And I couldn't believe I'd said that to her.

She grinned and said: "Yes, I am." And she laughed. And I laughed too.

And it struck me suddenly there were lots of things in life you had to know about which didn't feature in the Higher School Certificate. Lots of things *higher* than Higher School. And much, much higher than the Father in the Box.

Chapter Four

IT WASN'T JUST THE JOHNNIES May told me about. She told me how you didn't have to go all the way with a boy. You could do things that weren't going to turn out to be a problem later on. And she was very detailed. "Men," she said, "are easily satisfied when they're young and just starting out."

I couldn't see my mum ever telling me this sort of stuff. I wondered how many men May had had. Men, she said, liked to get about a bit, and were loudmouthed about it, but most of them settled down in the end. Women were usually the same about getting about – but they kept their mouths well shut. I thought hard about Mum. I couldn't imagine her with any other man before Dad. But then I couldn't imagine her with Dad either.

And I thought about Alan. May had jumped the gun about him and me. We'd not got past the touching stage and only a couple of times I'd let him get as far as my tuppence. But it's as well to be prepared and I was glad I'd been brought up to speed before I needed to know these things.

Him and me were actually doing alright. We'd go to the Odeon picture house on a Friday and a dance on the Saturday at the Palais, jitterbugging. And Mum kept asking me when I was planning to bring my young man home.

And then Alan started on about the same sort of thing. One Friday after we'd been to see Bette Davis in *The Little Foxes* in Leeds, and I'm wearing my nice winter coat with the suede collar, he takes me to the Kardomah in Briggate and says would I like to come round to his house for Sunday dinner? I suddenly had electric lights going on and off in my head. He said his dad would be staying home special that morning, not going off to the Duck and Drake as he usually did. And they had an indoor lav so I wouldn't have to traipse across the yard.

"More than *we've* got," I said. I had a sip of my *café au lait* in which the coffee was Camp Coffee with chicory, and not bad really, and the *lait* was condensed poured in a jug. I lit a cigarette.

"But it doesn't matter what you've got now," he said. "*We'll* have indoor as well, once we're wed." He put down his macaroon and waved his hands a bit.

I remembered what May told me about men. And I thought: Is this it? Is this all he wants? Pulled off a few times and he's wanting to settle? And I took a good look at him. He was really nice, two or three inches taller than me. Like I said, he had thick curly hair and quite good teeth. And he wasn't fat or spotty. And he was wearing a grey suit and a smart green tie. But was this what I wanted till death do us part?

He said: "I've got a good job. You know that."

I knew he did the same job as me but got paid more. A *little* bit more.

"It's regular and not bad pay and pretty safe as jobs go." Pretty safe? Doesn't he know there's a war on? What can you name that's pretty safe in a war?

I said: "Is this a proposal?"

He grinned. He said: "You can take it that way if you want." And he looked bloody pleased with himself.

Well, maybe it was seeing Bette Davis tearing lumps out of Herbert Marshall. But I couldn't stand it. I couldn't stand that smug thing that you often get with Anglicans who think *nice* is the same as *good*. And I said: "Tell your dad he can go to the Duck and Drake. Tell him he can get pissed as usual. I've got better things to do with my Sundays."

And his face dropped. And I thought: Oh God, what have I said? Because he wasn't a bad person and he'd treated me right and I should have treated him better. Also, I thought I'd let myself down saying "pissed". But it was a bit late now.

I said something like "We don't want to take things too fast" and "We're both very young." Though to be honest, most of the girls I'd left school with were engaged by now, half of them already wed. In the end, I stopped talking. It had all dried up inside me.

He said: "I'm sorry." He looked like he was going to cry.

I said: "You've nothing to be sorry about." I tried to laugh it off. I said: "You're a smashing boy, Alan. And I *am* very fond of you. But..." All the time I was thinking: No, no, no. This is not what I want. I wondered if I'd lose my job at Balfours. But I knew he wouldn't be vindictive. In a way, that was what was wrong with him.

Conversation sort of faded out after that. But it was early and I didn't want to go home yet. There was a newspaper lying on one of the seats and I picked it up to give me something to do. The truth was I couldn't usually bear reading the news, now the war had started. On the one hand, every newspaper was telling us how well England was doing: stopping the Jerries from invading us, getting fuel and food into the country in the face of the U-boats and battleships. But every day things were still getting worse. There were 30,000 school kids being taken out of Sheffield to country areas the Germans weren't as likely to bomb. Hospital patients were being moved out. Petrol rationed. Even theatres and cinemas closed for a while; but then George Bernard Shaw wrote to *The Times* saying it was a very bad thing and some of them opened up again.

The Lord Privy Seal's Office had sent out a daft warning that people should take shelter when the air raid sirens went off. I ask you! Housewives were being warned by the Mines Department to burn less this winter by having a fire in one room only, never using the oven for a single dish by itself, wrapping up hot water pipes to keep in the heat and sifting through the cinders for coal dust that could be used again.

The advertisements were the funniest. Rowntrees had a special cocoa that made your children not want to eat so much. And Jays, the furniture people, would replace your bomb-damaged furniture and give you three years to pay. I thought: With any luck, people will still be paying it off when the war's well over. But they probably wouldn't feel good about it.

After a bit, Alan said he didn't feel well and he'd take me home. We got on the train and set off. Usually we'd kiss and cuddle, but not tonight. Every so often, I thought: I could talk about the picture. It was very good. But not tonight. We got off in the city centre and I told him he didn't have to take me all the way, feeling sick and all. Then I looked for my bus.

There were three men standing at the stop. One of them was a tall, slim young man in a black pinstripe suit and a grey trilby who leaned against the bus shelter. The other two wore flat caps and one of them ate chips out of a newspaper.

The chip eater looked at me and said: "Ello darlin. I wouldn't mind takin *you* ome tonight." The other one laughed.

Then the chip eater walked right up to me and said: "Give us a kiss and I'll give you a chip." He held out the newspaper.

The other one said: "Give us a feel, more like."

I said: "We don't read the *News of the World* in *our* house."

The first one said: "Oooh, playin ard to get, are we?"

The second one said: "Too good for us. Is that what you think you are?"

And then the man in the trilby took it off and ran his hand through his wavy hair. It suddenly struck me he looked like Stewart Granger. Alan and I had seen Stewart Granger in *Convoy* the previous week and actually it wasn't much of a film. But I remembered *him*.

Stewart Granger said to me: "Can I be of any help, Miss?" His voice didn't really sound like Stewart's but at least he knew what an aitch was.

The chip eater repeated it as: "Can I be of any *elp*, Miss?" in a high-pitched voice and the other one said, "Piss off, mate, and leave the ladies to the lads."

Then Stewart punched the chip eater in the back of the neck and the man fell on his face with his chips all over the pavement. And Stewart kicked the other one in the stomach so he fell to his knees and was suddenly sick.

And suddenly the bus came round the corner and Stewart took my arm and we got on and Stewart said to the conductor: "There's an awful lot of drunks out tonight," and the conductor glanced at the lads on the pavement and nodded his head. Stewart asked me where I was going and I told him and he bought two tickets. I said: "Thanks, Stewart."

He said "My name's not Stewart. It's Denny. Denny Morrow."

And I told him it didn't really matter.

Chapter Five

THE GERMANS KILLED MY MUM. It was the first night of the big Blitz, 13 days before Christmas. The Stukas came over, wave after wave, and the Arches couldn't stand it. We heard the hits and we heard the brickwork collapse and it seemed everybody was screaming. Maybe even me. I don't know. Then suddenly it was the all-clear and we were coming out. We didn't know then that lots of the Arches people were killed – suffocated when the exploding bombs sucked out all the air. Suffocated. That's what it said in the *Sheffield Star*. Who'd've thought of that?

We were coming out of the Arches after the all-clear. We were crossing the road. It was still full blackout, but we could see everything because of the fires everywhere. We passed a burning tram in the middle of the street, its windows blown out and its insides melted. And Redgates Store was ablaze, all three storeys of it. I thought about the things I'd bought there, the knickers, the stockings. I thought of them charred and melted, like the insides of the tram.

Then this fire engine came clanging round the corner and it hit her. Sent her flying. I ran over, with May just behind. I knelt down and put an arm round her. Her head was red and mushy like squashed tomatoes – my fingers went straight through.

A man came up. He said: "I'm a doctor." He looked at her. He said: "She's dead."

I said: "I know." I thought: It doesn't take a doctor to tell me these things.

The fire engine stopped. The driver got out. He ran over to us. The doctor said again: "She's dead." The fireman was a big lad with broad shoulders and a lantern jaw. He put his face in his hands and burst into tears.

Another fireman ran over. He said: "We can't stop. There's a fire."

I said: "I know there's a fire. There's lots of fires." I said: "You'd better get on."

28

The first fireman said: "I can't drive. I *can't*."

I said to the second fireman: "You go on. Leave him with us."

A woman came running over. She said: "I'll find a phone box. I'll call the police."

The second fireman hesitated. Then he ran back to the fire engine, got in the driver's seat and they were off.

I said: "Thanks," but it was too late for him to hear it. I thought: Does anybody really need to phone? How many coppers and ambulances are out tonight dealing with the dying? I thought: It's too late for Mum. Better they put her on the "maybe later" list.

The fireman who'd been crying took off his helmet. He wiped his eyes. He said: "It was *my* fault."

I said: "No, it wasn't." I said: "It was the Germans' fault. Let's hope lots of Germans get killed tonight, sitting in their beds shouting *Heil Hitler!* Let's hope *our* bombs kill more than theirs."

He looked at me with a strange and terrible face. I got up and put my arms round him. I said: "Nobody blames you." I said: "There's fires. You've got to go and put them out." I said: "Find out where they are, where your mates are now. They'll not be far away. Go and help them."

He said: "But the police are coming." He said: "Yes. I might be able to do something."

I said: "Of course you'll do something." I said: "The police can find you OK. They can talk to you later."

He said: "They don't know my name."

"They know you're a fireman."

He said: "Yes. That's my job." He said: "Right. I'll find my mates. It can't be far."

I said: "Look after yourself." Then he was gone.

By now there was quite a crowd round my mum. Aunt May was standing over her. She'd put her coat over Mum's head. The doctor was still talking to somebody in the crowd saying: "Yes, we've got an ambulance coming. Somebody's gone to telephone. No, it's too late anyway." After a while, the people in the crowd drifted away. They wanted to get home. And they weren't missing much – there were bound to be other dead people along the way. Maybe some of them would be people they knew far better than they knew my mum.

Aunt May said: "Somebody better phone Algrave. Somebody better phone the pit and tell your dad."

It was strange, I thought, but neither of us was crying. It was only then I thought about my dad. I said: "We'll wait for the ambulance first."

So that took half an hour. Then the police brought us home and phoned the pit and the managers brought my dad up and told him, and they brought him home in a black Austin 10.

I hugged him. He hugged me back. May hugged him. She was crying by now. May wanted to stay but I said no. She made a pot of tea and went home, leaving the condensed milk on the table. We sat in the front room, him and me, and drank the tea. He was still covered in pit dust, with white circles round his eyes, like a glossy picture of Al Jolson. After a while he said: "It's bin a hard neet for thee."

"Not just for me," I said.

"No," he said, "that's reet." He said: "I've got a bottle." He went to the sideboard and brought out the Famous Grouse, about half full, and set it on the small deal table. He went into the kitchen and brought out two glasses. He poured us equal measures, what Denny would have called three fingers. We both drank.

He said: "I'll need thee more than ever now, girl."

I said: "What?"

He said: "Tha mother were a grand woman. She cared for us reet and proper." The way he used the word *us*, I knew it was that peculiar Yorkshire way, meaning *him*. I said nothing; I wanted to hear the whole thing.

"I know tha's got some sort o' job," he went on, "but that's not likely to last once the men come ome from t'war. And I know there's a lad tha's going with, though I don't ken much about him, and I expect tha'll be married someday, like any woman. But reet now, I need thee to tend my ome, to take tha mother's place."

And I laughed. I laughed so loud and sudden, it startled me. And I think it had the same effect on Dad. Maybe it was being in shock, a young woman who'd just seen her mother killed in the street. But I couldn't *stop* laughing. I was shaking so much, I spilled the whisky and I went into the kitchen, put a rag under the tap, came back in and cleaned it up. And I suddenly thought: I'm doing exactly what my dad wants – I'm keeping house already. And that made me laugh even more. I went back into the kitchen, bent over, put my head under the tap, splashed water all over my face, got a towel and wiped myself dry. I went back into the front room.

"Dad," I said, "I'm really sorry." And I told him what I planned to do.

And an hour later, when I got round to May's house with my suitcase, she said: "I was waiting up for you. I've tidied the back bedroom."

"Thank you, May," I said. And it was only then that I could cry.

Next morning the *Star* said: 600 people killed, 1,500 injured, 40,000 made homeless. That night, Mr Churchill came on the wireless. He said: "This is no time for ease and comfort. It is time to dare and endure." And I thought: Yes, yes, yes!

I had to walk to work next morning. I chose a black cotton costume with my overcoat. In Angel Street, everything was turned to rubble except the Car & General Insurance Company, a huge four-floor skeleton, its chimney stacks intact, the chimneys now blackened fingers stretching to the sky. But not hands up to surrender, I thought. No, not to bloody surrender! The width of High Street was a pile of bricks and girders, people doing things, shifting stuff. Doing their best. Nobody just standing around. Good, I thought, standing around doesn't do anybody any good. And at the Maples Hotel, people still being brought out on stretchers. Stay alive, I thought, stay alive. And Bramall Lane had been hit and United didn't know if they'd be able to play the next game there. And the Black Swan at Snig Hill destroyed. And the shops along the Moor.

The whole of one street I saw that morning was levelled: piles of bricks, bits of tables, doors, broken beds, an armchair with its springs sticking out. Well, I thought, no good repairing it now. And, you know, I couldn't think of the name of that street, though it was one I walked past every week of my life. And I can't now. Isn't that funny?

Chapter Six

IT WAS GETTING TO BE SPRING and I was leaving off my winter coat. By now, I'd got friendly with some of the girls in the office. There was one called Angela who stood out from the rest. She didn't just put files into folders. She did a lot of typing and giving out work and organising things. I don't say it was high-powered but it was more than *I* did. And she grew her hair in a bob. One day I went up to the canteen for a sandwich and Angela was there and she looked up and I took my sandwich over and sat with her. I sprinkled some powdered milk on my tea and watched it sink slowly.

"How are you finding it?" she asked. She was a tall woman in her late twenties, with pale skin and what May would call "good bone structure".

"It's alright," I said.

"Yes it is," she said. But her voice sounded as though she was mocking me.

"Except," I said – and then I hesitated because I wondered whether I should really say such a thing. I decided to go ahead. "I don't like Mr Lanchester touching my bum all the time." Mr Lanchester was the office manager, a small, plump, middle-aged man with a pencil moustache.

Angela laughed so much she spilt her tea. Then: "He doesn't touch *my* bum," she said.

I was surprised. I mean, Angela was a very attractive young woman. And Mr Lanchester was her boss. It seemed natural he would touch her bum. I waited for her to go on, but she didn't. So I plucked up courage. I said: "Why is that, then?" I expected her to say "I'd slap his face if he did" or something like that. There was something about her that showed she was a no-nonsense person.

She took off her glasses and put them on the table between us. "Put them on," she said.

I put them on. They were just plain glass.

"Men don't make passes at girls in glasses," she said. "Do you know why?"

"No."

"Because when you put on glasses, they think you're intelligent. And men are frightened of intelligent women."

That made it my turn to laugh. But suddenly I could see she was right. It was like when my mum said "Men don't want a brain box" but from the other side of the street, as it were. I said: "Where can I get some?"

"You can have these for a pound. I've got a spare pair in my desk."

"Give you ten shillings," I said.

"Done."

And I thought: *I'll* grow my hair in a bob.

*

But I never got chance to find out if Angela's glasses worked at Balfours. Next day, Mr Lanchester called me into his office. He had quite a small office with only one filing cabinet and two chairs. But Mr Lanchester's desk was big and covered with pens and blotting paper and a large notepad, and his chair was real leather, and that was big too. Must have been pre-war else the company would have jibbed at the coupons it took.

He waved me to the wooden chair in front of the desk and I sat down, pulling my cardy tight around me. I could see the folder in front of him had my name on it. In the six or seven months I'd worked at Balfours, reading upside down was one of the few skills I'd mastered. Or *mistressed* would be a better verb, I suppose. But there isn't such a word in our language.

Mr Lanchester said: "It's Josie, isn't it? Miss Cawthorne?"

I said: "Yes, Mr Lanchester." I was on best behaviour. I could've said: "If it isn't, you've got the wrong folder out." But I didn't.

He said: "Yes. Well..." He coughed. "And how long have you been with us?" He put his fingertips together.

"Six months," I said. What I didn't say was: "You can

look it up in your folder." What I didn't say was: "I've been here six months and I think I'm worth a raise in pay, ta very much." Not that it would have made any difference to anything. Because I knew why I was there.

He said: "You're a good worker. There's no doubt about it. You get on well with the other staff. Everyone speaks highly of you. Your timekeeping is excellent. But..."

"You're going to sack me."

He had the grace to look embarrassed. He said: "I'm embarrassed." He fiddled with his glasses a bit and scratched his nose. But maybe it was just an itch. "Yes, I'm letting you go," he said.

As if I was a prisoner!

"Why?"

There was a little bit of a silence. Then: "Mr Grantley..."

I thought: Looks like I've been wrong about Alan. He's got me the push.

Mr Lanchester went on: "... has told us he wants to leave. If he does so, it means he loses his reserve occupation status. He's a fit young man and will undoubtedly be called up."

"Oh no," I said.

"*Oh no* is right, Miss Cawthorne. I spoke to him at some length about his decision. He has, after all, been here for four years and is due for promotion. I might say it took some digging on my part and in the end some inquiries among other members of staff. But I now believe..." He fiddled with his glasses again. "...there are personal matters which, he feels, have made it difficult for him to stay."

"*Me.*"

"Well, yes."

I was thrilled. I thought: God, Alan is really in love with me. I caught myself smiling and covered my mouth with my hand. "Well," I said, "I can see you've got a problem."

"Yes," he said.

"Well," I said again, "I'll solve your problem, Mr Lanchester. I will resign. I will write you a letter of resignation this afternoon. I will give as my reason..." I thought about it. "... the recent tragic death of my mother

35

and the necessity of looking after my father who is also a person of reserved occupation."

"That would certainly avoid any embarrassment for either of us."

"And what I would like in return…"

"Yes?" I could see I'd got all his attention now. His hands were spread out on the desk.

"… is a reference referring to my reason for resigning and how sad you are to lose me. And you can write all the things you've just said about me: I'm a good worker, I get on well with everybody, my timekeeping is excellent, everyone speaks highly of me." I paused for breath. "I need a reference because, eventually, it's possible my father will remarry. In which case I would need to make myself available for employment once more. Obviously, we should all do what we can to help the war effort."

"Indeed."

"And then, Mr Lanchester…"

"Yes?"

"I would like two weeks' pay in lieu of notice."

"I don't see how we could give you lieu of notice, Miss Cawthorne, if you're resigning. I mean, if we sacked you, we could perhaps do that, but…"

I thought about it. "Might there not be a week's holiday pay owed to me? Also, I was eighteen a month ago. Might there not be an increment…?"

He began to write on his notepad.

Then I went back to my desk and I wrote my resignation letter in my best handwriting. And I went back into Mr Lanchester's office, but he was out. So I put the letter on his desk. And I wrote a letter to Alan and I slipped it into his drawer while he was still at lunch. I told him what a smashing person he was and I ended it *Love, Josie.*

The thing is: you can write *love* at the end of a letter and it doesn't really mean a thing.

*

When I got back to May's after work, she was just coming in the back door. She said: "I've had some trouble with the neighbours. They don't like me feeding the birds. They say it's illegal, which it is, on account of wasting good bread that should be feeding human beings to help kill Germans. But I said to them: if they report me, I'll have the Labour Party smash their windows. That shut them up."

When I told her what I'd done, she said: "You're a surprise and no mistake, our Josie."

"But I've done the right thing, haven't I, May?"

"I don't know if Denny Morrow is the right thing." She went in the kitchen and made a pot of tea.

I was shocked. I didn't see how May could have found out about Denny. Except she always seemed to know everything about everyone. "He might not be right for everybody, but he's right for me," I said in between sips. Then: "What's wrong with him anyway?"

"I'll not mince words. Denny Morrow is a crook. A black market fixer. A spiv, a wide boy who buys and sells dodgy stuff."

I said: "But he's not a pit owner."

She laughed. "No, he's not a pit owner."

"And he's not landed gentry."

"No, he's not that either."

I knew I'd nailed the two categories of real villains in May's view of the world. "So he can't be that bad, can he?"

"And where are you going to find a new job? Or are you just planning to be Denny's moll?"

My turn to laugh. "*Moll!* You've been watching too many pictures, May. Jimmy Cagney and Edward G Robinson. I'm nobody's moll and Denny's not a gangster."

After a while she said: "The one thing I know is this: it's no good telling young people anything. Especially not young *women*. They've all got to find out about men for themselves. Are you moving in with him?"

"I might be." In fact, I'd never discussed it with Denny.

"Well, at least I've taught you how to take precautions."

"Thanks to you, I can look after myself."

37

"But you'll always have a room back here with me."

"Thanks, May."

"Don't thank me. We're family. You never have to thank family."

"I'll pack some things, then. But I'll leave some things here as well."

And I thought: *I'm going to be with Denny!* And May switched on the wireless and it was Bing Crosby singing:

Do I want to be with you
As the years come and go?
Only forever...

And I thought: *That's an omen for me and Denny.*

May tried to pour herself another cup but there was nothing left in the pot. She put it down. She said: "But we all of us need a bolthole, a place we can get away to when times are bad. You just remember that."

And it turned out I *did* remember. Lots of times.

Stave III: Denny Morrow

When you wish upon a star, makes no difference who you are, anything your heart desires will come to you
...... Jesse McCartney, as sung in *Pinocchio*, 1940

He used to be a big shot.
...... Jerry Wald, Richard Macaulay and Robert Rossen, spoken by Gladys George, *The Roaring Twenties*, 1939

Chapter Seven

DENNY! WELL, I KNOW THIS IS THE BIT You've been waiting for, Father. Except that all time is eternally present to You, isn't it? So You know everything before it even happens. No surprises, eh? Maybe *I'm* the one that's been waiting to tell *You*, then.

Denny. Really that wasn't his name. It was Dennis. But he called himself Denny because... well, because he *was* a Denny. He was never really a Dennis.

Now, part of me is very concerned about what I say. I don't want to make it smutty or anything. But You know what it's like between a man and a woman; You know what it was like between Denny and me. You've seen it through the walls and through the ceiling, through my eyes and through Denny's eyes; and, if we didn't make sure the curtains were drawn, You've probably seen it through a nosy neighbour's eyes too. Well then.

I've got to say I don't like all this omniscience thing. I think it's off putting, knowing You see everything. That thing in Matthew about seeing every sparrow fall. But then I suppose it's *meant* to be off putting, gives us food for thought before we get on with doing things.

So You know what it was like, how I loved it, how I loved him too. You know all my feelings. It makes me want to blush. But it's down to You. You made me the way I am and there's no mistake about it. So I shouldn't really be ashamed. I shouldn't really tremble. But I do.

I'll just say all the things I want to say about Denny and get it over with and You can laugh at me if You like...

I loved it when he got my clothes off, when he took me in his arms, all the things he said to me and all the things I said to him. Though, if I'm honest, I remember best the things he *did*.

I loved the way he looked when he was naked. Not a muscle man, not a bodybuilder, not Johnny Weissmuller. I never wanted a Tarzan. Denny was slender and his ribs showed. I guess he was most like a lightweight boxer or a runner. Or something like that. I'd never been much interested in athletics, although I'd watched the Berlin Olympics on Pathé News.

I loved the way we touched and made love. I was always holding off that last bit with Alan, but I didn't hold anything back with Denny. I mean, I used the rubbers because I'm not so foolish. But I let him suggest it and show me how they were used and I acted like it was all new to me, that I'd never had myself a clever auntie.

I loved to go out with him, for a meal or dancing or to the pictures. I loved to see the other girls turn their heads. And I knew what they were thinking: *How's a little bitch like her landed a lad like him?* I loved the way he dressed – smart, confident, untroubled: the trilby hat, the suit, the cufflinks, the shiny bracelet on his wrist watch, the patent leather shoes. If I were a man, I thought, that's how *I'd* dress.

He had a husky voice, deep and manly. Call this silly if you like, but the lilt of him reminded me of John Donne, which I'd studied with the nuns. There was also a quietness to him. He never once raised his voice, not to me nor anybody else. He didn't need to.

And he was funny. And clever with it. He did a great impression of Mr Churchill, the lisp and the long drawn-out words. But he once said: "Churchill actually uses it. The lisp. The funny voice. You hear him on the wireless and you know who it is right off. That's clever."

And he was strong. Sometimes there might be a likely lad in the street, looking for trouble, sounding off about something, anything that might start a fight. And Denny would always take care of him. So the lad knew very quickly what was what and stopped doing whatever.

I remember one time we were dancing the Last Waltz at the Saturday dance, very slow, to Al Bowlly's "Goodnight Sweetheart"...

Goodnight, sweetheart, well it's time to go,
I hate to leave you, but I really must say:
Goodnight, sweetheart, goodnight...

And there was some lout on the edge of the floor, one of those types that hang around dances but can't get a girl, and he started to sing along to it. Very loud. Very drunk. Denny could see I didn't like it, it spoiled the mood, so he walked across to the lad, not hurried or upset in any way, and smiled, and touched his arm gently, and looked in his face from three inches away and said something really quiet that no one else could hear. And the lad started to say something but then his mate nudged him and whispered something in his ear. Then it was all apologies and smiles on the other lad's side. And Denny smiled too. Denny always smiled. But he never apologised.

I already knew what he could do, of course: I'd seen it with the two lads at the bus stop. I'd seen the power of him and the damage he could inflict. The lads in the dance hall hadn't seen that thing at the bus stop, but it was as if they knew instinctively what he was capable of. And him being respected by the men made all the girls fancy him more, I could tell.

By this time, I'd started buying my own make-up. Only a touch of powder for when my nose got red and sweaty, or my cheeks blushed. And I'd had my hair cut in a bob like Angela.

Officially, I was still living with May. But I was spending maybe two or three nights a week at Denny's. It was a four bedroom house over in Dore in a cul-de-sac with beech trees. The house had an indoor bathroom and lav. It had stained glass windows with butterfly patterns in the bedrooms and little angels – cherubim, that is – carved in the cornices. It had a drive and a garage. And a back garden with a pond full of carp (that's what Denny said they were) and a fruit cage with blackberries, raspberries, strawberries... But the fruit cage was going to ruin because Denny didn't bother to tend it and the fruit was over-ripe. The only thing outside that looked in good nick was the entrance to the underground Anderson shelter protected by its steel shield and a wall of soil.

Also, Denny didn't just have a wireless: he had a Decca

portable gramophone, which must have cost about £6, and a collection of records that included Glenn Miller, Crosby, Ambrose, Lew Stone and Arthur Tracey the Street Singer.

"This house is nice," I said the first time I saw it. "How'd you get enough to buy it?" I knew from May how Denny made his money, but I wanted him to come out with it and tell me.

"It belongs to a friend," he said, "and he's got to be away for a while so he said I could look after it for him."

"Is he on holiday?"

"Well, you could say that. He's not exactly in gainful employment. Though you could also say what he does is full-time."

"And how much did that motor cost you? Or does that belong to another friend?" Denny had picked me up in the middle of town in a black-and-red Bentley that I'd never seen the like of before.

"Same friend. He trusts me with everything. That's the 4¼ litre Mark V. It's very rare. Bentley stopped making them when war broke out. Mind you, I only use it for special occasions. Most times, I like to travel on buses. You can meet a lot of interesting people that way. The time I first met you, for instance."

And Denny had a telephone. Which was useful because May could always phone me from a call box if something was wrong. Which she did one evening.

"Josie," she said, "your dad's here. He's bothered about you. Seems he's been hearing things."

I groaned inside myself but I knew whatever it was had to be settled. "Keep him there. I'll catch the next bus," I said. I didn't want Dad being overfaced by a Bentley Mark V. I told Denny I'd be spending the night at May's. I put on a gabardine over my two-piece.

*

When I got there, Dad was looking moody, sat in an armchair in front of the gas fire. He got up as soon as I walked in the room. "What's this I've been earing about thee?" he said.

"I don't know," I said, "I'm not a mind reader."

He drew back his hand and I thought he was going to hit me. But then he thought better of it.

"What's this about a motor car?"

That's when I knew I'd done right by coming on the bus. I said nothing.

"I'm told tha's been gaddin about wi' a lad in a red-and-black motor car that's worth undreds."

"I don't know what you mean by gadding about."

"Oo's this lad?"

"His name's Denny and it's not his motor car. A friend of his lent it."

"E's got some rich mates then."

"Appen e as," said May. "I wish I ad some rich mates *myssen*." I'd noticed some time ago that May had two voices with two different sets of words: the voice the nuns had taught her and the voice she sometimes used with my dad. She moved easily between the two as circumstance dictated.

"And I ear tha's lost tha job," Dad went on.

"I'm looking for a new one."

"Tha's not gonna find it putterin about in a rich man's motor." Dad was shouting now.

"You don't raise your voice in *my* house," said May, raising her voice.

"That's as maybe. But what's for sure is I'm takin er ome and I'm doing it now."

"No, you're not," said May.

"She's my daughter," said Dad, "and I'll decide where she lives."

"I'll tell you what's for sure, Sam Cawthorne. I'll not have you in my house when you're in this condition. I can smell the drink on you. I can smell it from three feet away."

I thought: Nice one, May. I thought: Nice one, nuns!

Dad went quiet. May said: "Sit thyssen down again," and he did. She sat opposite him on the matching chair. "Now, Sam," she said, "you're acting like a piecan. Josie's a good lass and you know it. She's living in my house because she's not yet twenty years old and it wouldn't be right for a young lass to be living alone with a man, even if it is her father."

"I don't see..." Dad began.

"Yes, you *do* see, Sam. You're her father alright. But you don't have to act like you're in *The Barretts of Wimpole Street*."

I could see him wince. I never guessed he knew who the Barretts of Wimpole Street were, but he must have seen the film with Charles Laughton.

"Well..." he began.

"Well nothing," said May.

He was quiet.

She said: "I'll tell you what you've done, Sam. I happen to know Josie was planning to go out with her young man this evening to a Labour Party rally protesting about the profiteers that are making money out of this war. I don't know if you've seen the *Daily Mirror* this week..."

He nodded. He looked at his feet. "If this Denny is a Labour man..."

"So is Josie. I got them both to join."

"Aye. Well, appen tha's done right thing in that, May."

"Appen I do right thing in most things, Sam. Now, what have you got to say to Josie and me?"

"I'm sorry," he said. Eventually. I couldn't believe it.

"We all of us get upset at times," said May, "we all of us make mistakes." She picked his cap off the sideboard and gave it to him. "Now I'll wager you've got a shift tomorrow and you need the rest. Josie's perfectly fine staying with me."

"Spose so," he said and put on his cap.

I kissed him on the way out. After he'd gone, I said: "I've said it before, May. You're a wicked woman."

She shrugged. "God'll be the judge of that," she said.

Chapter Eight

IT WAS A MONDAY MORNING and I was in Denny's house looking through the *Star* for jobs. Not that I was keen for more filing, but I didn't want to be a kept woman either. That meant being somebody who couldn't make her own way in the world. But I'd been good at school, hadn't I?

Denny was out. I didn't know where. I'd never asked about his business and so far he'd told me nothing. I heard the postman coming up the drive and the letters hitting the mat in the hall. I went and picked them up. One was addressed to Denny and looked like a bill. One was addressed to The Occupier and looked like a government leaflet telling us to do something: sell our gold to the Treasury, or join the Auxiliary Fire Service or Dig for Victory. The third was addressed to Alonzo McIntyre Esquire.

I heard the Bentley outside and Denny opening the garage and I waited in the hall for him. I said: "Who's Alonzo McIntyre?"

He looked surprised, but only for a moment. He said: "The post must've come."

I handed him the letters. He said: "Alonzo is in the same business as me. He owns this house. You must have already figured out he's in chokey. He got collared for fencing." Denny paused and grinned. "Do you know what I'm talking about?"

"I know you don't mean sword-fighting. You mean he's in prison for receiving stolen property. How long before *you're* in prison too? Or have you already done time?"

"I've done Borstal. But that's all." He tapped the envelopes against his leg. "Alright, I can see we've got to have a talk. I know you've been putting it off and I've been putting it off too. Being honest isn't easy for me. I've not been honest for many years now."

We went in the lounge and we both sat down and I put on my glasses to show this was a serious talk. He started to tell me about himself. What I'm telling you now is how I remember it. It might not be exactly word for word, but the gist of it is right enough. And I want to get over the tone of it, how… what's the word? How *graceful* it was.

"First I want to tell you," he said, "why I'm not fighting in this war. Just so's you know if people ask."

"Alright," I said.

"I volunteered. I really did. But I've got his thing, this scar on my lungs. So the medics made me Grade F."

I tried to speak in a proper sentence but all I could say was: "How…?"

"I don't want to give you any sob story about my life, being a poor boy, starving hungry, beaten up by my dad, neglected by my drunken mum, because that's not what happened. I've had my troubles, yeh, but no more than anybody else.

"First, my parents loved me. My dad was a school teacher and my mum was a typist. And I'm an only child."

"I'm an only child too," I said.

"Yeh," he said, "I know." He went on: "They got killed. In a car crash. The son of a bitch driving the other car was pissed as a newt. He got sent down. But not for long enough. Anyway, water under the bridge.

"I was ten. My mum and dad, they didn't have any relatives that could look after me. My mum had an elder sister, but she was crippled and in her sixties. So they put me in an orphanage.

"That was rough. The other kids thought I was posh. Imagine. I guess I sounded posh because I talked like my dad, talked like a school teacher. Some of those other kids… I don't know how to say this because it sounds like I'm making it up… But some of those other kids could hardly talk, just went round grunting. When they wanted something, they grabbed it out of your hand. And they didn't know how to go to the lavatory, didn't know how to wipe their arses…" He stopped. "I'm sorry I said *arse* in front of you."

"Don't worry," I said, "some girls I know say *arse* as well."

He looked surprised by that. He went on: "And I was clever. I was reading *Just William* when the other kids were reading *Winnie the Pooh*. *Just William* made me laugh. That's how the other kids found out about it. So they called me Jackass because I was laughing at *Just William* and they got their crayons and drew all over my books.

"And I knew my times tables up to twelve when most of those kids couldn't add two and two. They gave me Chinese burns. And they punched me and kicked me all the time. In parts of the body that don't show through your clothes. And then... well, there's other things that I just won't talk about. When they got to twelve and thirteen, when boys start to be interested in girls... well, there weren't any girls in the orphanage. So they used to do things.... Well, I'm not going to talk about it. Like I said."

I reached out and touched his hand. He said: "And that's when I came down with pneumonia. In the orphanage. But I'm one of the lucky ones. I came through OK. The scar doesn't mean anything – except to the medics."

He took my hand and pressed it. He said: "Then I got rescued. It turned out I had an uncle on my mother's side. Uncle Ernest. He'd been a soldier for years and years and he'd been out of the country when my parents died. He retired from the King's Own Yorkshires and he came back to England and he dragged me out of that place and looked after me.

"Uncle Ernest was a good bloke. But he was a bit of a rough diamond. He was a crack shot and he'd kept his service rifle, which was illegal to start with, and he used to go out nights to the big estates round where we lived and poach game. Sometimes he'd have me go with him. Just for the exercise, he'd say, and just to show me how the rich own all the land."

"He'd get on well with my aunt May."

"In the end, the Fitzwilliam family came to a deal with him where they'd pay him regular money if he wouldn't go on their land anymore. But they still had trouble with poachers. So Uncle Ernest told them he'd sort out the other poachers if they doubled his money. And that's what he did. Poacher turned gamekeeper. Set a thief to catch one." He laughed. "That was a big lesson for me. *Three* big lessons. First, the thing about rich people owning everything. Second, they weren't so law-abiding that they couldn't come to a deal with you if it suited them. And third, you could be on both sides at once if you were smart enough."

I said: "Was it the poaching got you into Borstal? Was that your uncle Ernest?"

"That was my own stupid fault. I thought I was getting good at it. I went out one night on my own. Didn't tell him, though he must've guessed. Made a mess of it. Simple story. Wentworth Woodhouse. Fell over a tree root. Gun went off. Six gamekeepers on me like a ton of bricks. Lucky I didn't kill myself.

"It was the gun going off that got me Borstal. They considered me a dangerous character."

I reached for his hand again. "Was Borstal bad? Like the orphanage?"

"No. It was fine. I was a very good boy. I didn't even get a caning all the time I was there. And that's where I learned to box. There was this gym teacher called Mr Herbert. He liked to think boxing improved the character. Well, I think I've got to disagree with him there. But it kept me fit. And it bought me respect. Like with those two lads at the bus stop."

"Aunt May thinks you're a gangster."

"Al Capone, eh? That's not my style. More Al Bowlly, I like to think. More like a crooner than a criminal. I'll show you what I do." He stood up. "It's boring really." He went upstairs and came down with a suitcase. He put it on the carpet, knelt down beside it, opened it and tipped it up. A whole load of papers fell out.

"You know what these are?"

"Course I do. They're ration cards." I picked one up. It was buff-coloured and had *MF* on the front for *Ministry of Food*. Another type was green and said: *Issued to Safeguard Your Food Supply*; that was the children's version.

"No, they're not," said Denny.

"Course they are. I know a ration card when I see one."

"Only these don't come from the Ministry of Food. They were done for me by a lad named Aaron Bassett, a printer up in town." He thought a moment. "No, not for me. For Lonzo."

I dropped the one I was holding. I felt stupid. "You sell them," I said, "then…"

"Then somebody writes a false name in the new card and gets double the legal ration. Or three times the ration or four if you've got enough cards, or…"

"Or open a shop if you've got enough."

"Well, not open a shop exactly. But take the stuff round on a van: bacon and ham, sugar, loose tea, butter, sweets for the kids." He stopped. "Does that shock you?"

"No," I said.

"Anybody with a van can make a good living in the black market. But it doesn't have to come from fake ration cards. There's plenty of stuff comes direct from the farmers – they get more out of it than they do selling to the government. And it's easier to move stuff about in the blackout, or break into warehouses for that matter, or unload a ship at the docks. But I don't do any of that."

"You're just a spiv," I said, "a wideboy."

He nodded. "That's what I am. And I don't even make very much in the way of pounds sterling. I guess I've been kidding you a lot, making out how important I am. But I'm not rich and, like I said, I'm not Al Capone. But I could still get three years if any of this came out."

"And who's this Alonzo McIntyre? Apart from the man that owns our house? Is he a spiv too?"

"Oh no. Lonzo is more than that. He's part Scotch, part Eye-tie, part Mexican – no, don't ask! He's the Boss. Well, *my* boss. Boss of this manor anyway. He's been away for a couple of years like I said. But he's due out in two months which is why he's started getting post again. Things've been quiet while he's been away; now I shouldn't wonder they're going to get more lively. And we should be looking for a place of our own."

I thought: It's going to be difficult giving up the fruit cage. Then I thought: No, it's not. The further we get away from people like Lonzo the better.

I said: "I'd better go back to job-hunting." I picked the *Star* up off the carpet.

Chapter Nine

I SAW THIS ADVERTISEMENT in *The Star*: Women Wanted to Take Over the Balloon Barrage. It showed this woman wearing a cap and some sort of overalls or uniform (it wasn't a very good picture and she was kneeling down). I thought: Well, wonder how much they pay for that? And I wrote them a letter, making sure they knew I was a Miss so there'd never be any lost shifts on account of any kids.

We started looking at houses, Denny and me. The first one we looked at was a back-to-back with peeling wallpaper and the lavs were built in a line at the end of the road and everybody had to have a key to their own. "No," said Denny, "not for us." And I was glad he thought so.

The second was a two-up-two-down in Manor and we were only there two minutes when we could hear the neighbours next door having a row, going hammer-and-tongs at each other – and the language wasn't choice. "No," I said, and Denny grinned and said: "I bet they're noisy in bed as well." And he said it while the estate agent was stood with us and it made me blush.

Then we looked at a cottage out Dronfield way, and that wasn't bad at all. It was on farming land and the farmer's mum had lived there till she passed away a few months back. It wasn't big but it was lovely, with a kitchen, living room, bedroom and bathroom. The kitchen had an oak table and a gas cooker; the living room had a three-piece suite, the sofa and chairs in floral pattern covers, and a coal fire; and the bathroom had a coal-fired boiler and a lav. And I liked having trees and fields nearby, very different from what I'd been used to. But the rent was £4 a week and that was a blow. "Tell them we'll think about it," I said. I could see the estate agent this time was really surprised. Trouble was, we'd come out in Lonzo's Bentley so I guess they thought we had money to burn.

"Truth to tell," said Denny when he was driving us home, "I don't know what my income's gonna be when the gaffer comes back. He might have big plans for me and he might not. At least we've kept his house spick and span."

"Thanks to me," I said.

"Yeh, thanks to you. And it *could* make the difference. I could be going places in the organisation."

I said: "I don't know I like that. I don't know I like Lonzo Mack. I don't know I like the sort of organisation he runs. I've got used to what you do, Denny, and I'm not blaming you for it. But you can't spend your life on the wrong side of the law."

"No," he agreed, "but I might have to spend a bit of time yet before I make my pile and go straight."

*

When we got home I picked up the post and there was a letter addressed to me. I opened it and found I'd got an interview with the WAAF about being a Barrage Balloon Operator.

I rushed upstairs to tell Denny. He'd turned the back bedroom into a sort of gym – he'd got weights, a training bench to do sit-ups on, and four rubber mats "so my feet don't slip when I'm exercising". And he'd stuck Charles Atlas advertisements up on the walls: little comic strips about skinny men going to the beach and getting sand kicked all over them by big bullies. They were called things like "The Insult That Turned a Chump Into a Champ". I didn't really like this side of Denny – like I said, he was no muscle man, but he was slim and handsome like a proper athlete. I didn't want him to turn into a mountain.

When I went in, Denny was standing in his underpants lifting a set of dumbbells in each hand. He saw me and grinned. He said: "Come to admire me, then?"

I said: "I'm surprised you kept your pants on."

He said: "Oh, I like to keep my dignity when I'm training. But you can pull them down if you want."

"No," I said, "I've seen it all before." And I told him about the barrage balloons.

53

That actually made him put his dumbbells down. "You know you don't *have* to work."

"I know I'll soon be through the money Balfours gave me and I know we need to get a nice place of our own. Like that farmhouse. Anyway, it's helping the war."

"I suppose it is." He came over and put his arms round me.

I said: "Stop that." But I didn't really mean it. And I helped him undress me.

Afterwards, I said: "That bloody floor mat's filthy. I've got muck all over me." But I wasn't really upset. I said: "You can put your pants back on now."

*

So next day I got out my best charcoal grey two-piece, put on my lipstick, tucked Mr Lanchester's reference in my handbag, and got a bus to the Station Hotel in Rotherham, which was the Balloon HQ. I went through the foyer and showed my letter to a woman at the desk. She phoned somebody and said to me: "Right. Up the winding stairs and it's third suite on the left with a sign on the door that says: *Group Leader Cassidy*." So I said "Right" as well, and I did as I was told.

I found the room easily enough and knocked and a voice said "Come in" and I did. And there was this woman sat at a desk, surrounded by telephones and papers and wearing a blue uniform but bare headed, so her auburn hair tumbled messily over her shoulders. And, despite the hair, which I'd never seen before, I recognised her straight away.

"Sister Margaret Mary!" I said.

"Hello, Josie," she smiled and waved me to the canvas chair in front of her desk. "But it's not *Sister* anymore. It's Group Leader Christine Cassidy now."

I sat down. I said: "You're not a nun anymore!" Straightway, I thought: How could I say anything so stupid?

Christine laughed, but it wasn't unkind. "No," she said, as though she'd got the whole thing well rehearsed from having to repeat it so often: "I came to doubt my vocation. There were so many things: Hitler and the war being the biggest." She hesitated, then: "Also I persisted in the heresy that Charles Dickens was overrated and *David Copperfield* was not his best book."

So we could *both* laugh then. She said: "You want to be in Barrage Balloons Command. Well, it's not the sort of trade St Elfreda's prepared you for, but it's quite a sensible thing to do in the circumstances." Then her tone became more formal. "I understand you have a reference from your former employer."

I gave it to her. She studied it. "It says here you gave up your last job to look after your widowed father until such time as he might remarry. Do I take it he's getting married again?"

I thought for a moment about lying. But if I went along with the marriage thing, Christine would want to send a card saying *Congratulations*. I said: "No. It's a lie. There was an embarrassment."

She looked up, amused. "A boy?"

"He worked there."

Christine put a hand over her mouth, but I could see her eyes smile. Then: "Do you actually know what a barrage balloon is? And don't be insulted by the question. You'd be amazed how many people don't."

"It's a great big balloon up in the sky and it's connected to the ground by a steel cable and we put up lots of them so German bombers fly into the cables and crash."

"Good." She said it as though we might still be in class doing *Love's Labour's Lost* or something. "Barrage balloons can be flown as high as 5,000 feet. The aim is to stop any plane that comes in low or dive-bombers when they start to dive. But just to give you the technical detail: the balloons are about 18 yards long with a diameter of seven yards. That's three times the size of a cricket pitch, so they're hard to handle. The cables are attached with rope to steel rings on the ground and sometimes the ropes get worn, so that can be a dangerous problem too. The top of the balloon is filled with hydrogen so there's always the risk of fire if it gets out. We have to patch the balloons if they get torn – I seem to remember you failed Sewing, Josie."

I nearly jumped out of my seat. "No, I didn't. I got a pass. Just."

"Apologies. So school still stands you in good stead. That's nice to know. Now, some people don't like barrage balloons. And I don't just mean *Germans* don't like them. Can you guess why?"

I considered. "Because a barrage balloon can't read German or recognise a Swastika. They don't know who's enemy and who's friend. So it could be one of our own boys hits the cable and goes down."

"Got it in one. Would it surprise you to know that we probably bring down more of our own planes than we do of the Germans? Because it's true. Some people think the number of friendlies we bring down may be *six times* the number of hostiles. We've got no official figures – and some of us think that's the reason. Also some people believe putting up barrage balloons is the stupidest way to signal to the Luftwaffe that we've got something worth bombing underneath." She sighed. "But when you think of the numbers killed in any air raid over a big city, it still makes mathematical sense. Maybe." She waited as if to let me speak but I stayed quiet. She said: "I guess when people lose their vocation, they shouldn't look for something perfect to replace it."

Then she changed the subject. "There's lots of papers to fill in because it's not like you're starting just any job – you'll be in the armed forces. You get the uniform free and the pay's three shillings a day, which is two-thirds what the men get."

I did a bit of mental arithmetic, bearing in mind it wasn't one of my best results at school. "It's fifteen shillings," Christine interrupted – a bit prematurely, I thought. "That's for five days a week, though you'll have to work some weekends on rota."

We had a little silence then as though we neither of us

knew what to say. But she was giving me time to think, to consider. She often did this when we came to a thorny problem in Shakespeare – like the true nature of the relationship between Antonio and Bassanio in *The Merchant of Venice*. But this time I didn't need to consider.

"I want this job," I said, "I want it very much."

"Then you shall have it, Josie. I think you'll do very well here."

*

On the way home I found a phone box and dialled Denny. I said to him: "Phone the man and tell him we'll take the cottage."

Denny said: "That's great. Then I'll come over there and pick you up."

"Don't bother your pretty little head. I've got my bank book on me and I'm going to buy a bicycle. I'm going to need one to get to work."

Chapter Ten

I'D HAD A ROUGH DAY. First, the bike got a puncture. It was a three-speed Hercules Ladies' bike with a full chain guard, cost me all of £3. But I must have run over a piece of glass or something and I was stood by the roadside pumping away for nearly an hour. When I got to the balloon station in Attercliffe, there were nine people waiting for me. Well, when I say *waiting*, I don't mean they didn't start without me. I just mean they were very shirty about my being late.

We were inside the hangar repairing a couple of balloons. That meant blowing them up with this machine that looked like a giant vacuum cleaner, then cleaning off the silver paint and glue round the holes and gluing and painting new patches. The paint was poisonous so we had to go outside for twenty minutes at a time because we didn't have any masks or goggles or protective clothing. Only our uniforms, which scratched and made us look very masculine in trousers.

Also we had to paint blue and black stripes on the balloons for camouflage – so the Jerries wouldn't know where a balloon ended and the sky started. Or something like that. I thought this was nonsense, what with their being so big anyway that you couldn't really avoid them once you got close to them.

Half the team were men. The two corporals in charge were men. When it was lunch time, we sat on the grass, eating our sandwiches. I'd brought cheese and tomato. One woman – her name was Emmie – had brought dripping. "Dripping on bread is nourishing," she said, but the thought of it made me feel sick and I threw away my cheese and tomato half-eaten. One of the men – he was a lot older than me and going bald – said: "You don't want to waste stuff; there's a war on." So I said he was welcome to it and he picked it up, pulled out some bits of grass and ate it. I thought: Some people! But I didn't say anything.

In the afternoon we had the second balloon to do. So you can tell how whacked I felt when I cycled home. At this time, home was still in Dore because Lonzo still had a fortnight to do. But a lot of our stuff was already at Dronfield.

There was a car parked outside our house – a black Morris Minor. When I got in the living room, Denny was on the settee, and opposite him on the armchair was this big man in a green check jacket, green check waistcoat and brown corduroy trousers. Denny stood up. He said, "Josie, this is Gerry Tordoff. Gerry, this is Josie." I put out my hand and Gerry stood up too, smiled broadly, and shook it vigorously.

I gave Gerry the once-over through my clear-glass spectacles. He was about fifty years old, broad-faced with a florid complexion and good teeth – though they might have been false. He was also broad-shouldered and, though running to fat, looked like a man who could still take care of himself.

Denny said: "Gerry works for Mr McIntyre. He's come to see that we're alright..."

"Come to see the *house* is alright," Gerry corrected him.

"I hope you've found it *is*," I said.

"It checks out good," said Gerry.

"It checks out good," repeated Denny. He glanced at me and we both smiled like two people who know the difference between an adjective and an adverb.

I said: "I'll make a pot of tea."

Denny said: "We've already had something a bit stronger." That was when I saw the two whisky glasses.

"A cup of tea would still be great, Mrs Morrow," said Gerry. And I didn't correct him about us being married. That was the moment I realised I liked him – despite his passion for different-coloured trousers.

I went into the kitchen, lit the gas, boiled the kettle, made the tea, got out our Careless Talk Costs Lives tray, put out a small jug of real milk, a precious bowl of sugar, and three cups to make sure I would be part of any further conversation. Back in the living room, I got Gerry to pull out the small walnut table from the side of the Welsh dresser and I put the tray on the table and sat next to Denny on the settee. I said: "How many sugars, Mr Tordoff?"

"It's alright," said Denny, "anything you say to me is alright in front of Josie."

"Even the number of sugars you take." I couldn't resist it!

"She knows all about the ration books," said Denny.

And Gerry laughed. "Three, please," he said. "Sugar's good for you. It gives you energy." Then he looked back at Denny. He said: "There's two packages. I need to take one of them back."

"They're upstairs," said Denny.

"Tell me what I'm looking for and I'll fetch it," I said.

"No, it's alright," said Denny. He got up and walked smartly out of the room. Gerry and I drank our tea.

"How long have you known Denny?" I asked.

"Three, maybe four years, on and off. But I have to say he's kept *you* a secret. How long have you been hitched?"

"Seems like a lifetime," I said. "But it's only a few months."

"You're just what he needs and no mistake." There was a moment when I nearly blushed. Then Gerry said: "Somebody to keep house. If he's got one fault, it's that he's a very untidy boy."

I didn't know what to say to that. So I took another drink.

Then Denny came back in with the parcel in his hand. It was about the size of a big book, like an encyclopedia, and wrapped in lots of brown paper so you couldn't tell the shape. Gerry stood up and Denny gave it him.

"What's in that?" I asked.

"Best you don't know," said Denny.

"I'm afraid he's right about that," said Gerry, "Thanks for the tea, Mrs Morrow." And he shook my hand again. As he was going out, he said: "By the way, I don't know if you've heard – the Germans have invaded Russia."

Denny saw Gerry out. When he came back, he said: "Joe Stalin may be a son of a bitch, but now he's *our* son of a bitch. That's the best news since we got them back from Dunkirk."

I didn't really want to talk about Stalin. "What was it?" I asked. But he just stood, tight-lipped and smiling

I said: "It was a gun, wasn't it?"

He was still tight-lipped but not smiling anymore.

"So you're not a gangster? So you're not Al Capone? But you keep guns for people!"

"Just looking after it, Josie. It's all wrapped up like nobody's business. You saw that. I'm just looking after it..."

"For Lonzo."

"Of course for Lonzo. Like I'm looking after his house. Like I've not got much choice."

I said: "You've got to get away. From Lonzo. From all of it."

"Yeh, sure. Soon we'll be out of here, living in that lovely farmhouse..." He took me in his arms.

"Lovely farmhouse," I repeated. I let him kiss me. Then I said: "Your friend Gerry – he doesn't really think we're married, does he?" Then I answered my own question. "Of course he doesn't. I'm not even wearing a ring."

Chapter Eleven

AT THE BARRAGE BALLOON centre where I worked, there was a tall wire fence round the area and always a uniformed RAF lance corporal at the gate. His name was Hawkins and he was young and he had a toothbrush moustache. But when I got to work this particular day, there was a uniformed policeman there as well. OK, I thought as I wheeled my bike in, it can't be anything to do with me. Just keep your eyes front and don't walk too fast.

Both of them checked my ID even though Hawkins knew me by sight and didn't usually bother with it. "What's all this?" I asked and he sighed. The uniformed policeman said: "You'll find out about it soon enough, Miss." And Hawkins said: "There's a meeting in North Hangar," and he pointed to the main hangar where we had the admin section. As if I thought he might mean the Abbey in the Jane Austen novel!

When I got inside the hangar, the rest of the team had already arrived and were sat round on wooden chairs. Christine was there too – she now spent most of her time in her office on the site. Standing next to her was a young man in a light blue suit and navy blue tie who looked like John Mills in *Goodbye Mr Chips*. He had that thing of hair flicked over his forehead which I liked in John Mills, though I didn't reckon him half as nice as Robert Donat who was the star of the film.

Christine stepped forward and said: "OK, we're all here now." I was surprised she used an Americanism because she was usually very, very English and preferred *alright*. Maybe it showed she was nervous. "The gentleman by my side is Detective Inspector Peters from Sheffield CID." That brought what I can only describe as a sharp intake of breath from the dozen people sitting down. I still had to get to the front row for the one remaining seat. "Nearly standing room only," I said to Det Insp Peters when I was close enough, and I got a smile in return.

He then stepped forward and spoke to the room. "It's

actually Sergeant," he said, "Detective *Sergeant*." He turned to Christine: "But thank you, ma'am, for promoting me." That got a laugh and some people – including me – relaxed a bit. "The reason I'm here," he said, "is because there have been some disappearances from this barrage balloon unit." Then he corrected himself. "I don't mean *people* disappearing – I'm sure you'd all have noticed if that had happened. No, I mean things going missing."

"Theft," said Christine.

Again the intake of breath and people looked round at each other. Except me. Maybe I'd got used to the criminal world by now, but it didn't surprise me anymore that the people round me were thieving.

"Some paint," said Christine. And because, I guess, that didn't sound like anything too terrible: "Some tools as well."

One of the men put it into words: "That doesn't seem worth a real detective coming all the way out here, even if he *is* only a sergeant." More laughter.

Det Sgt Peters said: "The reason you've got plain clothes out here is the nature of your establishment. This is a sensitive area. If unauthorised personnel are finding it easy to get into these buildings, it might end up as something more serious than tea-leafing. Like spying or sabotage."

We all went silent then to show we took it seriously. But I don't think anybody really did. Somebody said: "If it's a security problem, isn't it up to the RAF to sort it out?"

Det Sgt Peters said: "If it's outsiders getting in here, then, yes, it is up to the RAF. But if it's insiders taking stuff out, that would widen the investigation. What CID can do is try to eliminate that possibility. One reason I'm here today is to warn you that you will for a while be under police surveillance. If you find a PC coming round to your house to ask questions, please understand it doesn't mean we think you're guilty of anything, only that we have to check up on everyone who works here. We may also be asking to search your premises."

"It's because of national security," Christine said.

One of our lads was called Tony and he fancied himself a

bit of a Tommy Handley like on the wireless. He shouted across to one of the other men: "Hey, Harry, what's this I've been hearing about you painting your Anderson shelter silver?" And Harry shouted back: "It's to confuse the German bombers."

"Well," said Christine as the laughter bubbled up again, "I know we *do* take this seriously and I know all of you will be co-operating with Detective *Sergeant* Peters and his men. I've already taken the liberty of giving him your names and addresses. We must get to the bottom of this matter as soon as possible. Thank you for your time." She and the detective exchanged glances. I could see she was biting her lip.

Then I started biting mine. The address Christine would have given the police was Aunt May's, but they'd soon find out I was never there. So they'd come back to me, their eyes full of suspicion, and I'd have to give them Alonzo McIntyre's address and... they'd be round to search it, wouldn't they? They'd be pretty stupid not to. And they'd find the forged ration cards and the brown paper parcels. Oh God, why did all this have to come up now? Another few weeks and we'd be moved to our cottage, and...

Alright, I thought, what do I do about it? I tell Denny right away. He moves the stuff out to wherever he's got a friend who'll take it over for now. Lonzo and Gerry need never know there was a problem. Denny won't like it, I thought, but it's not my fault, it's just...

It's just the Father in the Sky having a bit of a joke. Silver bloody paint!

That night, I told Denny what had happened. "No problem, sweetheart," he said. He made a phone call, bundled the stuff into the Bentley and drove off. Two hours later he was back.

"Where's it all gone?" I asked.

"Ahah!" he said, "ees better you know notheeng, seenyorita!" in a sort of Mexican accent which he must have picked up from a cowboy film. And he kissed me. Then he said: "This detective chap, don't wait for him to pick up on the address thing. Phone him up and tell him yourself. Even

better, go in to see him. Be friendly. It never hurts to have
friends in the force."

*

And that's what I did. It was my day off. I phoned first. I
said: "It's Josie Cawthorne." There was silence. "I was at the
meeting about the silver paint. I'm the one who came in late
and said: 'Standing room only'."

And yes, he remembered me! I said: "I've actually got
some information for you but I'd rather not talk over the
phone. Can I come into the station?"

He said: "I'll be on my break in an hour's time. Why
don't we have lunch?"

And I thought: Cheeky bugger! And I said: "Yes. That
would be nice."

We went to The Shakespeare pub, which was just a few
doors down from the police station. We both of us had fish
and chips and he had half of bitter and got me an Indian tonic
water. I said: "That address you have for me is wrong. I want
to give you my real one."

His left eyebrow shot up a bit. He put down his knife and
fork and took out his notebook and a fountain pen.

I took the pen and wrote my address in the book. I said: "I
hope you can read my writing."

He repeated the address. He said: "I think you have very
neat handwriting."

I said: "Thank you."

He said: "Why do you have two addresses?"

This was the moment of truth. I knew that once I told him
I was living with a man, I would be marked down as a fallen
woman and he wouldn't be paying me any more
compliments about my handwriting. But I couldn't see any
way out. I said: "I'm living with my fiancé. We can't marry
at the moment because I'm under 21 and my parents don't
like him. But we've applied to the courts..."

"Yes," he said, very man-of-the-worldish. But I could see
I'd bothered him. "Yes, I see. Well, thanks for telling me."

"And I realise," I said, "that I must tell my superior officer my correct address right away." I tried to look coy. "But it's all a bit embarrassing."

"Yes," he said, then quickly: "No, it's just one of those things." It was as though he was saying: We can still be friends. What was it Denny had said? It never hurts to have friends in the force. But pretty soon somebody at the nick would take a look at that address and the name of Alonzo McIntyre Esq would rear its ugly head. What a shame.

I offered to pay for my fish and chips but he wouldn't hear of it. When we got outside, there was a broad-shouldered man in a wide-brimmed trilby hat with a cigarette in his mouth passing by. Obviously another detective. He nodded to *my* detective and said: "Ey up, Jell."

"Ey up," said my detective.

"Jell?" I said, "What's that?"

My detective looked embarrassed. "It's a nick-name," he said. "Short for Jelly."

"That's a funny nick-name. How'd you get it?"

"One day," he said, "I'll tell you the full story."

But I could see that wasn't likely to happen. Shame. But never mind.

Chapter Twelve

I GOT BACK HOME at the end of a Friday and there was the black Morris Minor again. I walked into the lounge and there were Gerry and Denny pacing about over a small, squat man sitting in one of the armchairs. He wore glasses without rims and his thin black hair was plastered back from his forehead. His suit was charcoal grey and well cut, with slightly padded shoulders. I'd never seen a picture of Alonzo McIntyre Esq, but I didn't need to be told this was the man on the envelope.

"Hello, Mr McIntyre," I said, "I see you got out." And I walked across and held out my hand.

He raised his right arm by first raising his right shoulder and I got the impression that movement was painful. He took my hand and kissed the back of it. A slow kiss, a bit sloppy. Then there was a rumble of laughter deep in the caverns of his insides. He said: "I was told you were a lovely lady, Josie. Ah. A lady worth meeting." I couldn't place the accent, but his voice was as deep as his laugh and his pronunciation as slow as his movement. I guessed English was very much his second language. I remembered Denny talking about Lonzo's Italian, Scottish and Mexican blood. Though he didn't sound like anybody in a cowboy picture.

His skin was what I'd call dirty olive and his teeth would have been brilliant if they hadn't been chipped in a few places. It was difficult to tell how old he was, because men who can't move too well get fat early in life, and losing his hair might be no more than bad luck.

I noticed there was a bottle of whisky on the walnut table, already opened, and only a single glass. I said: "It looks like I'm down to make the tea again." I motioned to Gerry and Denny. "Won't you gentlemen sit down as well? You look very uncomfortable."

The Uncomfortable Ones sat. I went into the kitchen, made the tea and came back. I sat in the second armchair next to Lonzo and passed out the teas. I wondered what sort of conversation we'd have this time.

Lonzo's tea was black, no sugar. He didn't touch it. He said: "You got a cigarette, ah, Josie?"

I took another gulp from my tea, put it down, opened my handbag and held out the packet.

Lonzo took one. He said: "And a light?"

I took out my lighter – the one with *Love from Denny* inscribed on it – and lit the cigarette. I'd given Denny a cheap brass ring in exchange, to make him know I wasn't really *that* much under his spell; but I'd had his initials engraved on it so he wouldn't find it easy to give away.

Lonzo took a lung full of smoke, and blew it out in my direction. Then he looked at me hard and said: "Are you the one responsible, ah, for keeping my house so beautiful?"

"Well," I said, "I make Denny do a lot of the dusting."

This time the laughter was like a dam bursting and Gerry and Denny were forced to join in. I'd disliked Lonzo ever since I heard about him, but now I could feel the physical power of him, something that his slowness emphasised. He said: "I take it there's no chance of my keeping you on as housekeeper?"

Denny started to say something. "No," I said quickly, "we've already got a place lined up. Not as nice as this, of course."

"Of course. You young people need to be alone together. Not, ah, like the old men. Not like Gerry and me."

I could feel the heat coming from Gerry, but I pretended not to notice. Finally Lonzo said: "I'm staying in a hotel for a little while, doing business with, ah, a few professional friends. When you've been away a while, people sometimes take advantage, so I'm making sure this is not the case." Another pause. "But I intend to return soon. Denny, ah, tells me the coppers might be coming round to ask some questions but that all the problem stuff is out of the way."

"That's what he tells me too."

"He's a good boy, your Denny."

"That's why I chose him."

For the first time since I'd been in the room, Lonzo

looked at Denny. "You," he said, pointing the cigarette, "are a lucky young man. Don't let anybody tell you different." He turned back to me. "I don't suppose you've, ah, made him dust the Bentley too?"

I said: "I'm sure it'll be just as smart as when you last rode in it."

"I hope not. I'm a natural slob. That car's too good for me." Then he looked at Gerry. "OK, I'm ready to leave. The Morris Minor calls. Efficient and, ah, unremarkable. That kind of combination can be very useful." He crushed out the cigarette in his palm and shoved the stub in his jacket pocket. He said to Gerry: "Mr Chauffeur, you go out and check the car. Make sure it's good and ready." Gerry stood up and left the room. Lonzo looked at Denny again. "Hey, good boy. You go help him, OK?"

Denny hesitated. I looked across at him and nodded. He followed Gerry.

Lonzo waited maybe a minute. It seemed to me he might actually be counting the seconds. I drank some more tea. Then Lonzo put down his glass and jumped to his feet. Very fast. Very surprising. And he grabbed hold of my breast.

And I threw the tea in his face.

He shouted and stumbled and fell back into the armchair and pulled out a handkerchief and wiped his face. And then he did the Lonzo laugh again.

I'd drunk most of the tea already and all that had happened was the last dribble had splashed on the carpet. And it was nearly cold anyway.

And then Denny walked in. He said: "What happened? What's the commotion?"

"I spilt some tea on the carpet," I said, "and now I'll have to get a rag and wipe it. Silly me." And I went out to the kitchen.

When I got back, Lonzo had gone. I knelt down and patted the tea stain with the wet rag. Denny said: "You think I should've done more. You think I should have stood up to him more."

I said: "What was there to stand up about? You did

everything right."

"It's just," he said, "that I made out I was a big shot. I mean when we first met. Now you see I'm not. I'm just an errand boy. Lonzo wanted somebody to look after the place. Keep track of his business friends. It seemed OK. Money for nothing. I went to see him in Wakefield jail. Today was only the second time we've ever met. I've been stupid."

"Well, you're not stupid anymore." I grabbed his hand and kissed the back of it the way Lonzo kissed mine. "I never wanted Al Capone, remember?"

*

On the Monday, just before lunch, one of the secretaries came into the hangar. She said: "Can you come along to Christine's office? There's a phone call for you."

When I got there, I said to Christine: "Who is it?" I'd been so nervous I'd run most of the way. I thought: The only person who'd call me at work is Denny. Maybe something had gone wrong with him and Lonzo. Maybe he'd somehow found out what Lonzo did to me. Maybe Lonzo told him. Now I was about to pick up the receiver, my nerve failed me.

Christine said: "You'll be surprised to know who it is. But *I'm* not. Here, I'll leave you alone." And she went out.

"Is that Miss Cawthorne?" asked the voice of Det Sgt Peters.

I took a deep breath. "Yes, Sergeant."

"Let me ask you out to lunch again. You know I *do* have something I want to talk to you about. Something serious."

So. It wasn't what I thought. I had to stop myself laughing out loud. "Yes," I said. And there we were again, ninety minutes later, with the fish and chips and the half of bitter and the Indian tonic.

"You're not surprised," he said.

"No."

"You'll know what this is about."

"Better tell me."

"I did a check on that address you gave me."

"And you've found out it's owned by Lonzo Mack."

"And he came out of prison last week."

"I know. I met him on Friday." I reached out to touch my detective's arm, then thought better of it. "Look, it's like this. My boyfriend – my fiancé – has been looking after the house. That's all. Sort of managing things. A business arrangement."

"You know what Lonzo's business is? You know what Lonzo got sent down for?"

"I know he does black market. I know he got three years for receiving."

"No. It was conspiracy to cause grievous bodily harm. And it was *seven* years. He's out two years early on account of good behaviour."

I felt my blood run hot and cold. "No," I said, "there's a mistake."

"No," he said, "there's no mistake. And there's no mistake about what he does for a living. He does *anything*. Prostitutes. Drugs. Blags. Protection. He hurts people. Sometimes just to show he's in control. He went to prison because he set his boys on Billy Greenborough, a bookie that wouldn't pay his dues. Slashed his face top-to-bottom and left-to-right with razors. Billy isn't dead, but he might as well be. And there's at least two people Lonzo *has* actually killed, but we can't prove it."

"No, no," I said.

"Yes, yes," he said and he banged his fist twice on the table so that several people looked round at us to see what the commotion was about. Then he stopped. He stopped speaking too. And *I* couldn't think of anything to say.

Denny had lied to me. Oh God, oh God!

Chapter Thirteen

I GOT BACK ANGRY. Angry and scared. I let myself into Lonzo's house with what was really Lonzo's key, copied for Denny, who'd copied it for me. I was way down on what you might call Lonzo's key chain, and I wondered briefly if there were other people who had keys, people I didn't even know existed, people who could just walk in and... what? I thought: *Seven years for GBH.* I thought: *Shit!*

Denny was in the bath. Normally I'd go up and watch him naked, but today I wasn't in the mood. I made a mug of tea and sat in the lounge while I waited.

Denny came down in his blue fluffy dressing gown, a towel still in his hand, his hair still wet and skew-whiff. "Hello, luv," he said and flicked me with the towel and sat down.

I said: "Tell me about fencing, Denny. Tell me how people can get badly hurt from fencing. Is it because they take the little buttons off the swords?"

He looked at me as if I'd gone daft.

I said: "I know that Lonzo didn't go to jail for being a fence. He set his lads on a bookie and they cut him up badly and Lonzo got seven years."

Denny grunted. He said: "You've been talking to someone."

"Someone who told me the truth. Someone who doesn't lie to me like you do."

"OK. Now you know. But that doesn't alter..."

"Maybe it does. Maybe it alters everything. How many other lies have you told me?"

The muscles in his face tensed. At least he had the grace to avoid my eyes, to suddenly look down at his feet. At least he could still be embarrassed. Or was he just a good actor? "OK, I've lied to you. But only when it was necessary. I thought you'd leave me if you knew. Is that what you're going to do now?"

I thought: Fair question, Denny. I said: "I don't know. I

should leave you. But I don't know. One thing I *do* know is you've got to get away from him and from Gerry and from all the other dirtbags you're hanging about with. And you've got to do it now!"

"More easy said than done." He stood up, reached over to the mantelpiece, picked up the Park Drive, took a box of matches out of his dressing gown pocket and sat down again. I thought: He's giving himself time to think. Time to sort out an alibi.

He said: "OK, the lies. Yes, I've lied to you. I'm sorry. I promise I won't lie to you again."

I snorted.

He lit the cigarette, waved the match till it went out. I thought: More time, Denny? Can't you get it over with? Can't you tell me anything straight? He said: "When you're in with somebody like Lonzo, it's a life sentence. You don't just walk away. There. That sums it up. Are you happy now?"

"What other lies have you told me?"

"Not a lot. My dad really was a school teacher and my mum really was a typist. And they *were* really killed in a car crash."

"Why should I believe that now?"

"No reason. It's up to you. Oh yeh, I *wasn't* an only child. I had a brother. Tim."

"Where's he now?"

"Dead. Passed away. Gone to a better life. Tuberculosis. He was fourteen."

"And the orphanage?"

"It was pretty much like I told you. Only maybe the food was better than I made out."

"You didn't mention the food."

"Then it was *exactly* like I told you."

"We've not got on to Uncle Ernest yet."

"Alright. I never had an uncle Ernest. When I got out of the orphanage, I went anywhere I could go to find work. Not all those jobs were legal."

"Go on."

"You ever hear of the Badger Game?"

"Tell me about it."

"Usually it works like this: some nice looking bint – some nice looking *girl* – makes eyes at some middle-aged drunk slob and lures him into a flat. Then a couple of heavies come in and take his wallet. Mostly, the slob doesn't report it because he's got a wife and kids. So it's practically foolproof."

"And...?"

"Some lads I got to know went one better. Playing the queers. It's the same rumble but it's some nice looking *boy*. And the punter never complains. Because being queer is illegal, get it?"

"And you were the nice looking boy?"

"Oh, I never had to *do* anything, I was just the come-on. And I was under-age anyway. You know the sort of jail term you'd get if you were a man messing about with an under-age boy?"

"No. It's never been a subject that interested me."

"So nobody *ever* complains about that one."

"What about Borstal? Or did you make that up as well?"

"One day it all went wrong. The punter had a heart attack. I went to the flat downstairs and they dialled 999. Ambulance and police. So of course it all came out. The coppers wanted me to squeal on the other lads, but I wouldn't."

"Very loyal of you."

"Loyalty is one of my virtues."

"What about the boxing thing, then? And Mr Herbert, the gym teacher?"

"Yeh, I learned boxing in Borstal. But it wasn't the gym teacher that taught me how to put some lad out with a fist in the back of the neck. Or kick some bloke in the balls. No, it was the other lads that taught me."

"You've had a good education, then?"

"I've had the education I needed to get where I am today."

I thought: Right, where do I go from here? I couldn't

think of anything more to say.

But thought-reader Denny could. "Like I told you, being part of Lonzo's bunch is like being married – it's for life. The only way I could get out..."

I let his sentence hang. I didn't want to make anything easy for him.

"It would mean going on the run," he said.

"You mean from the police?"

"No, I don't. You're still not getting it. I mean on the run from Lonzo."

This was deep water for me. "How would we do that?"

"We change our names. Then we go somewhere – London, Manchester..." He paused. "... New York."

I laughed. "For that we'd need all sorts of papers. And there's a bloody war on, or have you forgotten?"

"They can be got. I'm in the business of forging stuff, remember? *You* couldn't tell the difference, could you?"

"Denny, those are *ration cards*. If we went to New York, we'd need passports, visas, birth certificates, vaccination certificates... I don't know what."

"OK, maybe New York's out of it. For now. Wait till Hitler's all over and done with and *then* we'll think about New York."

"And we can't go on the run from Lonzo because he'd get at us. Friends, relatives..."

"I'm an orphan, remember? And Lonzo only knows you as Josie. He doesn't even know your surname. There's nobody left for him to threaten."

OK, he'd got an answer to that one. Now, I thought, I'd really go ahead and put the kibosh on it. "And most of all, Denny, we'd need money."

"Right, luv. You said it. Got it in one. How does thirty thousand pounds sound?" A pause. "Look, Josie, you know what kind of ratbag Lonzo is. He'd cut your throat soon as look at you."

"I know what I've been told. Dope. Prostitutes. Robbery. Protection rackets."

"But that first one – that's where the money is. Dope. And

I'm not just talking Mary Warner. And I'm not just talking amphetamines, which is what the RAF give to their bomber pilots to keep them awake – and they pass the stuff on to people like Lonzo so they can make something on the side. I'm talking cocaine and heroin. That's the coming thing and that's where the money is. Lonzo's people can sell it on for big bucks – but then they've got a problem. It's explaining the money. It's the war that's done it. In the old days you could come back from Paris or Monte Carlo or somewhere and say you won it on roulette or the cards or whatever. But you can't do that in England. Especially now, when all the big races are cancelled. In England, you can't put a bet on two raindrops sliding down a window pane without having the coppers on you. So what do you do?"

"I don't know."

"You bank it. I don't mean you use a *real* bank. You bank it with friends…"

"Business friends. The kind Lonzo was talking about."

"Then you circulate it. But you have to do it slowly. It accumulates but it's not getting you any interest. And people have to be paid for keeping it, so it's actually costing you all the time. If you're Lonzo, it's going out in bits and dabs and you're not seeing the benefit right now. But you have to put up with that. You and me, on the other hand, are a different proposition. *We're* not under surveillance all the time from the coppers. If you and me were looking after it, well, it wouldn't cost us anything. First of all, we could open *lots* of small bank accounts, nice young married couple like us. Nobody'd get suspicious."

"Married?"

"Why not? We could have a dozen different names if we wanted. I can do us a dozen different birth certificates, driving licences, marriage certificates, all the ID we'd need."

"So would we really be married? Or would *all* the certificates be fakes?"

"Of course we'll really be married. That's what we both want, isn't it?"

I leaned across and kissed him.

"OK," he said. "Now we know where we are. But we needn't bank all of it. We'd keep a little bit at home, just to have a good time. In a suitcase under the bed. Or we could keep it in a few old socks and stick 'em up the chimney. As long as we didn't light a fire."

"We'd have to take them down for Christmas," I said.

"They could be our Christmas stockings."

We *both* laughed then. I said: "Where *is* this thirty thousand?"

"There's a man called Bill Netty. He runs a pub in Bradford. He's an ex-copper and he's even got a collection of truncheons and handcuffs hanging over the top of the bar like other pubs have horse brasses."

"You serious?"

"Oh yes. And all the other coppers go there for a late-night booze session every Friday. They lock the doors dead on half past ten, then they drink till midnight. And he's the man with the dough."

"And we're just planning to go in and take it off him?"

"Yeh. More or less."

"We go in after closing time when the CID are all in the snug, and we say: *Hello, Bill. We've come to take away Lonzo's thirty thousand pounds.* And he says: *Right you are. And he goes and gets the money box...*"

"Ah," said Denny. He got up and left the room. After a couple of minutes, he came back holding a brown paper parcel – like the one I'd seen him handing over to Gerry. "Go on. Open it."

I started tearing at the paper. Slowly a shape emerged. "I knew it was a gun all along," I said. I listened to my voice and how stupid I sounded.

"Not just a gun, Josie. It's a Ballester-Molina semi-automatic. Used a lot by the Argentine army. It's based on the American Colt."

I took it out of the wrapping. It was blue steel with a brown ridged grip. I stroked the grip. It was strangely satisfying. But there was something else in the parcel, like a small metal telescope without a lens.

Denny said: "That's a silencer. For when you want to be private."

"I guess there's a lot I don't know about guns and shooting people."

"Main thing about shooting people, Josie, is – hit them in the chest first. That puts them down. Then go for the head. That finishes it."

"Have *you* ever shot somebody?"

"Don't be daft. I read it in a cowboy story."

"So we're not going to kill him then? This Bill person?"

"Of course not. We're just going to frighten him."

I said: "It's not loaded, is it?"

"Would I be that stupid?"

I stood up, walked across the room, pointed it at the pouffe and pulled the trigger. It clicked harmlessly. "No, you're not that stupid." Then a thought occurred. "You told Lonzo and me you'd got rid of all the dodgy stuff, taken it out of the house…"

"Except this. I have a special hiding place for this."

"Well," I said, "you like to live dangerously."

"And so," he said, "do you."

Chapter Fourteen

WE HIRED A SMALL VAN and driver to take our stuff out to Dronfield. It was just a box of Denny's gym things, the All Dry battery portable wireless, the portable gramophone, a pair of extra chairs for the kitchen and a couple of suitcases. Even so, the van was full. Denny said it was my clothes taking up all the room.

I was just showing him the front door key to Lonzo's house, still attached to my key ring. I was going to tell him I was taking it as a souvenir to remind me never to go back to any place that Lonzo was involved with. Or something like that. Instead, I said: "Clothes? I don't bloody have any. You're always saying you prefer me without them."

"And so I do."

"And where's the gun?" I asked.

"In with the dumbbells."

"Hope it's safe, then."

"Safe as houses."

Denny went on ahead in the Bentley – Lonzo had said he could keep it till after the move. So there we were. Finally. Unpacking. In our own home, not Lonzo's. Well, *not* our own home, technically. We didn't own it any more than we'd owned the place in Dore. But we didn't have a gangster for a landlord.

First thing we did was take what I call a really practical tour of the house: I made us a cup of tea in the kitchen, then we lounged about on the armchairs in the living room, then I drew the curtains in the main bedroom and we made lots of love, then I had myself a hot bath with Denny watching me.

Then he said: "We should look around. See what's outside."

"It's just farmland. I didn't know you were a country boy. Maybe they'll let you milk the cows now and again."

He flicked a bath towel across my breasts. "Oww!" I said.

"Call it my criminal nature, Josie, but I like to know the ins-and-outs of a place. Just in case I've got to move out

79

quickly, make a getaway." And he laughed as though he'd made a good joke. Though he might just have been laughing about slapping me across the breasts.

So I got dressed again in slacks, sweater and windjammer jacket and we put on wellies and went for a walk. And it was lovely: hedges and birdsong and lots of big fields, though I'm going to have to stop there. I mean, I made a joke about what a townie Denny was, but I was just as bad myself. The only bird I knew to recognise was a robin redbreast and only then because they were always turning up on Christmas cards.

We'd been walking maybe fifteen minutes when we passed a clump of elm trees – those I *could* recognise – and turned a corner and nearly fell into a huge hole with columns of dirty white rock rising up in front of us six yards away on the other side.

"Elmwood Quarry," said Denny, "I knew it was round here somewhere."

"It's dangerous. They could put up a sign, at least."

Denny grinned. "Why? People who live round here know where it is and they know not to fall in. And they don't care about foreigners like us. I know a bit about quarries. I know that this quarry used to provide stones for Westminster Abbey. Any bit of a repair job and the Bishop was up here like a shot, signing the contracts."

"How long ago was that?"

"No idea. It's just something I read. I said I knew a *bit* about quarries, but not enough to write a book. Anyway, they've not been working it since the 19th century." He paused. "I like quarries."

"Why?"

"When I was a kid, I used to swim in quarries. Me and my mates. Stupid and dangerous, but it's what kids do. And even then I thought…"

"What?"

"It's a great place to hide things. No, not just *hide*. Throw away. Get rid of. Lose forever. I was a good swimmer when I was a kid. But the danger in quarries is: the water looks calm and peaceful on top, but there are currents below and holes and caves and places to get pulled down into and disappear till the Day of Judgement."

"In your case," I said, "the Day of Judgement itself might be the *real* thing you should worry about, not swimming in a quarry." And then the thought struck me. "You're not going to do that, are you? You're not going to strip off and jump in just to show me what a brave man you are?"

He turned and faced me and stepped up close. "No. Absolutely not. I told you: it's a kid thing, it's stupid. I was a stupid kid, but I've not been stupid for a long time now."

And he took me in his arms. And he hugged me and kissed me. It was a slow, lingering kiss.

And then suddenly he picked me up and pulled my legs up high against his chest. And I squealed. And he said: "Of course, I could always throw *you* in the quarry, Josie. If you ever got to be a nuisance. That might be fun."

And I squealed again. And he kissed me again. And it shut me up. And he went on kissing me, not letting up, not letting me breathe. When I finally broke away, I was breathless and panting and he put me down. And I staggered a bit.

"Careful," he said, "you don't want to go over the edge."

And I didn't. So I sat down instead and gulped some air back into my lungs. And after a while he put out a hand and pulled me to my feet and hugged me hard and we went back past the elm trees and back to our new home.

Chapter Fifteen

"MAY, YOU'RE NOT GOING TO LIKE what you're going to hear."

"Not for the first time," she said.

"I'm going to have to take a powder – you know what that means?"

"You're going to skedaddle out of here and never be heard of again. I've not heard that one outside a James Cagney film." She looked round her living room. "Well, you'd best sit down while you're still here."

We sat. It was early morning but I'd known she'd be up and dressed and ready for anything. Or nearly anything. That was May. I said: "Something's coming up that might be very bad for me if I stick around."

"Bad from the police?"

"If only! Well, bad from the police *alright*. But worse from certain people who would do me a lot more harm than the police."

"Denny's friends."

"They won't be his friends any more than they'll be mine once this thing happens."

"I'm guessing this thing involves large quantities of money."

"It has to. Otherwise we couldn't get far enough away. We might go to Manchester, London…" I left out New York. I didn't want her to laugh at me.

"Manchester!" she said. "London!" she said. She laughed anyway. "Brighton! Hey, why not try Brighton? I've been there twice and enjoyed it both times." She looked away. She clucked her tongue. "So. You're getting out of here and getting lost in some big city and your dad and me will never see you again. How will we know you're even alive?"

"I'll write. I'll write to *you*, and you pass the news on to Dad. I'll catch a train to somewhere and give you a different postmark each time."

"My! You *have* got it all worked out!"

"It's the only way Denny and me can be together and live a decent life."

May jumped to her feet. "Decent life!" she shouted. "This is never going to be a decent life for you, you fool! Oh, I thought you had brains as well as looks but I was wrong. I thought you were all grown-up but you're still a bloody schoolgirl!" She put her face in her hands and wept loudly.

"It's not as bad as all that, May…"

"Yes, it is!" She showed her crumpled, tear-stained face. "It's worse than anything else you could've thought of. If there's big money involved, do you really think crossing over the Pennines is going to stop people finding you?"

"We'll have new identities…"

"Don't tell me! You'll bleach your hair like Jean Harlow and Denny'll grow a moustache and pass for Errol Flynn. God, give me strength!" And she did something I'd never seen her do. She looked up to the heavens and brought her hands together in a gesture of silent prayer.

I was silent too. I took off my glasses and wiped them on my sleeve.

May sat down. She said: "But that's not the worst. No, it's not. That crackpot plan of hiding out in Manchester may be the *stupidest* thing but it's not the worst! You know what the worst is? It's leaving your family, your people. Your mum's dead, God rest her. I know you don't get along with your dad. And you and I have not always been so close. But we're the only kin you've got. And you don't leave kin!" She smashed her palm on the arm of her chair. Then she stopped. And when she spoke again, her tone was different, quieter. "Well, I suppose I know the reason for all this. It's the war. Mr Hitler and his bombers. He's changed the world. He's already destroyed half of Europe, now he's destroying us as well and he hasn't even crossed the Channel yet. Well, it's something we'll have to get used to."

I didn't say anything.

She said: "Alright, let's think how to make you safe. As safe as we can. Is there anybody in Denny's lot who knows your family name?"

"No. They know I'm Denny's Josie. That's all."

"Do they know about your barrage balloons? Can they trace you through that?"

"No, they don't. The only one…" I stopped because it hadn't occurred to me till now. "There's a detective. We had lunch. But he's a good man. He won't be blabbing anything about me."

"Good man, is he?" She smiled. "Another poor sod that's fallen for your charms! Well, I can't say I blame him."

I said: "It'll be alright, May."

She said: "No, it won't. But there's nothing can be done. Just make sure you stay safe, you daft little trollop. Dying is the last thing you ever want to do." And she reached over and took my hands in hers. And again it looked like praying.

*

When I got to the balloon centre, Hawkins at the gate, who never checked my ID unless there was a policeman there, said: "They've got him."

"Got who?"

"The bloke who was taking the tools and paint and stuff. It turned out to be Sturridge."

"Sturridge?" And then I placed him. It was the bald man who'd told me not to waste my cheese and tomato sandwich and then pulled the grass out of it and ate it himself. I thought about him: how could anybody steal from their workmates? And when there was a war on, too. But I stopped myself. Poor old bald Mr Sturridge would end up in clink. But whatever he did hardly compared with what Denny and I planned to do. No. I decided I wasn't going to be a whited sepulchre about Mr Sturridge. I said: "How did they know?"

"They went round to *his* house first. Apparently he'd got form for that sort of thing. They found the stuff on top of his wardrobe. Stupid place to hide it. Silly bugger."

So that's why the coppers never came round to Denny and me. They'd already got their man. Lucky for us. I couldn't imagine what Sgt Peters would have said if he'd found the Ballester-Molina semi-automatic in the broom cupboard or wherever.

Then I saw Christine. I thought: Well, it won't be long now and I'll never see her again. I said: "Christine, can I tell you something?" We were out in the hangar at the time.

"Something private?" she said.

I looked round me. I said: "Yes." We went into her office and sat down.

"Alright," she said.

I wanted to say goodbye, that was all. Like I'd done with May. But I couldn't get the words out. Maybe because she used to be a nun and she used to be my teacher. After a while I said: "I've got to go away."

"Why?"

"I can't say."

"Are you pregnant?"

"No!" I nearly shouted it out. "No, it's not that."

"Don't be offended. You'd be surprised how many Catholic girls…"

"No, I wouldn't. I've got May to tell me."

"Oh yes," Christine smiled, "I know a bit about your Aunt May. Well, if it's not that, what is it?"

I couldn't really say: My boyfriend and I are planning to rob a pub. I took a deep breath. "I can't tell you. But it will take a few weeks. I'm not sure how long. But it's not an abortion. No way." I thought: Why am I saying this? All this stuff about a few weeks? It's a lie. I'm going away forever. Why can't I just say goodbye, like I planned?

She said: "Is it leave you want? Compassionate leave?"

"What's that?" Though I knew exactly what it was.

"Well, if you had illness in the family. Your aunt May or your dad…"

I nearly said: "No, it's nothing like that." But I stopped myself. "Well…" I said.

"Well, it can't be your aunt May. I know she's still very active. In a lot of things. It must be your dad."

"Well…"

"He's an old man and he's suffered bereavement. Yes, I

85

can see that. I'm sure we can arrange something."

I stayed silent.

"After all," she said, "you're too good a worker to lose."

"Am I really?" It had never occurred to me before.

"A few weeks. A couple of months maybe. To help your father get over his grief. I'll see to that."

Tears welled up in my eyes and there was a choking sensation in my throat. I thought: I can't do this. I'm telling a lie. For no reason. I know I'm never coming back.

I started to say something but Christine interrupted. "I know I can fix this thing. But don't take too long, whatever it is."

"No," I said.

There was a moment's silence then Christine said: "By the way, we had a great night last night. A Stuka and a Heinkel 177. Crews all dead, I understand. And a Junker. All down to our little group."

"Good," I said, then I shouted: "Hurrah!" and waved my fist. It seemed a good way to get all that emotion out of me. Then I remembered Christine in her nun days. I decided to stop celebrating the deaths of our enemies. "I hope I've not offended you, Christine."

"No," she said, "I'm not offended at all." May was right. Hitler *had* changed the world.

Chapter Sixteen

I SAID TO DENNY: "You rented this car? Won't somebody remember you?" It was an Austin 7 four seater, black. The paintwork was scratched and it had a fusty smell.

He said: "I didn't rent it. I bought it. This morning. From somebody I never met before in my life. I paid cash."

"Where'd you get cash?"

"I've been saving for a rainy day. Or a nice investment. So that's what I've done: invested my rainy day money to get hold of some of Lonzo's loot. Speculate to accumulate. Now come on and get in."

I pulled open the door, shoved my brown leather handbag on the floor and squatted in the passenger seat. I was wearing a brown workaday dress with a light three-quarter length coat, which Denny said was good because it wouldn't stand out in a crowd. I hoped the fusty smell didn't rub off on me. Denny turned the key and we were away.

It was end-of-summer but the evenings were still light and warm. Bill Netty's pub was called The Trafalgar and it wasn't really in Bradford; it was some miles out in Great Horton, so it was a nice drive, trees and fields. I felt good about the chance to speed along country lanes. But I felt bloody *terrified* about what we were going to do.

*

We'd been in the Dronfield cottage for two weeks but we hadn't unpacked much of our stuff – only really the toothbrushes and work clothes. We were on tenterhooks. We were like two drunk people. We'd gone over it so many times.

Denny would say: "We get there an hour before ten-thirty closing. Obviously, a woman can't go in a pub by herself, else it would be noticed. When we're in, we sit in a corner, mind our business. I have a pint, you have a lemonade. Here," he'd open up the foolscap sheet with the plan he'd drawn and lay it on the kitchen table, "it's an oblong building, two rooms downstairs – lounge and public bar. Plus the Gents."

"I hope you know what you're talking about."

"I've been there eight times in the past four weeks, mostly lunchtimes – plus a couple of evenings, as you know. I've had a good look round. I've worn different clothes each time, so I won't be remembered. Different hats."

"Show me."

He always liked this bit. He'd put on his black bowler, then take it off and put on his blue check cap.

"Very smart," I'd say and he'd do it all again and we'd both laugh.

"Alright," I'd say, "now tell me what *I* do."

"Alright," he'd say, "there's two rooms upstairs – the bedroom and a storage room. Plus the Ladies. Half an hour before closing, you go up to the Ladies, lock yourself into a cubicle."

"How'd you find out where the Ladies was? I *hope* you didn't take some other girl."

"I wandered up there and had a quick peep and came down again looking very embarrassed." He smiled, so I realised once again what great teeth he had.

"Alright, Denny, pretend I've lost my memory. What's next?"

"I go to the Gents, then I come back and take our glasses to the bar and say goodnight. Two glasses, you see – I hand in two glasses. So Bill and his barmaid think you've left ahead of me. Psychological."

"*Very* psychological."

"Then the barmaid leaves and Bill locks the coppers in for an hour and a half."

"The barmaid *always* leaves?"

"Always. Because she's a respectable girl and she doesn't want to be involved in breaking the licensing laws. Right?"

"Right."

"So there's nobody going to come in and look in the Ladies. Because you don't get girl detectives, do you?"

"What about *Mrs* Netty?"

"Mrs Netty died eighteen months ago. She caught pneumonia after walking in the rain."

"So what happens if the lock-in goes on way after midnight?"

"It won't. My information is: Mr Netty is a bit of an old man these days. Maybe it's losing his wife so sudden. He still does the lock-in thing for old times' sake but there's an understanding it'll all be over by twelve. I've got a contact in CID who thinks I'm called Tony Venables and I'm a sales rep from Doncaster. Like I've always said, it's good to have friends on the Force."

"So let's suppose it all goes to plan, and I've parked myself in the Ladies. What do I do next?"

"You know what you've got to do."

"Tell me again. Pretend I've lost my memory again."

"You wait till Mr Bloody Netty has gone to bed…"

"So I'll have been in the lav two and a half hours at least."

"You're always going on about indoor lavs. You should be pleased. Then you go downstairs very quiet. Behind the bar in the lounge there's a set of hooks for the keys. You open the back door that leads outside. I'll be waiting and I come in on cue."

"It's too easy, Denny – too pat. Let's suppose it goes wrong. Let's suppose Bill catches me before I can get you in."

"Then you make out you're some stupid piece that doesn't know her knickers from her nylons and had a drop too much of the milk stout. And you get out of there fast. Or – you could always offer the bereaved man some tender loving care in exchange for a night's lodging."

"Thanks very much!"

"Either way, we think of a new plan. Well, that's life, isn't it? You got to take some chances. Don't worry. It'll turn out OK. I got a good feeling."

I nodded in spite of myself. There were more holes in Denny's plan than they have on a golf course. But there was something in me – something stupid, maybe, or something plain bad – that made me want to go through with it.

I remembered Christine when she was still Sister Margaret Mary. For some reason I can't recall – because it wasn't on the curriculum – we'd been talking about Balzac's *Thérèse Raquin*. And I said I couldn't believe the lovers went through with killing her husband because it was obviously going to go hopelessly wrong. And Christine said it was a *folie à deux*. That meant two people getting together to convince themselves that a mad scheme was really sensible. Now I knew exactly what she meant.

Chapter Seventeen

WE DID IT MORE OR LESS as we planned it. We got to
The Trafalgar at quarter past nine. We found a little table in a
corner of the lounge. Denny got his pint and my lemonade
and a packet of crisps. The place wasn't packed yet but it
looked as if it would be in the next ten minutes. And it was.

By ten o'clock, all the blinds were drawn anyway because
of the blackout.

Most people in the room, as far as I could tell, were
talking about cricket – there was a local league in the area
and a whole bunch of teams set to play the following day.
One of the teams was Trafalgar Tykes, who regularly used
the pitch behind the pub. There was a red-headed woman at
the next table and she was saying to her mousey friend that
some of the players were in the public bar, and she was
thinking of joining them. But the friend was saying how the
public bar was a bit rough and how the call-up had taken
away all the nice-looking lads and left all the fat middle-aged
farts who couldn't play cricket anyway. "My old dad can run
faster than they can," she said.

Other people were talking about the rationing and about
what Mr Churchill had said on the wireless last night or the
night before about the sacrifices we all had to make.
"Baloney," said an old fella sat near the bar, and somebody
else told him to watch his language. The old man said:
"Baloney isn't bad language," and there was a bit of an
argument about that. Finally he said: "Mr Churchill is all
well and good, but fine words butter no parsnips," and
someone else said you could only butter parsnips these days
if you saved all your coupons. And everybody laughed.

I thought: How is it that we're all in a terrible war and
people can still talk about fat cricketers and parsnips? And
then I thought: How is it we're all in this terrible war and
Denny and I are going to rob the pub tonight?

We had one bad moment. Denny had brought a leather
shopping bag with a zip on it to keep the Ballester-Molina in,

and he put it down under the table. And then, for half a minute, he couldn't find it.

A fat woman in an imitation mink jacket, who was sat on his right, said: "Is this your bag?" and held it up. She said: "You should keep it under your own table."

Denny laughed. He said: "I must have kicked it over to your side by accident."

"Well," she said, "you should be more careful."

"I will in future," he said. He laughed again and he took the bag off her.

And that was about the only time he said anything. When it got to ten o'clock, I nodded to him, reached for my handbag and started walking over to the stairs. Then I realised I'd got the wrong bag. I was carrying the one with the gun. I thought: What will I do? Shall I go back and get my handbag? But then I thought: This whole business is about not being noticed. If I turn and go back, people will remember it. So I just went on up the stairs and into the Ladies.

The red-headed woman's mousey friend was washing her hands in front of a mirror. She looked up when I came in. She said: "I think this war will go on for twenty years."

I said: "No, it won't. Not now Stalin's in it."

She said: "Huh. That Stalin is Hitler's friend, isn't he? He'll go over to Hitler's side again soon as it suits him."

I said: "The Americans might come in."

She said: "What side will they be on?"

I said: "Well, I don't know for sure, but I'm hopeful." Then I held open the door for her and she went out.

I looked across at the line of eight cubicles. Seven of the doors were open and the cubicles empty. The furthest one had its door shut. I couldn't see any legs under it. I gave it a gentle push and it swung open and, yes, there was nobody there. I went inside, pushed the bolt shut, sat on the lav. I thought whether I should pee right away? But no, the best thing was to wait until I *had* to do it. There were bound to be a lot of women coming up in the next half hour. Last pee before going home – for safety's sake. If they could hear *me* peeing, they were less likely to bang on the door or shout at me to hurry up or anything. The thought of anybody trying to hurry me made me nervous. What would I do? Shout back and tell them I was doing my best?

I then thought about how it looked from outside. Even if I wasn't peeing, I should have my knickers down, otherwise it looked weird. So I started pulling them down and then I remembered I had that stupid big leather bag rather than the dinky one I should have brought up. That would look really strange if I left it on the floor. In the end, I stuffed it behind a pipe at the back of the lav. And then I waited.

And it happened just the way I thought it would. I counted the chatter and the footsteps and I reckoned maybe eighteen women, but spaced out enough so as not to trouble me. Then it was quiet. I won't say *silent* because I could hear some noise from the coppers downstairs but it wasn't anything loud or frantic. They'd been drinking all evening and probably half the day, anyway, and they were a bit over it by now. An early start tomorrow for some of them.

This was the bad part. Nothing to do but sit and wait. I kept looking at my wrist watch. I had my pee, and then I thought that, because it was supposed to be empty now, I'd best pull up my knickers and sit side-saddle with my feet up so nobody could see I was there. The whole plan depended on Mr Netty *not* coming in to check after lights out. But supposing he did? I'd better make myself as small as possible.

Time passed. And passed. But eventually I could see it was ten past midnight. But Mr Netty didn't come in. Neither, as far as I could hear, did he even come upstairs. So. Problem. There was Denny, waiting patiently out back, and I was still sat on the lav. Should I risk going down anyway? What would happen if Mr Netty saw me? What if there were other people still there, lying around drunk?

And then I remembered: I'd got the gun. Why not give it a go?

I got up and only then I realised how stiff I was from sitting in that silly position for so long. Never mind. I got the bag and opened it and took out the gun. The silencer wasn't there – Denny must still have it in his coat pocket. Never mind.

I drew back the bolt on the cubicle door and went out. I saw my reflection in the mirror. Josie the gun girl. I looked stupid, as though I didn't know how to hold the thing. Well, I'd better get that right. I'd been to the pictures enough times seeing men carrying guns. I'd just have to think like a man for a bit. I put down the bag and practised my poses. I said things in a whisper like "Don't make any false moves" and "Keep your hands where I can see them". Then I laughed. Then I pulled open the door to the landing. Then I started down the stairs, holding the gun in my right hand, holding the bag in my left. When I got to the bottom, I could see the lights in the public bar were out but the lounge lights were still on. So Mr Netty must still be in the lounge. There I was, still without the keys I needed. And there was Mr Netty between me and the back door where Denny was waiting. Damn fool plan, Denny! Everything's gone wrong! *Except* I had the gun. I walked very slowly and quietly into the lounge.

Mr Netty was sat at one of the tables nearest the bar and he had a bottle of Johnnie Walker in front of him and a tumbler half-full of the stuff in his hand. He didn't look like much: a balding middle-aged man running to fat. He didn't see me at first, maybe because I'd been so quiet, maybe because he was drunk. Suddenly I felt sorry for him. Here he was, a man who'd lost his wife, and he was about to get a Ballester-Molina in the face. But then he'd been a bent copper, hadn't he, making friends with people like Lonzo? What was the phrase Lonzo had used? *Business friends.* So I better toughen up.

I kicked the side of the bar to get his attention. I held the gun out in front of me with both hands. I said: "Don't make any false moves."

Mr Netty looked up. He put down the glass. He said: "Bloody fucking hell!" and jumped to his feet. The bottle fell off the table, landed with a crash and shattered.

94

I said: "Keep your hands where I can see them."

He said: "What's this about?"

I said: "Thirty thousand pounds. I want it."

He said: "Where would *I* get thirty thousand pounds?"

I said: "From Mr McIntyre."

He said: "I don't know any Mr McIntyre."

I said: "Maybe you call him Lonzo."

He went quiet. For maybe a minute. Then: "I don't know what you're talking about."

I said: "Yes, you do." I walked towards him.

He said: "No, I don't."

I didn't know what to say. I didn't want to get caught in one of those children's games of *yes and no*. So I just kept quiet and walked closer. I could feel sweat on my nose.

Then he said: "You don't know how to use that thing."

I remembered then I'd pulled the trigger in our living room when I was testing to see if it was loaded. You actually don't need to know very much to pull a trigger.

He said: "You've still got the safety catch on."

I nearly looked to check, but stopped myself. I knew we were playing *upper hand* to see which of us had got it. This was much more of a grown-up game and I was happy to go with it. After all, I was the one with the gun, safety catch or not. And I knew the best way to test it. I lifted my hands so that the gun was pointing about three feet above his head. And I pulled the trigger.

This time it was loaded. And the safety catch was off, no matter what Mr Netty said.

Kearrrrrrrraaaaaaaaaaaaaaackkkk!!!!!!

The bullet hit the ceiling and took down a lot of plaster. What a bang! Good job The Trafalgar was out in the country! But I hadn't reckoned on the recoil and it nearly knocked me off my feet. I fell back against the bar. I thought: How come I never see John Wayne fall over when he shoots somebody?

I wasn't sure then what exactly happened. Maybe Mr Netty had tried to jump me and fallen over. Maybe he just fell over because of the loud bang and the fact that he was very scared. Anyway, he was lying in what midwives call a foetal position on the floor and holding his leg and moaning.

He said: "Look what you've done, you fucking idiot! I've twisted it!"

I said: "Get up!"

He said: "I can't. I've twisted my leg!"

By now the sweat was running all down my face. I realised I'd done everything I could, short of shooting Mr Netty. Then there was a really loud sound of glass breaking and wood splintering and in less than a minute Denny was in the room. He said: "I heard the bang. You OK, kid?"

Mr Netty shouted: "OK? She's a fucking nut case!"

I said: "He's drunk half a bottle of Johnnie Walker." I said: "Mind where you walk. There's glass all over the floor."

"OK," said Denny, "give me the gun." And I did.

Chapter Eighteen

"OK, MR NETTY," SAID DENNY, "or may I call you Bill?"

Mr Netty said nothing, just kept holding his leg.

"Josie," said Denny, "help Mr Netty to a chair. And give him a cushion."

I got hold of Mr Netty by his left arm and got him to his feet, though he was pretty heavy. Then I put my arm round him for support. I could see one of the chairs near the bar already had a cushion on it and I helped him across, being careful to avoid the broken glass, and sat him down. It seemed to take an age. He still said nothing.

I said: "I'm sorry you hurt your leg."

Mr Netty said: "Thanks." I couldn't tell if he was being sincere. His face had gone from red to pale so I could see he was sobering up.

"Now, Mr Netty," said Denny, "I want to know where you keep the money that our mutual friend Mr McIntyre has entrusted to your safe keeping." He took out the silencer and screwed it on to the gun barrel.

Mr Netty said nothing.

"Please, Mr Netty, let's not play games, eh? You can see I've got a gun in my hand. You know it's loaded because it's already taken down a part of your ceiling. So you know we're not kidding."

Mr Netty said nothing

I could feel my sweat had turned cold. I thought: What happens if he doesn't talk? Is Denny going to shoot him? Then I thought: No, no, Denny wouldn't kill anybody. Anyway, it wouldn't get us the money. Then I thought: Is Denny going to torture Mr Netty? I knew quite a bit about the Inquisition and their particular methods of torture, but Mr Netty didn't have any racks or iron maidens lying about in the Lounge. It's a funny thing that the Church has never actually condemned the Inquisition in so many words – a thought that suddenly came to me that very moment.

I went across to Denny. I said: "We've got to talk."

He said: "Not just now."

I said: "Yes. Just now." I was trying to keep my voice down so that Mr Netty wouldn't get the wrong idea, think we were going soft or anything. Finally I got Denny to come with me as far as the doorway and I whispered to him. I said: "What are you going to do?"

He whispered: "Scare him a bit."

I said: "But we're not going to do anything bad to him, are we?"

Denny said: "I thought I might hit him a couple of times. With the gun."

I said: "You can't do that. He's already injured."

Denny said: "OK. I'll just mention it to him. We can hope it doesn't come to that. "

Then we walked back to where Mr Netty was sat.

Denny said to him: "There's got to be a strongbox. In a safe. I don't want to spend the next couple of hours turning over all these nice reproductions of paintings you've got in your establishment, looking for that safe. I don't have time to waste." He waved the gun in the air to indicate the dozen or so paintings on the walls of the Lounge.

"Constables," said Mr Netty.

"What?" said Denny.

"Constables. It's a joke. This is a police pub, right? So it's Constables in the Lounge."

I looked round at the walls more carefully than I'd done before and I could see he was right. Reproductions, of course. I went up close and had a better look. There were three that I knew from sessions Sister Margaret Mary used to do with us: the view of Salisbury Cathedral with a rainbow; the Haywain; and The Cornfield with what I'd always thought was a sleeping boy – but now I could see he was drinking water from the stream.

"For fuck's sake!" said Denny.

"And in the Public Bar," said Mr Netty, "we've got film stars. Some of them in colour: Betty Grable, Ginger Rogers, Claudette Colbert. More for the men, you see."

What *I* could see was that Mr Netty was a cool customer once the Johnnie Walker wore off. "Why won't you tell us?" I said, "Is it because you're afraid of Lonzo Mack?" I'd got sick of calling him Mr McIntyre.

Mr Netty said nothing.

"Look," I said, "you've been hurt. You put up a fight. You've been knocked about and your leg's hurt. You did your best. Lonzo can see that."

Mr Netty sighed. He said: "It won't do you any good, lady."

"Why?"

"Because you've not got the combination. And neither have I."

"You're a liar," said Denny.

"No, I'm not."

I said: "I don't think he is."

"OK," said Denny. He said: "I don't need the combination. I can open it without. It's just gonna take longer is all."

I looked hard at him. "You're telling me you're a safecracker as well as everything else?"

"A Peterman," said Mr Netty. "That's what we call them in the Force."

"I'm a Peterman," said Denny.

"Alright," said Mr Netty, "it's behind the Betty Grable, where she's looking over her shoulder and sticking her bottom out."

Denny handed me the gun. He said: "Don't take any crap from him!" and legged it to the Public Bar.

When he'd gone, Mr Netty said: "You don't look like the sort of woman who'd shoot me."

"How do you know the sort of woman who'd shoot you? I've already fired this gun once tonight."

"Shooting at a ceiling is one thing. Shooting at a man is something else again."

"Maybe I'll just shoot you in your good leg. That'll impress Lonzo even more."

And then Mr Netty laughed. And Denny returned. "OK,"

he said, "I've found it."

*

I'm not going to take you through every detail of the rest of it. For one thing, I wouldn't be able to explain properly how Denny got the safe open. We got Mr Netty into the Public Bar with the usual hard work on my part. Then Denny did his amazing stuff with the combination lock, moving the dial with his fingers, putting his ear up against it, holding his breath, waiting for the clicks. It was just like David Niven in *Raffles*. Except for the length of time it took and Denny swearing all the while, which quite embarrassed me in front of Mr Netty. Afterwards we got the handcuffs that Mr Netty kept over the bar and we cuffed him hand and foot to a big oak chair.

When we got back to Dronfield, it was daylight. Mr Churchill was on the wireless again, but I can't remember what he said.

Chapter Nineteen

I NEVER KNEW THERE WAS SO MUCH MONEY as £30,000. I mean, I'd never thought how it might look, counted out in piles on a tabletop. We'd got fives and tens and ones and we counted it four times. Not that we thought we'd got it wrong the first three, but we wanted to enjoy the feel of it, the notes slipping noiselessly into the piles, so elegant, so nice. I loved the big white tens and fives with their squirly Gothic writing.

That night I threw away my glasses and bleached my hair. I knew how to do it – I'd read an article about Hollywood's platinum blondes and I knew they used bleach and ammonia. There was something in the chemist shops called Light Top, which they kept under the counter so respectable women could be discreet about it. But I just went in and asked for it in a loud voice. I mean, if you want something, you shouldn't be afraid to ask. That's always been my motto. Anyway, if you suddenly turn into Carole Lombard, people aren't going to be fooled that you've looked that way all along.

So then we put the money in two suitcases – one for me, one for Denny. "If disaster strikes one of us, the other one can still get away with some cash," said Denny.

I said: "I don't want to get away if you don't get away too."

That was when he showed me the ring he'd bought from Woolworths. "Make it a lot easier if people think we're married," he said.

"And we soon will be," I said. I put my head against his shoulder. Then I said: "See you wear the ring I bought *you*."

He said: "*Men* don't wear wedding rings."

I took mine off. I said: "It's both of us or neither."

He sighed. "OK," he said.

We packed what little stuff we'd kept with us and put everything into the Austin 7, the money in the boot, the clothes and stuff on the back seat. Then Denny drove into Derbyshire. "Buxton's nice," he said. "Quiet."

What Denny had done was make us up some identifiation papers. He'd got his forger friend Aaron Bassett to do him a driving licence under five different names – Patrick Ryan, Tim Jones, Andrew McGregor, Paul Graham and Philip Davis. "I wanted one of each," he told me, "Irish, Scotch, Welsh and two English, just to be fair to everyone. I'm a patriotic sort of person."

He'd also got marriage certificates for all the men's names and I was down on those as Margaret Matheson, Genevieve Brady, Clementine Weston, Joan Semple and Theresa Patchett. "Theresa Patchett?" I said. "What sort of name is that?"

"Very ordinary," he said. "Lots of Theresa Patchetts in the world. And it's nothing like Josie Cawthorne. Lots of people take up an alias and they keep the same initials or the same Christian name or something like that. Dead stupid."

We booked in at a B&B. The room was nice but nothing special. But it had a lav next door to our room which is always useful.

*

This was Denny's plan. We went down to the local branch of Lloyds, asked to see the manager, said we wanted to open an account. This is how it went:

Manager: "Good morning to you. I understand you wish to open an account, Mr...?"

Denny: "Patrick Ryan. This is my wife Margaret."

Manager: "Good morning to *you*, Mrs Ryan."

Me: "Good morning." I twisted the ring round my finger a bit so he didn't have to strain too hard to see it.

Denny: "The thing is: my wife and I are only just married."

Me: "I used to be called Matheson. I still can't get used to my new name."

Manager: "Ahah! Then congratulations to the both of you." He hesitated. "Actually, I think the proper thing is to say congratulations to the husband and wish good luck to the wife."

Denny: "Never mind."

Manager: "Fine."

I kicked Denny gently. The manager, on the other side of his desk, couldn't see it. I thought Denny was being too abrupt.

He took the hint. He said: "My grandmother has died..."

Manager: "I'm very sorry to hear that."

Denny: "Thanks." He coughed. He was deliberately slowing down a bit. He sighed as though recalling good times with his gran. He wiped one eye. He said: "She left us a considerable sum of money. Five thousand pounds to be exact."

The manager looked impressed. He said: "Ahah," again.

"My grandma," said Denny, "her name was Alice. A very old fashioned name." He offered another sigh.

Manager: "Indeed."

"And she had very old fashioned ways. For instance, she kept her life savings in a suitcase in the attic."

"Well!" said the manager, suitably shocked.

"And this is the suitcase." Denny picked it up off the floor, placed it on the manager's desk, flicked the catches, and opened the lid.

"Good Lord!" said the manager.

Denny and I had had a long talk about this, just how we were going to do it. I mean, if you've got a suitcase full of money, it's bound to cause a shock, however you go about showing it. So it's best to get the shock out of the way as soon as possible. I said to the manager: "I've never seen so much money before," which was almost true, "but *you* must see this sort of sum every day."

The manager said: "Well, yes, I do." He was obviously pleased to be regarded as a financial man of the world and he smiled broadly. He also looked at my blonde hair in such a way that I could see he warmed to it.

Denny said: "Grandma Alice lived in Birmingham. Sparkbrook, actually." One of Denny's talents was for the clever little detail when lying.

"I don't know Birmingham very well," said the manager. But, of course, he could always look up Sparkbrook on the map afterwards.

"We don't like Birmingham," said Denny, "we prefer to live in the country now we've got a bit of money. We're staying in a bed and breakfast at the moment, but we're looking for a place near here. I don't suppose you know of anything?"

The manager mentioned a salubrious part of Buxton but I don't remember the name now. And he mentioned an estate agent just across the road.

"We'll certainly look in there," I said and I brushed my blonde hair back over my ears. "Won't we, Pat?"

"Yes, Margaret. We certainly will." And we did. And we got some nice photos of nice houses. Just in case the manager checked.

He asked for all the identification, of course, and Denny showed him the driving licence and the marriage certificate. And the manager took our money and gave us a bank book.

"Make it a joint account so my wife can draw on it too," said Denny. "These are dangerous times and death is always there in the background."

The manager agreed. "Will you also need a cheque book?" he asked.

Denny and I looked at each other. "Yes," I said, "we should." It took about twenty minutes to issue one with both our names.

Denny said: "You know, I still keep thinking about Grandma Alice."

"I do too," I said, "though of course I hardly knew her, if I'm honest."

And the bank manager smiled and shook our hands on the way out.

*

And we motored out of Buxton the very next day. And there's no point telling you about the other banks: the

Midland in Barnsley, Barclays in Huddersfield, Westminster in York and National Provincial in Manchester. Because it was all the same, word for word, and all the managers liked my blonde hair.

Chapter Twenty

WE WERE STAYING IN A B&B a few hundred yards from York Minster and I got Denny to come with me to look round it. "Of course," I told him, "it's a Catholic Cathedral, stolen from us by Henry VIII and built on since then quite a lot, but it's still lovely."

He nodded. He said: "All property is theft in the end." At least he took off his hat when we went in.

Afterwards we sat in a pub and ate bubble and squeak and I had a gin and lemonade and Denny suddenly said: "I don't know what's happened to Aaron Bassett."

"Why should anything have happened to Aaron?"

"I've been trying to phone him but he doesn't answer. Truth is, I still owe him for those papers he did for me."

"Maybe he's busy."

"Nobody's too busy to take your money."

"Maybe he's got a girlfriend."

"If he's got a girlfriend, he'll be needing money all the more. I left a message saying when I'd ring again to make sure he was in. No, I'm scared, Josie. I reckon there's something wrong. I really do."

I felt a chill go down my spine. I had a little shiver and took another sip of my gin. But I couldn't see what Denny was driving at. "Are you thinking Lonzo has done something to him? But why should he? First of all, he's got no reason to think your Aaron was anything to do with what we did to Bill Netty."

Denny stroked his moustache. He was growing one just like May had predicted. And I didn't like it. I mean, Errol Flynn is fine in that sort of moustache, but not Stewart Granger, no way. Denny said: "He knows Aaron does forgeries for me. For all of us. He knows we'd be needing that sort of thing if we're going to hide the money. Oh, Lonzo will have thought ahead. So if he gets his claws into Aaron and Aaron starts to remember the names he did for the documents…"

It still seemed far-fetched to me. But I could see Denny was bothered and I never liked it when he was bothered. It cast a real shadow over York Minster and the whole day. "So what do we do?"

"You mean what do *I* do? Well, I think I've got to go back, see if there's any damage, cover our tracks if there is."

"Don't be silly. That's the worst, most dangerous thing you could do. Anyway…" A horrible thought had occurred to me. "You're not going to do anything bad, are you? You're not going to do anything bad to your mate Aaron?"

He grinned. "Course not, stupid. No. But I've got to know if things have gone bad so I can work out a new plan."

I wasn't convinced and I kept on arguing all the way back to the B&B. But I could see he'd got this bee in his bonnet. "If you do go back, you'll be careful?"

"I'm always careful."

"You should let your moustache grow a bit more. Maybe wear glasses."

"I'll buy some first thing. Might even grow a beard."

So I punched him on the arm – not hard – and we ended on a laugh. But I still didn't like it.

*

The holiday mood had suddenly evaporated and that night I thought about what I'd do when Denny went away. Then I remembered Christine and what she'd said about compassionate leave. I never knew how seriously she'd meant it. But I thought I'd better give her a call.

And that's what I did next morning. "You can come back tomorrow if you want," she said, no hesitation. "All I have to do is fill in some papers."

I thought: She's too good to me – I don't deserve it. Then I thought: Am I likely to be spotted if I do go back? Bleaching my hair and ditching the glasses had made a huge difference to my looks. And I'd started pencilling my eyebrows – I thought they looked more elegant than the normal hairy things. Though I vowed I'd never shave mine off like

Marlene Dietrich – that would be unnatural. And I'd changed the way I dressed – bright patterned dresses now, instead of dark two-piece costumes. I'd just that week bought a light blue floral print flare dress with a sweetheart neck and an orange polka dot dress with a fluted hem. I'd even taken to high heels, which I'd never liked before. So I wasn't just acting like a different person – I'd *become* one. I put it all down to Denny. And all those dodgy clothing coupons.

I kept reminding myself Lonzo only knew my first name and we'd only met once. And he didn't know anything about where I worked or the people I'd be living with. Even if he found out about the farmer's cottage, we'd left no clue there to show him where we'd gone. Alright, then!

We paid the landlady at the B&B and packed our suitcases. We still had most of the £5,000 we'd kept with us for spending money. Denny had tied up the tenners, fivers and ones separately with rubber bands. "Now," he said, when we were getting ready to go, "you keep the money and you keep the bank books." He handed them to me. "Then if anything happens to me, you can draw the whole shebang...."

"Stop it!" I said. "Don't talk that way. You're going to be careful, remember?"

"That's right." He gave me a big hug and I nearly cried.

I said: "There's another thing I want you to leave with me. Leave the gun."

He pulled away. "You're not planning to shoot anybody?"

"No. But I want to make sure *you* don't shoot anybody either."

He laughed. "OK. I'll even leave you the bullets as well. Just in case."

He kissed me, but a serious going away kiss this time, not a passionate one. He said: "If you're going back to the barrage balloons, that's where I'll call you when I know better what's happening."

I said: "That's where I'll be. Defending our country and our future."

He said: "And that's where *I'll* be. I'll be defending our

future too."

It was a good thought to end on and he kissed me again. I wondered what May would say when I arrived on her doorstep.

Chapter Twenty-one

I SHOULD'VE KNOWN what she'd say. When I got back two days later, she said: "Thank God!" and hugged me and pulled me inside. She said: "You're not still on the run, then?"

I said: "Hiding in plain sight."

She said: "Best thing to do." And she never asked me anything more. I unpacked in my old room and we had a whisky and a cigarette while we listened to the wireless. It was mainly dance bands with some war news every half hour. The trouble with war news is: you want to believe it, but you know the people running it want you to believe it as well. So it's a bit strange.

When I went to bed, I had a look at the money and the bank books again. Denny had packed them in a brown paper bag and stuck it down with sticky tape. I thought: Here I am, rich beyond my wildest dreams. And I can't touch it.

Two reasons I didn't want to fettle about with our ill-gotten gains. First, because maybe Lonzo had got wind of the bank accounts from Aaron Bassett and knew enough to home in as soon as anybody took the cash out. I couldn't think how he might know such things – but if Denny was afraid of it, it must be possible. Second, I felt guilty in a very Catholic way. What does it profit a man if he gain the world and lose his soul? What would it profit me if I gained £30,000 and lost Denny?

And then I took out the gun. That was also wrapped up in brown paper with sticky tape. And the cartridges came in a little cardboard box. And the silencer was there too. I put everything in a spare handbag and I put the handbag at the back of my wardrobe. Out of sight, out of mind.

*

Next morning I was back at the Hangar. L/Cpl Hawkins on the gate did a double-take and wolf-whistled. "Well," he said, "if it ain't Mae West!" I wasn't much pleased, what with Mae West being a rather crude figure as far as I was concerned, and about a million years older than me. But I let it go and gave him a smile. I could see it made his day.

Christine was also taken aback. "I needed a change," I said.

"Yes," she said, "you certainly got it."

So I had to go through a morning of being ogled by the men and getting disapproving looks from the women. But after that, the novelty faded and we got on with the job.

I thought: I'm safe. I'm back with my workmates. I'm winning the war. But I wondered how Denny was doing. And I wondered *what* he was doing.

*

Second night back, I visited my dad. He was sitting in his vest and trousers, having tea in the kitchen with a small, dark-haired woman in a pinafore.

"Josie," he said, "this is Dora."

I said: "Hello, Dora."

Dad said: "I'm sure you two will get along like a house on fire."

I said I was sure we would. Dora looked less certain. We talked about the pit, how Algrave was hitting record highs in output and how there was plenty of overtime. We talked about the war, how the Americans were bound to come in eventually. And we talked about jitterbugging and I pretended I didn't know what it was. "I suppose," said Dora, "it's alright for coloured people." I just ran a hand through my hair and smiled. I didn't stay beyond half past nine because I didn't want to know if Dora was staying the night.

*

That's how life passed. Work and home to May and wireless in the evenings. There was more bombing in Sheffield and Leeds but not as bad as it had been – only a hundred or so killed. May and I started going out to The Castle, which was a pub a few streets away. I'd noticed how it was getting a bit more usual to see women in pubs without a man by their side, I guess on account of the war. But we always drank milk stout. I think May thought we might get a bad reputation if we swigged whisky.

And then I was at work, reading the *Star*. And there was a little piece on page five, like a single column with a small headline:

Body in
Burnt Car
Mystery

and another little headline underneath:

Identity of
Man Still
Unknown

The paper said the car was found on a piece of waste ground near Dronfield and it was an Austin 7.

All my insides and outsides went hot and cold and hot again. And I made myself read the rest of the story. But there was nothing else in the six short paragraphs that meant anything, only police officers saying an investigation was going on and appealing for information. And I put the paper down and I was sick all over the hangar floor. Some of the women helped me out and took me to the Ladies and helped me clean myself up. I said: "It must be one of my fish paste sandwiches." And one of the women said: "Fish paste can be very funny sometimes. You don't know where they've caught the fish."

When I clocked off, I went to Christine's office and asked to use the phone. I rang the number Det Sgt Peters had given me and I asked for him by name. When he came to the phone, I said: "It's Josie Cawthorne."

"Oh yes," he said, "I *do* still remember you."

"Well, I read something in the paper. That car fire out at Dronfield."

He had to think hard before he knew what I was talking about.

"I'm wondering about the body they found. You see, I know someone who had an Austin 7 and I've not seen them lately. I know I'm being silly, but I wondered if you could tell me anything else about it." Suddenly I felt sick again. "I wondered if you knew who the dead man was by now."

He said: "No, I don't think we do." But then he said: "Where are you? Can I ring you back in the next half hour?" And I said I was at work, repeated the number and put the phone down. I said to Christine: "Can I hang on for a bit?"

She said: "Fine. Helping police with inquiries, are we? Or just renewing our acquaintance with Mr Peters?"

I laughed. "Both. Sort of."

When the call came back, Christine left the room. The sergeant said: "There's still no identification. I'm afraid the only thing left of the victim was his bones."

"Right," I said.

"We only know it was a man because of the shape of the pelvis."

"Of course."

"But there's one funny thing."

"Go on."

"Well, I'm looking in the envelope as we speak. I mean – we usually make up a box of the victim's effects. But in this case, there's only enough to go in one envelope. Only one thing, actually. I'm looking at it right now. It's a ring."

I didn't say anything.

"It's a brass ring like it might be a small curtain ring or something. But it's got an engraving."

I thought: Dear God, please don't let it be DM. But what else could it be?

Det Sgt Peters said: "The inscription looks like D something. Does that ring any bells?"

I said: "No, it doesn't." I said: "Now I think about it, the person I know didn't drive an Austin, after all. He drove a Morris Minor. This has all been very silly of me. I'm terribly sorry for wasting your time."

And I hung up.

Chapter Twenty-two

ON THE WAY BACK TO MAY'S, I stopped at the Off Licence and bought half a bottle of Johnnie Walker. The lad in the shop said: "You giving a party, lady? Can *I* come?"

I said: "You wouldn't like it. It's a wake."

He said: "I've been to some good wakes in my time."

I just about managed to stuff the bottle all the way into my handbag. It made the bike a bit hard to balance so I was longer getting home. When I got back, I took a tumbler out of the kitchen cupboard. I said to May: "I'm going straight to my room. I've got some serious thinking to do."

"Hmm," she said: "Be sure to take some water with it."

Up in my room, I lay on the bed and poured myself three fingers. I sipped it. I wanted to get drunk – really drunk – but not too fast. I really *did* want to think, but I knew it was going to be more painful than anything I'd had to think about in my whole life. I needed painkillers.

The Germans killed my mum. But the Germans were a long way off. Maybe we could kill a few with our barrage balloons but it wasn't that satisfying. Lonzo Mack killed Denny as sure as God made little apples. Maybe he didn't pull the trigger himself or use the knife or tighten the wire round his neck or whatever. But Lonzo did it. Right now I didn't know for certain where Lonzo was – maybe he was still at the house in Dore. Anyway, I knew he was a lot nearer than the Germans. And I had a gun. All I had to do was find him without him finding me.

OK, I knew what Lonzo was into: the drugs, the prostitutes, the protection rackets. But I didn't know how to get close to him, close enough to pull out the Ballester-Molina and put a bullet in his brain.

And was I just being daft? Was I already so drunk – I took another sip of the whisky – that I'd kidded myself into being the moll in a gangster picture? Maybe all I'd get would be grapefruit in my face from Jimmy Cagney. The thought of it made me laugh. But only for a moment.

I'd fired the gun twice already – once when it wasn't loaded and once to bring down a bit of Bill Netty's ceiling. I knew I could do it physically – aim along the barrel and pull the trigger – but could I really do it to a human being, even one as vicious as Lonzo? I had a word with You, Father. Do You remember that? I lay on the bed and I said: "Can I do it, Lord?" Looking back, I don't know what I was really asking. Was I saying "Am I really brave enough to pull that trigger?" Or "Am I going to get away from the police afterwards?" (I didn't fancy being hanged.) Or was I saying: "Will You forgive me and let me into Your Heaven when all's said and done?" Anyway, You didn't answer. I said: "OK, God, stay schtum. No Comment. That's what You always do anyway."

But then I felt bad about saying that. You're still God and You have the right to remain silent. It isn't going to be taken down and used in evidence. And I knew I was, in a way, *cursing* God and it is always a bad thing to curse God. Ester Petheridge had told me all about St Jerome – how he got Job's wife all wrong. In the Old Testament, Job's wife tells him to bless God. But Ester said this was all hooey. The old Jewish scribes knew it was a terrible sin to curse God, and even to write about somebody doing it was pretty dangerous. So they wrote *bless* instead of *curse*. And all those ancient Hebrews understood what was really meant. But when Jerome came to translate it into Latin, he'd got no idea and he translated it literally. As a result, Catholics today think Job's wife is a pretty nice person. But the Jews and the Protestants know different.

Then I spilt some of the whisky on my pillow and I had to take off the pillow case and I left it on the floor to dry.

Had Lonzo gone back to Dore, to the big garden with the fruit cage, after all? If so, maybe I could watch out for him, keeping out of his way, and wait for my chance. But it would be nice to know beforehand, so I could be sure I wasn't wasting my time. Who could I go to, to find out? Sorry, I mean *whom*. I thought about Det Sgt Peters. But that was too dangerous. For him as well as for me. No, it would have to be…

Of course! Aaron Bassett, Denny's forger. If Lonzo had leaned on him to get the gen on Denny, Aaron would sure as hell know where he was. Or have a good idea. So that was the first step.

I reached across for the bottle on the floor, and overbalanced and knocked it over. I jumped to my feet and set the bottle upright and tried to dry the rug with my hankie. *Fuck*, I said under my breath.

Then I just sat on the rug with my back against the side of the bed. I let my head loll on the counterpane. I wondered how much I'd drunk. I looked at the Johnnie Walker and it was about three-quarters empty but that didn't mean anything. I didn't know how much I'd actually spilled. I was probably still OK. Not so drunk that May would have to have words.

So I had my plan, more or less. I would find Aaron Bassett. I would go to see him and find out all he knew about Lonzo. I would track Lonzo down, no matter where he was. And I would kill him.

It would be like Job's wife in reverse. Some people might remember me as an evil woman who committed murder, but really I would be a saint, a crusader, doing something good in this world. Something that needed to be done.

I got to my feet. The room swam a little. I said under my breath: "Be still, room." But it didn't seem to hear me.

After a second or two, I fell face down on the bed. And I slept. Until May woke me with a cup of strong tea in the morning. And yes, Father, I know what sort of sleep it was. The sleep of the self-righteous.

Chapter Twenty-three

I LOOKED UP AARON BASSETT in the Leeds telephone directory. It said *A. Bassett (Printer)* and gave his address on York Road. I arranged an early finish with Christine ("The others will be saying you're my favourite," she said) and caught the bus. Aaron's business was one of those titchy little shops that you could pass by on a rainy day without noticing. The glass-fronted door said *Open*. A bell rang when I opened it and a man came out right away, wiping his hands on a dirty rag. There was that smell I knew must be printer's ink and it wasn't unpleasant.

"Yes?" he said. He was a lanky young man with untidy hair and crooked teeth.

"Do you do posters and notices and things?"

"Of course we do, luv. I'm a printer." He showed even more of those teeth in what I took to be a friendly grin.

"Do you do ration cards and forged driving licences?"

The teeth disappeared from view and he stopped wiping his hands.

I said: "You did some work for Denny Morrow. I need to know about that."

"Well," he said, "you're a woman so you're not the law."

"I'm more of an *in*-law. I'm Denny's girl. He's gone missing. I think he's dead."

His face showed shock. I considered and decided it was genuine. He went across to the door, locked it and turned the *Open* sign to *Closed*. "Better come int' back," he said.

I followed him into a workshop where a press was humming away and stacking up quarto size sheets that all said *Maudie's Café Menu*. There were two metal chairs. He motioned me to one of them and sat on the other.

I said: "You did ration cards and a driving licence and a marriage certificate for Denny."

"Who's saying I did?"

"Not me. Not to anybody outside this room." I hesitated. "I think you were Denny's friend." I paused again. "*Are*

Denny's friend."

"Everybody's Denny's friend. He's a popular lad." He started to grin again but stopped it half-way. "Are you really saying you think he's dead?"

"He had a bust-up with a man called Alonzo McIntyre…"

"Oh shit!" he said. Then: "Sorry for my language."

"Don't worry about your language. Tell me about Lonzo. Has he been round with his heavies? Or sent anybody?"

"Nobody's come round. Why would they? I do work for Denny, I do work for Lonzo, I do work for lots of people. They all know me. They all know each other. They've got no reason to get heavy with me."

I considered how much I could say. But I liked Aaron the way I liked Gerry Tordoff. They might be crooks, but I trusted them not to be vicious. I thought: More fool you if you're wrong. I said: "Denny took some money off Lonzo. *We* took some money. A lot of money. A man called Bill Netty…"

"Shit," he said again. This time he didn't apologise.

"That's right. That's how bad it is between Denny and Lonzo. Between Lonzo and me."

"I heard about the Netty thing. But it was only rumours. I didn't know Denny was in on it." He stopped. He laughed. "But that's Denny. Bigger than life." He stopped laughing. "I mean he was always a great lad."

"I know. I loved him."

We had the sort of silence that meant we'd run out of things to say. And the press stopped too. He said: "I've got to collate the menus." I nodded and stayed put. The truth is I'd hit a brick wall and I didn't know where to go next. But then I thought: He's a printer. Why not get something printed while I'm here? When I thought about it, when I thought about the slippery road I was on, there were a couple of things I might need. Things that might serve me well if the rain got heavier. When he'd finished his menus, I said: "I've got a job for you. I'll pay alright. I'm not asking favours."

"You'll not get a better printer."

"I want a birth certificate. Can you do that?"

119

He nodded. "I can do anything." He sat down again. "I can copy the basic document easy enough. And I can print the registration district on top. Where do you want to be born?"

"Far away from here." I had a think. "Croydon."

"Where's that?"

"I think it's in Surrey. I'll find out and let you know."

"OK. I'll do all the top printing: the registration district, the county and the registrar's name. I'll make up the name and print *Deputy* so it'll be hard to check." He grinned again. "How old do you want to be?"

"What do you mean?"

"It's the stamp. Tell me when you want to be born and I'll see you get the right stamp with the proper king's head on it."

I was only 19. I thought: Wouldn't it be useful to be over 21? I said: "I want to be born in 1916. That's..." I remembered my history lesson even though I only got a Credit in the exams. "...George the Fifth."

Aaron wrote it down in pencil on a scrap of paper. "I know a few stamp collectors. And George the fifth won't be expensive." He said: "You'll have to fill in the top bit yourself. In proper handwriting. The date and the entry number. Nobody ever checks the entry number. And the registrar's signature. Make sure it's *good* handwriting. If you make a mistake, you'll have to start again and that means printing a new document."

"More expense."

"That's right."

"I'll be careful, then." I went on: "And I want a driving licence. I can't drive but I might learn and then it would be useful." I knew from my experience with the banks that a driving licence could get you a long way.

We went on for a bit about the details of the licence, made a date for me to come back, then I left to catch my bus. I sat on the top deck so I could smoke. And I thought: New birth certificate, new name. Something positive. And it came into my head all of a sudden: *Gloria Mundi*. But I couldn't spell it that way on the certificate. I compromised. *Gloria Mundy.* There. That sounded real. Our Gloria, Mrs Mundy's little lamb.

Chapter Twenty-four

I OWED CHRISTINE AN AWFUL LOT. Was it only a few weeks past when I'd been set on running away with Denny and taking Lonzo's money and spending the rest of my days on the lam from a bunch of gangsters? Now I couldn't bear to look at the bag with the five thousand pounds in it or open the bank books with their neat handwritten inscriptions of the amazing wealth Denny and I had spread out on the table top when we'd come back from Bill Netty's pub in a sort of frenzy. Was it just because I feared Lonzo would track me down if I made any move to get the cash out of the banks? Or was it Catholic guilt and penitence – that I blamed myself for going along with the madness, for being part of the crazy process that had ended up with Denny being killed? Either way, I didn't want to touch it.

Folie a deux. That was it. Christine had been the person who gave me the words all those years ago. And, when I'd been a real-life victim of that very same thing and told her I was going away, she'd never questioned me or made any sign that she recognised the fever that possessed me. All she'd done was give me a second chance, a way to get back when it all went wrong. Compassionate leave to look after my dad? No, *I* was the one that needed the compassion and the looking after and Christine had somehow recognised that. She'd treated me like the prodigal who deserved a break.

And I thought I'd make it up to her – well, at least do something nice to show my appreciation. *How Green Was My Valley* was playing at the Leeds Gaumont with Walter Pidgeon and Maureen O'Hara. I'd always thought from the way she talked that Christine was Welsh, so I thought it was just the film for her. So I asked her to come along and we went on a Saturday afternoon. And it wasn't bad if you can forget that Maureen O'Hara is obviously an Irish American who was more at home with John Wayne than with Walter.

Afterwards, we went to the Khardomah in Briggate, the same one I'd been to with Alan what seemed like a century ago, and we had Eccles cakes.

I said: "Did it seem real, then? Is that what life is like in the Valleys?"

She looked confused. "I don't know."

So then we established she was from Devon and knew absolutely nothing about Wales except she'd seen *The Corn is Green* with Emlyn Williams on stage in London four years ago. She thought he was very attractive.

"Well," I said, "you're full of surprises."

"No, I'm not. You're just full of assumptions. Still, I *did* enjoy it. Yes."

"Thanks for having me back," I said.

"Thanks for *being* back." She reached out and touched my hand and kept her own hand on top of mine for just a half minute more than was comfortable. She said: "I do appreciate you, Josie. I always have done. The first time I saw you, I thought: What a beautiful young girl. Now, there's someone who'll go far. And then I realised how clever you were, how sensitive."

"You brought it out in me." All the time I was saying this, I thought: What a disappointment I'd be to her if she knew what my life was really like: the lies, the terrors, the stupidity. I was glad she didn't have any way of finding out. I said: "You don't really know me, Christine. You may think you do..."

She put her hand on mine again. "We none of us know each other. We all of us just think we do. But we all of us have secrets." She took her hand away and touched her eye and I realised she was crying. Well, not full blubbing, not like a kid, just a small tear or two.

I felt my stomach muscles tighten. I felt my mind glaze over just that little bit. I realised I didn't know what to say next, what was coming up in the conversation. I thought I might mention Walter Pidgeon but I couldn't remember any scene he'd been in. I said: "I thought that Roddy McDowall was good. He's so young but..."

And she said: "And *you're* so young, Josie. You think you're so grown-up, but you're not. You've got your whole life ahead. Decisions to be made, choices..." Her voice tailed off. Then she said: "Never forget that."

"I won't."

And finally Christine said: "I love you, Josie. I think you're the most beautiful girl I've ever met."

And I picked up what was left of my Eccles cake and took a bite. After a minute I said: "I love you too, Christine. We're friends. We always will be."

She said: "That's not what I mean."

Awful silence. She put her hand on mine again and I took mine away. "I know what you mean," I said, "and I say we're friends. I say we always will be." I picked up my tea and sipped what was left. It was cold. The room was cold. There was rain on the window pane. I thought: *It's the end of summer*.

Christine stood up. She said: "I think I ought to go."

I said: "We'll catch the bus."

She said: "No, I think I'd better go. I think I'd better go now." She put some coins on the table. She said: "That's for the waitress." And she walked out.

*

I thought: The one thing I don't want, the one thing I really don't want to do, is to go down to the bus station and find she's still there and stand in the queue and not know what to say to her or even whether to say anything at all.

A part of me cursed You, Father. Even though I knew it was a mortal sin. What on earth were You doing to take my friend away like this? What happened to Denny had nearly destroyed me. But then I'd thought how there was at least some justice in it, some pattern in the Universe. After all, we'd sinned, the both of us. Fornication. Theft. Bearing False Witness, if you count the forged documents. And we'd been punished. When I thought of it afterwards, it was almost as if I'd been expecting it, as if I'd been tempting You. But this! It was out of the blue. What point did You think You were making? Alright, maybe it was a test – a terrible test. Maybe it would lead to something that would change things, show me You were still on my side, at least a little bit. But I couldn't see any good coming out of it.

I wandered into Briggate. I pulled up my coat collar against the rain. I had a scarf in my pocket and I tied it round my head. I walked up to Headrow.

And then I saw there was an exhibition of Piero Della Francesca at the Art Gallery. I was astonished. I thought every valuable painting in England had by now been stashed in a coal mine somewhere to prevent bomb damage. It was startling to think that my dad might be working next door to a Leonardo or a Landseer without knowing it.

I knew from school days Christine was a great lover of Renaissance painting and I thought what a shame it was we'd wasted our money on a stupid film when she wasn't even Welsh.

So I went inside and bought a guide because I didn't know Piero very well. It was impressive if you like that sort of thing. They had the *Nativity* with the Angels playing lutes, the *Madonna and Child Enthroned* with four of the Angels, luteless by now. They had *Saint Monica* with her scroll, *Saint John the Evangelist* with his red robe and open book, and *Saint Nicholas of Tolentino*, but I didn't know much about him. I was very taken with *The Battle Between Constantine and Maxentius* with its rearing horses and long lances; but it was badly damaged in the centre with the paint decayed or eroded. I also have to say I wasn't so keen on the *Madonna of Senigallia* where Mary and the Angels seemed to have the same face and Jesus seemed a bit big and too old to still be being carried around by his mum.

I wondered how we'd got all these paintings – I didn't suppose Mussolini had decided to loan them to us. Well, I thought, I wouldn't be too unhappy to know we'd stolen them.

After a while, I had a sit down on one of the couches they had there and I wondered if it would be alright to catch a bus by now. Or there might even be a train. There were more trains running these days – Christine had said it was a sign we were winning the war. I took off the head scarf and looked down at my feet. And then a woman's voice said: "You look like a right whore with all your bleach, Josie Cawthorne."

I looked up, startled. A tall woman was standing in front of me. She had her jet black hair piled high, a skirt that stopped four inches above the knee and a blouse cut so low it looked as though her breasts were fighting with each other. It took me a moment to pull myself together. Then I said; "So do you, Ester Petheridge."

"That's because I *am* one," she said.

Chapter Twenty-five

WE WENT ROUND THE GALLERY together. There were some minor Constables I hadn't got round to seeing – I suddenly remembered Bill Netty's joke and covered my mouth to prevent me laughing out loud – and even more minor Gainsboroughs. No coal mines for them! Ester agreed with me about the Pieros. "Pieros at the end of the pier," she said. But she added: "I'm glad the bombers didn't get the Art Gallery like they got the Museum."

"Did you know," she said when we got to a very pink nude by some artist I'd never heard of, "that in the Middle Ages and early Renaissance, there was a big controversy about belly buttons?"

"No," I said, "I didn't." I was struck by the way Ester could mix what sounded like high academic stuff with vulgar talk at the drop of... well, whatever it was she liked to drop. I realised I had never got the hang of her when we were at school and I still didn't have a clue. "Tell me about it," I said.

"Did Adam have a navel? Did Eve have a navel? After all, neither of them was born of woman so they didn't need one. But some people said: God can foresee everything and he doesn't change his mind very easily, especially when it comes to the archetypal designs that he'd already spent so much time thinking about. So it was obvious he'd give Adam and Eve navels in anticipation of their offspring and for future use thereof.

"It was a real source of dispute among the intelligentsia of the time. And it affected all the artists. When you got a big political issue like that, nobody knew who was going to win and nobody wanted to end up on the wrong side – especially artists, who depended on clerical patronage.

"So they invented the giant fig leaf. Instead of having a fig leaf to cover the basic rude parts, they painted these huge fig leaves to cover their navels as well – if they *had* navels, which was left open to question."

127

"That's fascinating," I said. Ester looked at me hard as if I might be teasing her. But I wasn't. I was enormously impressed.

She said: "It's interesting to see which side of the fence some people jumped. I mean, not *everybody* hid behind a giant fig leaf."

"No. I get that."

"Durer was *for* the navel. Just look at his *Adam and Eve* some time. But he came from a rich family so he didn't need to worry."

"Yes, I *will* look." When she lapsed into silence, I thought about Michelangelo. I knew he was funny about some things – he didn't know how to paint women at all and they all came out like men with breasts. But I couldn't remember a single one of his navels. I thought it best to be honest about my failure. "What did Michelangelo do?"

"Oh, he's definitely *for* the navel in the *Creation of Man* – you know, God and His pointy finger. But you look at his *Fall of Man* and he's gone all fuzzy. Adam and Eve are sort of half-turned away from you so you can't really see. Failure of nerve, I'd say."

"Failure of nerve is a bad thing," I said.

"Yes," she said. "Mind you, the Proddies have their own daft buggers too. Did you know that miners aren't allowed to work on the same shift as their sons?"

"Is that in case there's a disaster?"

"Is it buggery! It's only in places where they've got pithead baths. It's because of Leviticus. I don't suppose you've read Leviticus?"

"No."

"It's Old Testament. The Third Book. That's the thing about us Catholics – we never read the Old Testament, except the Ten Commandments."

"Except you."

"Except me. I like to do things I'm not expected to do." She grinned. "You probably realised that by now. So. Moses comes down from the mountain and he's not just got his Ten Commandments, oh no! He's brought back a whole big book of what God expects from us, God's instructions on how we're all supposed to live.

"And one thing you must never do is uncover the nakedness of your father, which counts the same as the nakedness of your mother, whatever that means. And so, when pithead baths started, the bosses decided that miners who were father and son could never be on the same shift because they might see each other naked. It's true. Ask that aunt of yours."

"I won't bother. I believe you."

"Well," she said, "it's nice to know I can still teach you a few things." Then: "Let's get out of here and get ourselves a drink. I mean a *real* drink."

"It's not opening hours yet."

"I know a place," she said and beckoned with her finger. I thought about it for just a second. Then I followed.

*

It was called The Knights of the Golden Sun and it was tucked away on a side street off Westgate. "It's a club," said Ester, "there's no closing time here." She knocked on a narrow wooden door and the door opened and a big man in a bomber jacket gave her the once-over. "Hello, Ester," he said and nodded. "Don't forget to sign in."

We walked down half a dozen steps to a desk in front of an arch. There was a quarto size register open on the desktop and a fountain pen chained to a heavy-looking silver inkpot. Ester signed: *Neville Chamberlain*. I signed: *Betty Grable*.

"Good choice," she said.

We sat down at a heavy, round, wrought-iron table with two heavy, round, wrought-iron chairs either side. I glanced round the room. It was medium-sized with two large windows that let in plenty of daylight. Which was just as well, considering the only inside lights were six bare but dim bulbs attached to metal holders six feet up the walls. Those walls were covered in a dirty green-striped wallpaper. When I finally looked at the clientèle, I realised we were the only women there.

"We're the only women here," I said. I kept my gaze firmly on her, not wanting to make eye contact with the men.

"I should hope so. It's reassuring to know most women have better taste. But don't worry about it. I'm known here. So are my friends. Nobody's going to mess with me or with anybody who comes in with me." A waiter in a white jacket came over and Ester said: "A bottle of your best Chateau Doncaster, *garçon*."

I said: "What?"

"Well," said Ester, "you wouldn't expect real French stuff with the Nazis running the vineyards these days."

It came in a metal bucket with two glasses. She handed over two pound notes and four half crowns.

"Two pound ten!" I said.

"When you're living the high life, you don't count the cost, Josie. Sorry, I mean *Betty*. Anyway, I'm supporting local industry." She poured two generous glasses. "Now ask all your questions and we can get them over with."

I took a deep breath. "Are you really a whore?"

"Whore, tom, brass, prostitute. Yes, I am. Here's the story. In a few hurried words. Like Pathé News.

"I got pregnant. I was sent to live with the nuns. There were lots of other girls like me. Lots of penance to get through. They stripped us naked every day just to get a free show. They had us scrub the floors, wash the dishes, clean the lavatories.

"I had a boy. I wasn't allowed to give him a name. Not officially. But I called him David because the world to me is always Goliath. Somebody adopted him. Gone to a good home. Like a lucky stray dog. So I packed my bag and got out. I didn't go back to my parents because they had no use for me and I had no use for them.

"Anyway, I learned more than cleaning lavatories. I learned how to do things with men and avoid having a baby. It wasn't the nuns taught me such things, it was the other girls. Though it came a bit late for all of us. So I scraped a living whoring on a casual basis. Then I got lucky. I met a decent pimp and got myself organised.

"So there's me and this other girl. We share the men and we share a flat. This pimp owns it. We pay him rent for the flat and he pays rent for some other convenient places where we can take our men – because it would be stupid to bring work home. He lets us have twenty-five per cent of everything we take.

"There's just one problem. This other girl's moving out. She's getting married, for God's sake. Would you believe it? OK. The cock crows. End of Pathé News. Now what about you?" Ester took a gulp of the Pinot.

"Alright. In a few words. Very boring. Had a fling with a great fella. Lost him. Had a good job. But I don't think I can go back there. Something happened today…"

Ester arched an eyebrow. "Something just now? Just before I turned up?"

"Yes."

"Well," she took another sip, "sounds like Fate. Though I don't suppose I can get you to join me in my new career? Not even with a flat share?"

"No, I don't think so. But thanks for asking."

"Well, I didn't really think you would. But you've got the hair for it, so I thought I'd ask. It would've been good news for Gerry. He's started to worry."

"Gerry?"

"He's the man I mentioned. My minder. My twenty-five-per cent. He's called Gerry Tordoff."

Sometimes you read in books that the earth moved – and usually it's connected with sex. But now I felt it and it had nothing to do with sex at all. Now I knew, Father. Now I knew what point You were making. Something that would lead to something, something that would lead me to Lonzo Mack. I said: "You still a Catholic, Ester? You still believe in miracles?"

"Only now and again," she said.

Stave IV: Ester Petheridge

A cigarette that bears a lipstick's traces, an airline ticket to romantic places. Oh, how the ghost of you clings! These foolish things remind me of you.

..... Eric Maschwitz, *These Foolish Things*, 1936

Look now, you are king in the chapel. But I will be queen in my own kitchen.

.....Richard Llewllyn, spoken by Maureen O'Hara,
How Green Was My Valley, 1941

Chapter Twenty-six

I HAD TO BE STRAIGHT with Ester. As straight as I could be. Next day, which was Sunday, I caught a couple of buses to her home in the early evening to tell her what was what. The flat was impressive – a basement in a cul-de-sac off Kirkgate, just a mile from Leeds City Centre. "Close enough to the Big Bad World," she said, "but sufficiently underground to be safe from the bombers. Well, *pretty* safe."

It was amazing. There were two bedrooms, a lounge with a gas fire, a good-sized bathroom and lav, and a kitchen with a gas range and pantry. And a telephone. It didn't quite cost the Earth – only half the Hebrides and two continents.

Even more impressive was Ester's car, parked outside: a two-seater low-slung convertible sports car painted bright red. She said: "It was a gift from a man friend. Really. It's an Alfa Romeo and the man told me it had a supercharged 2.9 litre engine. Though I've no idea what that means. Except it's fast off the mark."

"It's great," I said. "Aren't you afraid of somebody nicking it?"

"Oh no. Like I told you in the Golden Sun, people know I've got friends. A professional wouldn't even consider it and an amateur would get caught in an hour. It's a pretty flashy car, right? Only a fool would steal a flashy car."

"And the flat is great too. And yes, I want to live here. But your first hunch was right. I'm not into…" I hesitated.

"Prostitution?" she said.

"Yes," I said. "Will your Gerry person be OK with that?"

"Sure he will. He's a teddy bear. As long as you pay your share of the rent."

"I thought people like that…"

"Pimps, you mean?"

"Yes, I *do* mean pimps. I thought they were thugs, scavengers, the scum of the earth."

"Well, some of them are. But some whores are bitches and *I'm* not. Gerry's OK. I can't say he's a father figure because I can't stand my fucking father. No, he's more like an uncle, really."

Yes, I wanted that flat share with Ester. Yes, I wanted to meet Gerry Tordoff again and hope he didn't recognise me with my blonde hair and without my glasses. Yes, I wanted to find out the latest on Lonzo, though I hadn't worked out how. Yes. Crazy really.

"OK," she said, "what's the deal?"

"First thing I have to tell you: I don't want anybody round here to know my real name or anything about me. My new name is Gloria."

Ester's eyebrows rose three inches. I wondered if she was offended, so I said quickly: "My full name – though I don't expect to use it in mixed company – is Gloria Mundy."

That made her laugh, loud and long. I said: "I'll split the rent 50-50. Oh yes, I can afford it." I was thinking of the £5,000 that Denny had left me with.

More eyebrows from Ester. "I didn't know barrage balloons paid that much."

"I've had a legacy recently."

She snorted. "Of course you did. And I'm the Virgin Mary with candlesticks where my tits should be." She brought a new bottle of wine out of the pantry – this one had more of a kick and she referred to it as *Eau de Dearne* – and two glasses out of the sideboard and we sat in plush armchairs and drank it. "A shame it's still autumn," said Ester, "the wine would be colder in winter."

"It's good," I said.

"It's *OK*," she said. She brought out an ashtray and a teak box full of cigarettes. We sat and drank and smoked. She turned on the wireless. It was a band but I couldn't recognise which one. Then: "If you're paying half the rent, Gerry will be perfectly OK with that. I'll just have to work harder, which means more money, which is OK by me as well."

It was then she said: "There's something else you should know about. You know what the Badger Game is?"

"Yes. It means picking up men and robbing them."

I thought she suddenly looked at me with new respect.

"Yeh, that's exactly what it means. Gerry summed it up. He said the great thing about it was: I didn't have to have sex with anybody. Just kid them along. I thought that was a lot better than some of the things I'd been doing."

"So tell me about it."

"Why?"

"Just because I don't want to be part of it doesn't mean I don't find it interesting."

She laughed. *"Doesn't mean I don't find it interesting!"* she mimicked. Then: "God, you're the funny one, Josie. You were so quiet at school. Such a swot. I was always the trouble-maker, getting the Mother Superior's slipper across my bum. But even then... Maybe it was *because* you were so quiet. That's what made me wonder about you. OK, we'll make a deal."

By now I'd got the impression she liked the word *deal*. Maybe it was the American sound of it. "What sort of deal?"

"I'll tell you about the Badger Game and you tell me about this great *fella* you mentioned. And what you mean by a *fling*. I know you were good at English. So was I. Words. They're everything, aren't they? They tell you so much about people. What words they use, what words they *don't* use."

"In the beginning..." I said.

"For ever and ever. Amen." She took another drink. "Twenty years ago, the girls used to advertise in the newspapers. *Learning the Charleston,* that's what they called it. Dance lessons. Everybody knew it was sex they were selling, but nobody was bothered as long as they didn't use rude words. These days it's *jitterbugging*. Only some of us are doing more than just selling sex. Because selling it to the sort of creeps who'd buy it in the first place is a nasty business sometimes. Some girls would rather spring a trap. Get the suckers into the spider's web and sting them. If that's what spiders do. Or bite their heads off. Whichever it is.

"I'm a bit more high-class than the jitterbugs. I go round the big hotels – the Queens in City Square or the Golden Lion in Briggate – and I make myself known. I mean, I don't *do* much. I don't do a strip on the bar or anything. I just

135

sit in a corner in my best gown with a glass of champagne and I read the *Times* or the *Telegraph*. But I'm a woman alone, see? Pretty soon there's some chap asking whether I've read such and such a thing about the war and isn't it terrible news? And then it's, would I like another glass? And I always say: 'Well, I don't want to have too much. It might make me tipsy in the taxi home.' Oh, they love that!

"And at some point, I say 'Gosh, is that the time? I should be home by now.' And they offer to drive me. Well, I should think so! If the mark hasn't got a car, he's not worth my time, is he? So then I've got to decide – do I treat him as a regular punter? Or do I tip the wink to Gerry – a quick phone call from the lobby – and we take him for everything in his wallet?"

"How do you decide?" I was enjoying it. I was kind of living it along with Ester.

"Two things – first, has he really got so much cash as to make him irresistible to Gerry? Second, is he maybe not a bad joe and I take pity on him and just give him the regular service? Actually," she pursed her lips, "I'm pretty kind-hearted if they're nice. But some of the bastards…

"So we go wherever it is that Gerry's got a place sorted that night and we go in and… I never let it go too far if it's a Badger. I mean, a zip undone is all you need.

"Then Gerry bursts in. And I say 'Oh my God, it's my husband! I thought he was away in Nova Scotia for the fishing' or something like that. And Gerry's a bit elderly for a donnybrook if truth were known, but he's no slouch when it comes to scaring people. Anyway, he's got righteousness on his side, OK? He's the wronged husband. So the mark is pretty worried and it's not long before he offers to pay for any *misunderstanding*. And a chap like that is usually carrying a lot of money, believe me."

"And what if he isn't?"

"Then he can *get* some. Remember we've got his wallet by now – I mean *Gerry* has. So we know his name, we know where he lives. We've probably got his cheque book. *Ipso facto*, if you remember your Latin."

I should have been disgusted. Really, I should. But I was thrilled. It was like watching Bogart and Cagney and Edward G all in the same movie. And with a woman as lead. Who would it be? Bette? Barbara Stanwyck? They didn't do women like that at the pictures.

So then Ester said: "Truth or dare. Your turn this time. Tell me about the dreamboat, tell me about Mr Right."

"Well, he was very good looking."

"Of course he was. What did he do for a living?"

"He was a spiv." I could see Ester was impressed yet again. "And there was plenty of stuff he wouldn't tell me about. And he'd been to Borstal."

She whistled under her breath. "And what do you mean by *fling*? That's the word you used when we were in the Knights."

"I mean we went all the way. I mean it was like we were married."

"Except he didn't marry you."

"He died. He was killed in a car crash." I was appalled by telling such a lie. But it couldn't be helped.

There was silence then. Finally Ester said: "I didn't realise. I'm an idiot. I'm a cow."

"You're not so bad. But I'm not going to tell you anything else."

"In that case, it'll have to be *dare* instead of *truth*. Listen." I listened. It was Hutch singing "These Foolish Things". "Dance with me," said Ester.

Again I got that tight feeling in my stomach. But I got up, put down my glass and stubbed my cigarette in the ashtray. You know, Father, it's a very sad, slow song and we just held each other and – I don't know – sort of wobbled round the room.

A cigarette that bears a lipstick's traces
An airline ticket to romantic places
These foolish things remind me of you
The winds of March that make my heart a dancer
A telephone that rings but who's to answer?
Oh, how the ghost of you clings!

And the thought of Denny filled me.

"Are you OK to stay the night?" asked Ester and I pulled away. "Don't worry," she said, "I'm not a Lezzie. Or only when somebody pays me."

"Yes, alright," I said. "Aunt May knows I'm with friends."

"Yes. It's nice to find a friend, isn't it?"

And I had to agree. Although I was using my friend to help me get to kill someone.

"And you *do know*," said Ester, "that Hutch is screwing half the countesses and duchesses in England, don't you? Even though he's as black as the ace of spades."

Chapter Twenty-seven

ON MONDAY MORNING I got up at half past five, ran down to Leeds bus station and had to catch two separate buses to get to the Barrage Balloon centre.

OK. Call me Miss Ditherer, Miss Can't-Make-Up-Her-Mind, Miss Scatterbrain. But I'd realised I couldn't walk out on the job after all. If anything, I needed it more than ever. I needed something solid, unchanging, predictable in what was now a precarious life.

Also, I didn't want to run out on Christine. I'd been shocked when she made a pass at me, but I didn't want to do the dirty on her. She'd been a good friend to me and that was how it should stay.

And I managed to arrive at the usual time. And I managed to say "good morning" to her in what I hoped was a cheerful, chirpy way – a lot more cheerful and chirpy, actually, than I normally was. She said "good morning" too. But I could see she didn't know whether to smile or not. So I smiled double for the both of us. But I didn't keep up too much eye contact because I didn't want her to read the wrong message into things.

And the day was like any other day. Better than some. We'd brought down another Stuka and a Heinkel the previous night – I *think* that's what Christine said when she "addressed the troops" but I wasn't really taking it in. I didn't have my regular sandwiches, just four pieces of bread with a scrape of margarine and an apple that I'd stolen from Ester's pantry.

The only thing that was at all different was that there was a new guard on the perimeter fence who actually asked to see my identification papers. Lance Corporal Hawkins, who usually did the job, had been promoted to full Corporal and was now something of an *aide de camp* to Christine. He didn't seem to do much actually – just sort of followed her around and stood, all straight-backed and self-important, occasionally brushing his moustache with his index finger.

We did all the usual things like sewing and mending (Christine always referred to damaged balloons as the "casualties") and I then accompanied one of the other male troops in the truck when we took two of the balloons back to their strategic sites.

At end of day I made a special point of saying "goodnight" to Christine and making some silly comment about how the weather was getting colder as we moved into winter. It wasn't the most profound or insightful remark but she managed to agree that the days were drawing in. And this time she smiled. So I knew that *she* knew that everything between us was OK. Job done.

Two buses later I got home to Ester. I use the word "home" because that was how I now thought of it, though I had to get across to see May that evening to explain what I was doing – or enough of what I was doing that would keep her from worrying too much.

Ester said: "I hope you're planning to be in *tomorrow* night. Gerry wants to give you the once-over. And it would be a good idea if you brought the rent along."

"Right," I said as though it was a very ordinary moment. "Will all in oncers do?" and I laughed. But my heart was thumping.

*

I went back to May. I didn't tell her much, just that I was planning to share a flat with an old friend. But I guess I'd got her into the state where she'd long ago decided not to ask. I filled my suitcase with all the needfuls. And I'd bought a big black leather document case with a lock and key. After all, I had lots of documents to take with me: the bank books, the forged papers Denny had got us, and now the birth certificate and driving licence that Aaron sold me. And it also had room for the Ballester-Molina and the wad of notes Denny had left me.

"I'm going to have to leave you my bicycle," I said to May, "It's got to be buses if I'm living in Leeds."

"Half the world away," said May. Then: "Be sure to take

plenty of exercise to make up for all this sitting around."

"Don't worry," I said, "I'm intending to stay healthy."

And so I was.

*

On the first bus back, I thought a lot about Gerry and whether he'd recognise me. No glasses, bobbed hair left to grow, dark hair bleached (weekly now), cheeks powdered, eye-brows pencilled, and I'd started making my thin lips into a bow shape with my lipstick. Also, I'd got that different wardrobe of pretty dresses – though I'd realised by now they were a lot too summery and sweet for this time of year and maybe I should have bought something more slinky like the gowns Ester wore for her hotel jaunts. But I guess *they'd* never have been warm enough anyway. And I could always borrow from her if I wanted. Also, as You probably noticed around this time, Father, I'd started to talk differently. I said *OK* for *Alright* and used stuff I'd picked up from going to the pictures (I mean *going to the movies*) like: *Son-of-a-Gun* for *Gosh!* and *Buddy* for *Friend*.

That's how clever I was, Father! That's how smart and on top of things! I bet You were laughing all the time.

*

Gerry was pretty much the way I remembered him. He still wore corduroy trousers, though these were black – and they came with a blue sports jacket. So it wasn't quite so unnerving. "Hello..." he said as he came through the door, showing those great teeth.

"Gloria," I said and offered my hand.

"Hello, Gloria," he said and shook it firmly.

Ester motioned us to sit down and we all did. Gerry said: "Does Gloria know about...?"

"Oh yes," I said, "I know it all."

Gerry's eyebrows went up just like Ester's usually did.

"She knows all she has to know," said Ester, "nothing

141

more, nothing less."

"You know Ester's on the game, then?"

"But *she's* not, Gerry. *Gloria's* not. And she doesn't want to be. So I don't want you thinking you might get her to volunteer. I don't want to encourage competition." Ester had raised her voice at this point.

"What Ester does for a living is her own business," I said.

"Very commendable attitude," said Gerry. I thought he was looking at me in a strange sort of way and I had a sudden fear that he'd recognised me. But then he smiled again. He said: "Well, money's money, wherever it comes from. And if you've got the moolah for a place like this, that's fine by me. Did you bring it?"

I handed over a month's rent in lowest legal tender.

Gerry counted it. "Ready cash, just how I like it," he said. Then: "Where'd you two meet?"

"At school," we said simultaneously.

"That's good," he said, "school friends are loyal, they stick with you. Not like business friends."

I remembered Lonzo had used this phrase and I wondered if a canny Gerry had twigged who I was and was prodding me to get a reaction. Then I thought: Don't be stupid. You're getting panicky over nothing.

He smiled again. Yes, I thought, he's wearing false teeth alright – the gums are too pink. I smiled too, to show him *I* wasn't. Crisis over.

Ester gave him a shot of whisky and we chatted about the war the way people used to talk about the weather. "Can't see it changing," said Gerry. "Can't see the Yanks coming in. Lots of Germans in America. Lindbergh is a big agitator for staying neutral. Flying the Atlantic by himself is one thing, coming over with a load of troops is something else again. Anyway, there's nothing for them to fight for over here. They think we've lost already. And if we manage to win, so will the Russians. Roosevelt won't want that."

I was actually impressed with Gerry's analysis. My overview of the intelligence of gangsters and pimps generally shot right up.

But Ester was having none of it. "You're spreading despondency, Gerry. You ought to be arrested."

"I ought to be arrested for lots of things," he said, and finished his drink and got up. "Well, nice to meet you, Gloria. I'm sure we'll get along just great. So long, Ester." He hesitated a moment as he went through the door. "School, eh? Best years of our lives! All of us." And then he was gone.

I'd made it! I was in with Gerry just as he was in with Lonzo. The only problem was how to jump the next hurdle without falling on my bum.

Chapter Twenty-eight

CHRISTINE CAME IN. "There's a call for you."

"Who?"

"The boyfriend."

Of course, I knew who she meant. *Whom.* I couldn't tell whether she was disapproving or not.

I followed her to her office. When I picked up the phone, I said: "Hello, Detective Sergeant Peters."

"Wrong," he said.

"Oh?" I said.

"Now it's Detective *Inspector*. I'm a DI."

"Gosh," I said. "Promoted! How nice!" I was thinking: What in hell is he doing ringing me again? The time when I had a sort of half-crush on the Det Sgt had passed long ago. Now I considered him a nuisance. Especially at a time when I was planning a murder and not getting very far with it.

"I'm sorry to disturb you," he said.

"That's OK." Not what I was really thinking.

"I wanted to see you again."

"Oh?"

"I have certain information."

"Right."

"Which you might consider," he paused dramatically, "worth hearing."

"I'm sure I would but…" I wasn't in the mood to spend another fish-and-chip lunch with him, going over the various criminals I might know, especially if it included Denny. I said: "In that case, let's make it dinner." I meant dinner in the southern sense of a full-blown evening meal where he could entertain me with *Duck à l'orange* or some such.

"Right," he said, "where do you suggest?"

"How about *Maison Française*? It's in Leeds." This was a restaurant frequented – and recommended – by Ester.

"Alright," he said, "when?"

"Tomorrow night. Will you pick me up?" I was thinking: He's already done that.

"Yes," he said, "I *do* have a car."

At that point I thought maybe I was overdoing the indifference. After all, a good meal can't be bad as long as there isn't any expectation of a favour in return. I said: "It shouldn't be difficult. I'm living in Leeds right now."

He said: "Oh."

I didn't give him the full address. I had suddenly visualised him checking the location on PROTA, the Police Rota of Prostitutes' Addresses that still occupied my fantasies. I hoped to God there wasn't any such thing. I said: "I'll be at the railway station. Maybe about seven o'clock."

"Seven will be fine."

"I expect you'll have to book."

"I'll book."

Well, I thought as I hung up, this is a turn-up. I thought: I wonder what Ester will think about it? In the event, Ester laughed like a drain. She said: "I don't know where that French place gets its stuff. Maybe they have people smuggle in the pâté from Calais, but it's much more likely they smuggle horsemeat from Birmingham. The French have always been partial to horsemeat."

*

The weather was cold and I put on my tweed overcoat. It was getting on for Christmas – though, because of the blackout, there were no Christmas trees with fairy lights in the city centre. It had started to rain and I put on a headscarf. He arrived on time, driving a four-door Austin 8, which is a pretty small car to expect four people to share. Still, it was OK for the two of us.

And when we got to the restaurant, he had done all the things he should. We were greeted by a waiter whose accent was like Maurice Chevalier's. There was a table for two set aside. The restaurant was small enough to be cosy, with reproductions of posters by Lautrec and ballerina pictures by Degas among big, blown-up, black-and-white photos of de Gaulle. It was certainly a different world from the British

Restaurants set up by Mr Churchill, where you got mainly sausages with mashed potato or minced beef with parsnips and you sat next to the radiator to keep warm.

When we got to the table, he held the chair out for me. And when I sat down and took off the scarf, he stepped back suddenly. It was only then I realised this was the first time he'd seen my bleach blonde look. Well, let him get used to it.

He asked me what I wanted to drink and I said orange juice for starters, so he ordered two of those. When we picked up the menus, he could actually read a bit of French, though his pronunciation wasn't great.

The fact that it was a French restaurant didn't save it from British Law. So we couldn't have a meat or fish starter followed by fish or meat for the main course. We both started with some sort of vegetable soup; then he had *bœuf bourguignon* and I managed *coq* without the *vin*. I kept remembering what Ester had told me in addition to the horsemeat thing – that I could expect the occasional dog if things were really bad. She called it *chien à manger*. That made me giggle a bit, which is never a good thing when you're out on a date. But I always say if something tastes good, it *is* good; so I didn't really care.

While I was sipping my soup, I took a good look at my detective friend. I thought how right I was thinking he looked like John Mills, even now when I was seeing him in electric light at night time.

And he *talked* like John Mills – ordinary, everyday. We had to cover the war, of course; but he had nothing much to say except it had been going on for three years now. As if I couldn't count. Then he said: "I volunteered, you know." And I wondered where I'd heard that before. He said: "Because I was a policeman, they thought I was more useful catching deserters." He laughed. And it came to me that Denny had said a similar thing, although in his case it was a scar on the lung that kept him out. Suddenly I thought of all the men who'd stayed home for whatever reason having to explain it to the women they fancied. First thing they had to say, really, first question that would have come into any

146

woman's head.

I suddenly realised something else. I said: "I don't even know your Christian name."

"Robert," he said.

"Bob or Bobby?"

"No, never Bobby. Not for a policeman. It better be Bob."

So he didn't want to be treated like a policeman all the time. But he didn't start on the real stuff, the information that might be "worth hearing", until the main course. Then he said: "Denny Morrow. He was your fiancé, wasn't he?"

"Yes."

"I hope you don't mind me talking about him."

"No."

"There was a ring. I mean, you phoned me about the body in the car and I didn't understand what it was all about. Then, a bit later, I worried because you might think I was pestering you. I didn't want you to be bothered by me. I still don't."

I didn't say anything.

"There was a strange ring. It had initials on it. DM. I guess the ring belonged to Denny Morrow. Or you thought it did."

"But I was wrong, remember? I'd got the wrong make of car."

"Look, I'm not trying to cause trouble for you. That's why I wanted to talk away from the station."

"Go on, then."

"Where is Denny Morrow now?"

"I don't know. We split up."

"I'm sorry to hear it. In that case, what made you think he might be dead?"

"I told you..."

"... that you remembered the wrong type of car. But I don't believe it. I think you recognised the ring and the initials are Denny Morrow's. *Were* his, if he's dead."

I thought for a mad moment I might argue with him over the grammar because the initials were *still* Denny's even if he *had* been murdered. But I stopped myself. I'd made a mistake agreeing to this meeting. *I* was the one being stupid, not Bob Peters. And I didn't want to make a bigger fool of myself.

He said: "There are things I can tell you about Denny Morrow."

Tears started in my eyes. "If you're going to tell me he was a crook and he'd been to Borstal, I know all that. And we both know he worked for Alonzo McIntyre. And we both know the sort of man Alonzo McIntyre is. And now Denny's left me, I guess I'm just another fallen woman."

When I said the words *fallen woman*, I raised my voice and several people at nearby tables turned their heads.

Bob Peters didn't bat an eyelid. He passed me a handkerchief and I blew my nose. Noisily.

"Denny Morrow wasn't his real name. Did you know that?"

"Sure. I knew it was Dennis. I suppose he thought Denny was kind of racy. He was a kind of racy person." I hoped Bob Peters took it the way I intended – that *he* was a pretty dull one.

"His real name was Dennis Morgan."

That hit me. I was going to say something but didn't. I bit my lip. I remembered Denny saying some people who used an alias were stupid enough to keep their own initials. I now realised he was joking about himself. A joke within a joke. A lie within a lie.

"And he'd also called himself Donald Michaels. Yes, he went to Borstal. Yes, he also got done for Actual Bodily Harm. And his previous included six months in Wakefield jail for safe-cracking, first offence. And yes, he was already married. With a son called Paul who is now six years old."

This time I bit my *tongue*. There was blood in my mouth and I used Bob's handkerchief to wipe it away. "Well," I said, "I loved him. And I still love him now he's dead." It was the best I could do and this time I made sure I said it quietly.

There was a silence between us of maybe a couple of minutes. Then Bob said: "I've upset you, but I needed to know how much you knew. I'm sorry I had to do it. I believe you when you say you still love Denny and I know you'd tell me if you knew for certain he was dead. I guess I'm not such a great detective." He wiped his mouth on a napkin. "And I guess you won't want to stay for the sweet."

I thought about it. I said: "Yes, I will. I think I'll have the *charlotte russe*. Though God knows what's really in it. And I'd like a liqueur with my coffee. Maybe a Benedictine if they have it." And I said: "It's real French coffee here, you know. I don't know where they get it."

He didn't rise to the bait, but he looked just as surprised as he did when he saw my blonde hair. He said: "OK."

"And," I said, "you can tell me something about yourself. Are you married?"

"I used to be. I'm divorced."

"What happened?"

"She didn't like the long hours and the fact that most people don't like policemen anyway. She took off with an able seaman."

"Sensible girl. Any children?"

"None."

"Right. Now you can tell me why people call you Jelly."

Chapter Twenty-nine

HE SMILED SHEEPISHLY and brushed at that lick of hair to push it back in place. "Well," he said, "it's not because I'm soft or wobbly." Then he stopped and I realised *he'd* realised he'd made a double entendre. Or something like that. And he was embarrassed.

"Go on," I said.

"Well," he said again, "one morning two years ago, I was having my hair cut in this place off Church Street in Sheffield. It's run by a man called Formby, like the comedian." He laughed. "Though I don't suppose you need to know that."

"Never mind," I said.

"OK. A man came running in and said he thought there was a bomb in the Cathedral. Actually, it wasn't *in* the Cathedral at all, it was just outside. And we'd been getting threatening phone calls and letters at the station. It seemed there was this weird IRA unit. That's the Irish Republican Army."

"I know what it is."

"And they were targeting Anglican churches. Something about Protestants stealing their churches from Catholics."

I remembered with a shock my lecturing Denny about Henry VIII when we stayed in York.

"So," Bob went on, "I got up and ran out and got straight up to the Cathedral. I still had the barber's towel round my neck. And there, just outside the main door, was what we police call a suspicious package.

"So I took a good look round. There's a saying in the Force: *Always use your eyes*. Because a lot of people don't. They turn up and make a quick judgement without taking it all in."

"I can understand that."

"OK. So word had spread that there might be a bomb. You know how this sort of thing starts. But, people being what they are, instead of keeping clear, they were milling around. I'd managed to get through the crowd and I saw this brown paper parcel. It wasn't just tied up with string. It had black duct tape. And I picked it up. My Lord! It was hot!

"And then I spotted this pick-pocket I knew pretty well. Harry Dowd. I shouted: 'Hey, Harry, can you get me a fire bucket?' He couldn't hear what I said, so he ran over. And this made the crowd come forward as well. I said to him: 'Harry, I need a bucket of water. Can you get one from the greengrocer?' Because there was a greengrocer's shop just across the road. Martins, I think it was called. And then I said to him: 'Warn the crowd to get back. Will you? I think it's a bomb alright.'

"So he ran back, waving his arms and shouting to people to keep back. And they went back about a yard. And Harry ran into the greengrocer's and I picked up the bomb."

He stopped to get his breath and I had a chance to say something, but I didn't. By now, I was as breathless as he was.

He went on: "The parcel was getting hotter. If I said it was as hot as a newly boiled kettle, you might think I was exaggerating. But that's what I thought. I actually dropped it.

"Anyway, there was only one thing I could think of to do. I took out my pen knife. which I always carried with me, and I started to cut the tape and the string. And I unwrapped it. And inside there was something like a large sausage wrapped in greaseproof paper. I thought: My God, if it turns out to be somebody's packed lunch, I'll be a laughing stock.

"But it wasn't. It was dynamite. Gelignite. Jelly. Whatever you want to call it. It was yellow and soft. It looked like some kind of sickly sweet, like a stick of kiddy's rock that had gone wrong.

"And there were more. There were nine in all. Well, I thought, I've hit the jackpot this time. And then I thought: What the hell good is it if Catholics ever get their churches back but they're all turned into rubble?"

He laughed. I laughed. He said: "I took them out, one by one, and put them in a row along the pavement. About five or six inches between each one. So if one went off, maybe the others wouldn't go as well.

"One of the sticks had a fuse in it. So I used my penknife and cut the fuse out. I didn't know this was a daft thing to do. Because if you grate against the gelignite with a knife, it might go off. And any one of those sticks could have gone off if it rubbed against a piece of grit on the pavement.

"Also in the parcel was a red balloon and inside the balloon was a cylinder which I pulled apart and got acid burns on my hands. I actually cried out with the pain. And then Harry came back with the bucket of water. He saw the burns. He said: 'Dip your hands in this, Mr Peters.' And I did. And it was very soothing.

"And Harry said: 'They phoned the Fire Brigade from Martins.' And then I put the sticks into the water and I thought: That's all I can do until the Fire Brigade comes along. And I went back to the crowd and said: 'Keep back until the Fire Brigade get here.' And fifteen minutes later they arrived. Good lads, all of them."

I said: "Yes, I know." And I remembered the lad I'd hugged as my mum lay dead in the street. And he was crying. But Bob Peters hadn't cried.

Bob said: "I don't know exactly what the Fire Brigade did. But none of the sticks went off, thank God. So they saved the Cathedral. Shame the Jerries came along later on and had a go at it. Anyway, Harry Dowd and some of his less than respectable friends bought me a pint on the back of it. *Several* pints, actually."

"You should have got a medal," I said. "You're a hero."

"Well, I did get a medal. The King's Police Medal."

"You never told me that." As soon as I said it, I felt stupid. Of course, he never told me about it. Because real heroes don't talk about how brave they are. Not even with girls they fancy.

I said: "I'd like to see that medal."

His eyebrows went up. "Why? Don't you believe me?"

"Of course I believe you. I'm just saying I'd like to see it sometime. I'm saying you should invite me to come round to your house."

And I reached across the table. And this time I didn't just *touch* his hand, I grabbed it hard and held on to it as long as I could without looking too soppy.

Chapter Thirty

I LET BOB DRIVE ME to the end of the street. I'd not quite given up my worries about a prostitute address list. I said: "I can't ask you in because of my flatmate." And he said: "Fine." And I kissed him. Just a little one, not quite on the lips. And I said: "You've got my phone number at work." And I got out of the car and let myself into the flat. There was another car I recognised parked next to Ester's.

You probably wonder, Father, why I don't go on about what it's like having a prostitute for a flat share. Well, I guess it's no different from having an accountant or a waitress, I guess. Except she worked nights. So she'd get back at, say, eleven o'clock and we'd have a glass or two of wine and she'd ask me how my day was and I'd say "OK" and I'd ask her how it went for her and she'd say "OK" and that was that. I don't think Ester was very much interested in barrage balloons. And, if I was interested in what *she* did, I guess I didn't like to show it. So there.

But one night she'd come home with a cut on her head and I'd got out the TCP and some cotton wool and, naturally, asked how it happened. "Well," she said, "the mark got a bit shirty when Gerry came in, and he lashed out, didn't he? And he was wearing this stupid gold ring with a diamond in it, and it cut me. And Gerry gave him a right going-over. And we took the ring, which Gerry told him would pay for my medical expenses. And Gerry got his wallet too with a roll of notes and his name and address and – would you believe it – a picture of his wife and kid. So it won't be the last he hears of it. So it's been a good night. Profitable."

Gerry was a puzzle. Ester had called him a teddy bear and I have to say: up to now he was always polite and friendly with me. But he was also a pimp and a gangster and for that sort of work you had to be hard. And he obviously didn't mind showing on occasion how hard he could be. Maybe it was his liking for corduroy that had made me think he was a bit soft.

But anyway. This particular night I got back from seeing Bob, Gerry was inside, having a cuppa. "Hello, Gloria. Hope you've had a good night out," he said. He put his cup on the small table and stood up. "Gotta be going now. Ester's given me your rent, so that's OK. And I'm sure you women have lots of girlish things to talk about. Thanks for the tea." He put on a grey fedora that was lying on the table and buttoned his gabardine. "Next time I come, I'll bring a bottle of bubbly and we can wish each other a merry Christmas." And he smiled his famous smile and was gone.

"Well," said Ester, "how did it go?"

"You mean the date? Nothing much to tell."

"Of course I mean the date. How far did he get?"

"Not very far. Not really up to the starting line."

"Oh, come on! You've got that look about you. I know *something* happened."

"Well, he's a nice bloke. Not as boring as I thought."

"Well, that's progress. Have a fag and I'll bring out the hooch."

So we sat and smoked and drank. I said: "How was *your* fella, then? The father of your son?" After I said it, I wondered if I'd made a mistake.

She snorted. "His name was Richard. He had lots of freckles. Freckles all over him. You wouldn't think a man could have so many freckles in so many out-of-the-way places."

"Do you hate him?"

"Why should I hate him?"

"He left you in trouble."

"No, *I* was the one split with *him*. I didn't want him bringing up my child."

"But David had to be adopted."

"Had to? I don't know if I believe in *had to*. Thing is: I didn't want Richard bringing him up and I didn't want *me* bringing him up either."

"Why not?"

"Because of the kind of person he was. Because of the kind of person *I* am."

"What kind of person was he?"

"Very good looking. If you like freckles. Bit stupid. Oh God, *so* stupid."

I thought a bit before I asked the obvious question. "And what kind of person do you think *you* are?"

"I'm nasty. I'm selfish. I'm as hard as the nails they hammered into Jesus. Actually, let's not beat about the bush. I'm damned."

I was shocked. "Are you still a Catholic?"

"You asked me that before. And the real answer is: I am when it suits me. I'll live a long, bad life and probably confess it all when I'm 93." She took a puff of her cigarette. "Don't get me wrong. I do like people – I like *you*, for instance – but I don't *love* people. You can see the difference, can't you? It's a doctrinal difference. Except my son. I love him well enough not to go near him. Don't you see? Don't you get it?

"Oh, Josie," she said, using my real name for the first time in a while, "you should have been here in March. That would have taught you what life's really like. We had nine air raids. *Nine over two days.* I didn't bother to count them, I just read it in the *Yorkshire Post* afterwards. We were bound to be bombed, weren't we? We've got Avro, where they make the Lancaster bombers. We've got Barnbow where they make armaments. Of course we'd be bombed.

"It was a weekend, Friday night. Big night for me in *my* trade. I was getting myself ready for work when I heard them coming over. I talk about being safe here, underground, and I'm glad of it. Little Aladdin's cave, this is. But I didn't *feel* safe, not that night. Listen, I'm ashamed to admit it. But I hid under the bed. Don't laugh."

"No, I'm not laughing."

"I don't know why I did it. That stupid bed is only wood and springs and a shabby little mattress and it wasn't going to save me if they dropped something heavy on top of me. There were 40 bombers – that was in the *Post* too – and they dropped the incendiaries first and then the high explosives.

"I went round afterwards to look at the wreckage. The

Town Hall. The Museum in Park Row, though I'd never been inside it – museums are for old people. Kirkgate Market, where you could still get silk stockings if you knew who to ask. And the Post Office. And the Quarry Hill flats. And worst of all, the Hotel Metropole, which was a good area for me – nice clientèle."

Ester poured us both another drink so the bottle was empty. She took it into the kitchen and dropped it into a bin. When she came back, I said: "If you're as hard as you make out, what would you do to the bastards that flattened the Town Hall and killed a lot of people?"

"I'd crucify them. Two nails in each hand."

"But it's war, isn't it? Our side are doing the same to them when they get the chance."

"Good for our side, then. Let's do more of it. That's how I feel."

"Yes," I said, "so do I." And I told her about my mum being killed in the street. Just to show her I too knew what life was about. Then I said: "Is there anybody else you'd actually want to kill? I mean other than the Germans?"

She thought about it. "No. Not really. I couldn't be bothered."

"Not even the nuns who took your baby?"

"Not even them. I told you – he's got a better chance where he is than back here with me. He's probably in America, somewhere they don't have to worry about bombers. Now wouldn't that be great, to be in America right now?"

I emptied my glass and Ester emptied hers. "What if I told you I was planning to kill somebody? Somebody who really deserves it, just as much as those Germans?"

She snorted again. "I'd say you've got a right nerve going out with a policeman."

"Yes, I've got nerve alright. But would you help me, Ester?"

"Only if I thought we'd get away with it."

"It's a man called Alonzo McIntyre."

"Never heard of him."

157

"Gerry knows him."

She became very quiet then. She must have been thinking *that* was the reason I was living with her. Which it was. I realised I was pretty drunk and I think Ester was too. Anyway, I could pass it all off as a joke tomorrow morning.

After a bit, Ester turned on the wireless. It was some crooner, but I couldn't think who, though it might have been Al Bowlly, who'd been killed in a bombing in London in April. I picked up the empty glasses, took them through to the kitchen, rinsed them under the tap, put them upside down on the draining board. Then the music stopped. There was just a man's voice now, talking loud and rapidly. I couldn't make out the words but I guessed it was a news bulletin.

As I wiped my hands on the tea towel, Ester appeared in the doorway. She looked shocked. She said: "You were always good at geography."

"No, I wasn't."

"Well, better than me." She took a deep breath. "Have you ever heard of Pearl Harbour?"

Chapter Thirty-one

THE AMERICANS WERE IN THE WAR! We were so excited, we went down to the Crown and Anchor after work – all twelve of us – and I had two gin and tonics. "Good job you're not riding your bike going home!" said Christine.

Corporal Hawkins was drinking pints of mild. He got up and sang a song called "Yankee Doodle Dandy". It went:

I'm a Yankee Doodle Dandy,
I'm a Yankee, do or die;
A real live nephew of my Uncle Sam,
Born on the Fourth of July.
I've got a Yankee Doodle sweetheart,
She's my Yankee Doodle joy.

I'd never heard it before and it made no sense to me. But everybody joined in the chorus once we'd learned the words. Corporal Hawkins had a terrible voice. Afterwards he kissed Christine, which I thought was cheeky, but she didn't seem to mind. It was one of those times.

Two bus rides later, I lurched into the flat. Ester and Gerry were sitting in the lounge drinking. I'd obviously been too drunk to notice his car this time. Gerry said: "Hello, Josie."

"Hello Gerry," I said. And then my blood ran cold. I looked hard at Ester.

"She didn't tell me," said Gerry. "She's been a good friend to you. School friends are always the best. No, she didn't *have* to tell me. I've got eyes, haven't I? You think a bottle of bleach and a few dabs of lipstick are going to fool me?"

"I guess not." I sat down.

Gerry poured me a glass of champagne from the bottle he'd obviously brought. He raised his own glass. "And losing the specs didn't fool me either," he said. And he swigged it down.

"I'd rather have tea," I said.

Gerry nodded to Ester and she went into the kitchen. I

heard her pour water into the kettle.

"What's your game these days?" said Gerry.

"I don't have one."

"Because," said Gerry, "I've been asking myself that question ever since I met *Gloria*. I asked: Why should Josie Whatever-she's-called come back into my life? After stealing £30,000 from my employer, Mr McIntyre? Oh, it could have been a wild coincidence. Such things do happen in life. But suppose it's not? Supposing she's shacked up with Ester, my number one girl, because she wants to get to me?"

I decided I couldn't be in any worse trouble than I was. I said: "Lonzo Mack killed my Denny. I intend to kill Lonzo Mack."

And he laughed. He laughed so hard, he had to take out a handkerchief and wipe his eyes and blow his nose. "So," he said when he'd calmed down, "little Josie the miner's daughter, the convent girl – see, I know that much about you – is going to kill the evil Lonzo Mack, the biggest gangster in Yorkshire? Maybe in the whole North of England?" He put away the handkerchief. "How?"

"I have a gun."

He rolled his eyes and snapped his fingers. "Of course you do! You shot a hole in Bill Netty's ceiling!" And he laughed again. "But how, Josie, my girl, did you plan to get at Lonzo?"

"I don't know," I said, "I hadn't got that far." And I burst into tears.

Ester came back in and put the tea in front of me. I wiped my eyes on my hand. "Thanks," I said, and: "You're my friend, Ester. Really. I didn't mean to do anything to hurt you."

"Forget it," she said. Then: "Is this Lonzo prick the one you were talking about last night? Somebody who's just as bad as the Germans?"

I nodded. Ester said to Gerry: "She asked me to help her kill someone, someone who deserved it. I said I'd give it some thought."

"Well," said Gerry, "that makes *three* of us that'd like to see Lonzo dead."

*

I sat there. I said nothing. It seemed like hours. But it wasn't. I suppose it was about two minutes. It was Ester who broke the silence. "Fuck!" she said. Then: "That's fucking hilarious."

"Why?" I asked, not meaning *Why is it fucking hilarious?* but why did Gerry want Lonzo dead?

"First," he said, "I want you to know I had nothing to do with what happened to Denny. I liked Denny. We got on OK. But he was crazy going after Lonzo's money. *You* were crazy, the both of you. You must've known that."

"*Folie a deux*," I said.

"What?" said Gerry.

"Forget it," said Ester.

"I didn't know anything about it till it was well over. I didn't know about the heist, I didn't know about Denny and you being involved, I didn't know Denny had been picked up. I didn't..." He hesitated.

"You can tell me what they did to him," I said.

"No, I can't. Because I wasn't there. But you know the kind of heavies Lonzo uses. They wanted to know where the money was. Obviously. And they wanted to know where *you* were. *Who* you were. And they didn't get any of that."

"Denny was a brave man," I said.

"Yes, he was." Gerry looked at Ester then back at me. "And finally they wanted to hurt him, they wanted to make an example."

"Well," said Ester, "I don't want to hear the details even if *she* does." That was the first time I'd known Ester show weakness.

"OK," said Gerry, "Denny is dead. And Lonzo is still alive. And I, for one, could live without him."

"Why?" asked Ester.

"Now the Yanks are coming in, the whole drug scene is going to change. These GIs are flush with drugs: cocaine,

161

heroin, you name it. They're all called Mario and Gianni and they've all got brothers and uncles in the Mafia. Lonzo wants to get in on that. He wants more than just getting in – he wants control. First, because the GIs will be a big source. Second, because he doesn't want other people flooding the market. Do you get it? If there's an ocean of Yankee dope out there, the price goes down – splash! Lonzo doesn't want that."

"And what do *you* want?" said Ester.

"I want *out*," said Gerry. "I'm getting too old for gang war. Understand? It's not just a flood of drugs we're gonna get from the Yanks, it's a flood of guns too. And bombs. It'll be like Chicago in the twenties. I don't want to be an Al Capone."

"Neither did Denny," I said. "But he said he couldn't get shut of Lonzo. Couldn't get away."

"And I can't either." He took another gulp of his drink. "Myself, I'm very happy with a few nice girls like Ester. I know how to do a bit of the heavy stuff when it's necessary. But I'm not into gang war. Yes, I want out!"

"If we're going to kill this Lonzo," said Ester, "we need to know where he's going to be and when and how we can get at him."

"Yes," I said, "that's what I should've been finding out. I've wasted so much time."

"Maybe you're just not the type," said Gerry, "It's OK pulling a trigger when you're pointing at the ceiling."

I'd had those doubts myself, Father, as You know. But I didn't have them anymore. Not after I'd heard how Denny faced death for me. I said: "I can do it. I *will* do it."

"Fine," said Gerry. "Now I'll tell you the where and when."

And he pulled some papers out of his jacket pocket.

*

"Well," said Ester, "haven't *you* been a busy boy?" She'd sat down again by now and poured herself another glass.

162

Gerry said: "There's a drop that Lonzo has to make, handing over big cash to one of his suppliers. The date is a week on Friday. I know because I arranged it. And it's got to be in some out-of-the-way place the coppers don't know about.

"Well, one good thing about this war is that we've got lots of places dotted about the countryside that nobody's living in anymore, but there's still enough cover to provide a bit of privacy. Some Heinkel or Stuka or Dormer comes out of Leeds or Sheffield or Manchester and it's still got a couple of bombs on board so the pilot drops them over a few isolated houses on the way home. That's the sort of place I'm talking about. Look, I've got a map."

He took it out of his pocket and spread it on the table. It was drawn in red and blue crayon so it wasn't exactly *Mappa Mundi*. But it was big enough to see details and the road names were written in clear block capitals. He stubbed the map with his index finger. "It's a farmhouse. It's badly damaged but still standing. There's a roof and two floors and it's not going to fall down just because somebody breathes hard. I've arranged date and time with Lonzo…"

"But not with the other bloke," said Ester.

"Obviously not. And when Lonzo turns up, Josie, he'll find you waiting for him. With that big Argentine gun."

"Is it on a bus route?" I said.

"Is it on a *what*?" said Gerry. His voice had suddenly risen.

"She can't drive," said Ester. "Never mind. That's where *I* come in."

"But you can't drive the Alfa," I said, "it's too flashy. It'll be noticed."

"It doesn't matter," said Gerry, "because the farmhouse is just down the road from the barrage balloon site. She'll be picking you up from work. That was my idea."

"What could be more innocent?" said Ester. "I can show off the car to all your work mates. What sort of killers advertise themselves like that?"

"Got it in one," said Gerry.

"Just one thing," said Ester. "What's in it for me? I don't want to sound mercenary but I am, after all, a whore. You get your freedom and Josie gets her revenge. What do I get?"

"You get the flat," said Gerry. "Permanent hundred per cent ownership."

"It's a deal," said Ester quickly.

But something else – something very obvious – had now occurred to me. "Lonzo won't be alone, will he? He'll have bodyguards."

Gerry scratched his nose. "He usually settles for one minder. Somebody he really trusts. Somebody who drives him. *Me*. But I won't be there this particular day because something will crop up at the last minute. And Lonzo will have to drive himself because it's too important for him to miss out on and too late for him to get a substitute."

I said: "But if you *do* duck out, doesn't that put you in the frame with Lonzo's business friends?"

"No," said Gerry, "it actually gives me an alibi. I've arranged to be arrested."

I remembered again what Denny had said about it being useful to have friends on the Force.

"OK," said Ester, "I think we know what we're doing. I think it's time for a seasonal toast. Come on, Josie, you can manage one glass at least."

And so I did. And Ester proposed the toast. It was Tiny Tim's. "Merry Christmas, God bless us every one."

Chapter Thirty-two

THE FRIDAY AFTER NEXT came round soon enough. There was talk about going for another drink after work, the men in particular having got into a habit, but I said I couldn't because my flatmate was picking me up in her car.

"You should learn to drive," said one of the corporals, and I agreed that I should. "What sort of car?" he asked. And when I told him, he whistled. So I knew he'd be sticking around those few extra minutes to see the sights.

And she was dead on time. And she parked just across the road from our wire fence and got out and sort of stood there like... well, like Vivien Leigh as Scarlett O'Hara, standing at the top of the stairs at Tara. But, unlike Vivien, she wore trousers ("It's too cold for skirts," she said when we discussed the whole thing beforehand). But they weren't anything like the trousers I wore for uniform. They were shiny black and looked as if they were painted on her legs. And she wore a man's white shirt with the collar turned up and it was unbuttoned "down to her belly-button" said Christine, though not quite with complete truth. And her hair was piled high like Carmen Miranda in *Down Argentine Way* with Don Ameche.

But it was the car that impressed the men. I'm not like Ester: I can't go on about supercharged 2.9 litre engines. But I will say: it was smarter than smart, with four lights at the front and shiny spokes on the wheels. Because of its long nose, it looked like the head of a Labrador – or maybe an elongated raindrop. No, change that. Because it was red, it was more like an elongated drop of blood.

The men charged over and surrounded it. They started touching the chassis (as Ester later described it) and kicking the wheels (but quite gently, said Ester) and generally giving it the eye. Even the women were impressed, though I think the women were more taken with Ester's clothes than with her car. So we made an impression. I remembered what Ester had said to Gerry and me: "What sort of killers advertise

165

themselves like that?" This little show was our alibi.

We got inside and Ester started off to enthusiastic waves and shouts and wolf whistles. I'd never really thought what sort of driver Ester might be, but now I was impressed. There was no hesitation about her – but no risk-taking either. She drove fast but with skill. No, I think a better word is love. She drove with *love*. It was as though she was putting a pet horse through its exercises, caressing and cajoling, though of course I've never ridden a horse and I'm only imagining.

As we smoothed our way along those country lanes, I got out the crayon map that Gerry had made and tried to guide her. "I've already looked at it," she said, "and I've worked it out."

Within fifteen minutes, we'd come to the ruined farmhouse, victim of Mr Goering's Luftwaffe. It was pretty much as Gerry had described it: badly damaged but still standing, a roof and two floors. Scaffolding holding it up OK, so it wasn't going to fall down when somebody breathed. Tucked a bit away from the road, so it was a little bit private.

"We need to park," said Ester, "some way away from here. Somewhere where we can watch out for Lonzo's car and not be seen." We soon found the place – a field of stubble about a hundred yards away. I got out and opened the five-bar gate and Ester drove in. She shouted: "Get the stuff out of the boot." There were two parcels. I carried them back to the passenger seat. One was our tea – two sandwiches of black market chicken and a flask of black coffee. And a flashlight to eat them by because we'd turned off the headlights and it was pretty dark by now. The other was the loaded Ballester Molina – which Ester now referred to as the Ballbuster – and its silencer, stashed in my black leather document case. We knew Lonzo was due in the next half hour and we waited without talking.

After twenty minutes I said: "Supposing he comes from another direction?"

"This is the *only* direction. Unless he's practising for the Monte Carlo Rally, which isn't likely to be held again for several years."

"Suppose he's not coming straight from home?" I tried to think what he might have been doing. "He could have gone shopping or something."

"Yeh," said Ester. "He could have gone down to Woolworths to buy a golliwog for his baby granddaughter. Now just keep quiet and watch like I told you to."

Ten or twelve minutes later, a car came by. We knew from Gerry that Lonzo was driving a Morris Minor these days, like Gerry himself. I remembered Lonzo calling Gerry's car "efficient and unremarkable" so it was a natural for what Lonzo was doing. Trouble was: it was now so dark it could have been anything. But we heard the motor stop after half a minute.

"That's the one," said Ester. "We don't want to lose you, Josie, but we think you ought to go."

I picked up the case containing the gun. I opened the car door. I shivered. I zipped up my windjammer.

"Good luck," said Ester. "I'll still be here when it's over."

"I should bloody well think so," I said, shut the door very gently and walked towards the farmhouse.

*

I didn't use the flashlight for obvious reasons. I just hoped my eyes would get used to the dark very quickly. And I didn't take the gun out of the case, but I did undo the fastening so I could grab it pretty fast. I remembered what Denny had said: Aim for the chest first to stop them; then the head to finish them off.

And then I bumped into something and there was a bit of a clang. I worked out I'd kicked some piece of scaffolding lying about that wasn't joined up with the rest. A voice shouted: "Who's there? Is that you, Kenny?"

Lonzo's voice! Booming as usual from the deep canyon of his chest! And I wasn't going to pretend to be Kenny, whoever *he* was. I just stood very quietly, hoping Lonzo would think a rabbit made the noise. Or something like that. I

167

mean, I was a townie and so was Lonzo as far as I knew. There were lots of sounds in the country that didn't make any sense to *our* ears. I hoped it wouldn't bother him enough to... to *what*? Was Lonzo carrying a gun? Would Gerry have been carrying a gun if he'd gone along with Lonzo? Of course he would. And that meant Lonzo by himself would be carrying one. Ah well.

But Lonzo's voice had told me one useful thing: he was above me, on the first floor. Why he had to go upstairs in that God-forsaken wreck, I didn't know. Maybe he felt safer higher up. Maybe his eyes got used to the dark faster than mine and he wanted to scan the horizon now and again to check on who was coming to see him. And it meant whoever might come to visit him had to go upstairs too and that would make a noise. Moral: Stay where you are, Josie.

Then a flashlight came on above me. My ceiling – Lonzo's floor – lit up. And Lonzo's weird voice shouted: "Hey, hey, Mr Kenny! Be a good boy, now, ah, don't play games! Don't try taking advantage of an old man!"

I stayed still. Lonzo shouted: "I've, ah, got a gun, Mr Kenny! You don't think I'd come out here without my equaliser? Now show yourself, or I'll think you're not, ah, *my* Mr Kenny after all!" And Lonzo switched off his light.

And then a funny thing happened. Another clang. From maybe a few yards away. Maybe, I thought, this time it really *was* a rabbit banging into the scaffolding. And then:

Kearrrrrrrraaaaaaaaaaaaaaaackkkk!!!!!!

Lonzo had fired his gun. And, just like the gunfire in Bill Netty's pub, it nearly deafened me. And suddenly there was a God-almighty shout from above. And I remembered the second shock that night with Bill Netty: the recoil! The bloody recoil!

And next instant the crash of a body. And I switched on my flash and looked round the room... and there he was. Lying on the concrete floor face down, about three yards away from me. Not moving.

I reckoned he'd fired the gun towards the noise. And he'd been at the top of the stairs. Stairs that didn't have a bannister anymore. And the recoil had shot him into space and he'd landed on his head.

Oh, please, God, how I *hoped* he'd landed on his head!

I went across to look at him. I held my Ballbuster to his head. I turned him over. It was Lonzo alright – the olive skin and broken teeth. But now there was blood. Like my mother's blood the night of the fire engine. In death, he looked stupid. As though any sense that might have lingered inside his head had flown away. Like his soul. And I knelt down and felt his pulse and there was none. And I put my hand under his shirt and felt for his heartbeat. And there was none. And I didn't know what to do.

And then Ester came in. She was now wearing her full-length winter coat. "Sorry," she said. "Sorry about the noise."

"What are you doing here?" I said. "You're supposed to stay with the car."

"I wanted a pee," she said, "so I went in the field and then I thought: Now that I'm out of the car, maybe I should come and help."

"That noise?" I said. "That was you?"

"Sorry," she said again. Then she took in the body. "Is that him?"

"Yes, it's him."

"Is he dead?"

"Yes, he's dead."

"That's wonderful," she said, "we didn't even have to kill him."

"Oh yes, we killed him. He was scared, He fired his gun. He fell. *We* scared him. *We* killed him. I'm not having you say we didn't kill him. I'm proud we killed him."

"But if he was trying to kill *us*, it was self-defence."

"No. *We* were trying to kill *him*. It was us."

"OK," said Ester, "we should take his gun."

"Why?"

"Because by himself he's just a stupid man who fell off a staircase or something. If he's got a gun, that makes it suspicious."

"OK, we'll take the gun."

"It's the right thing to do. Nobody will ever look for a bullet if they don't know about the gun." She picked it up and hugged it to her breast. "It's just like *your* gun."

I had a look and it was. "Yes," I said, "I remember now. There were always two guns."

"And he was delivering money, remember? Lots of money. We should take that away too."

"Why?"

"Same reason. Also we could use it to pay our bills."

"You want us to go through his pockets?"

"*I'll* do it if you want." And she did. And she found an envelope. It was stuffed with tens and twenties.

I stood up and stretched. I felt very tired.

"Well," said Ester, "I don't know what to say."

"What do you mean?"

"I mean here's a dead man and he might well be a Catholic. You told me he was part Mexican and most of *them* are Catholics. But he's dead and there isn't any priest here."

"I should hope not."

"It shouldn't happen like that."

"Look," I said, "we were all set to kill him ten minutes ago. And then we robbed him. And now you want to say a prayer for him. Is this one of those times when you're still a Catholic?"

"It must be," she said. In the end, she said: "Holy Mary, Mother of God, pray for us sinners, now and at the hour of our death. Amen."

And I said: "Honest, there are times I really don't get you at all."

Chapter Thirty-three

BOB PETERS LIVED in a semi on a busy road in Attercliffe, north of Sheffield, and he had an indoor lav and a telephone. I let him pick me up at Leeds station again and drive me. It wasn't that I was worried about the address this time; I just didn't want him to see the Alfa and ask me what my flatmate did for a living.

His hall had an umbrella stand and coat hooks with only one overcoat and one jacket on the wall and there were unopened letters on the bottom stairs.

"Only bills," he said as he took my tweed coat.

"You should always pay promptly," I said. "It helps the war effort."

There was a reproduction of Constable's *The Cornfield* in the living room. I was able to tell him that it might look as though the boy was asleep, but when you looked at it close up, he was drinking water from the stream.

"I'd never noticed that," he said.

I sat at his table in the living room while he messed about in the kitchen, bringing in a tablecloth, then plates, knives and forks. "I know you like meat," he said, "so I've done Spam, peas and chips."

"Lovely," I said.

While we were eating, I asked him about work, but he wasn't forthcoming. "It's difficult to talk about. I mean, there's prosecutions pending and all sorts of legal restrictions. I know it's silly but, as far as my superiors are concerned, you might be a criminal who would use the information." Then he said: "What's *your* work like?"

"Well," I said, "it's difficult to talk about. As far as my superiors are concerned, you might be a German."

And he laughed. And I laughed too. And after that it went a lot easier and we managed to talk about books and films. And to my surprise, he'd actually read *The Ragged Trousered Philanthropists*, but didn't think much of it. "Too many abstract ideas," he said, "not enough good characters.

171

Otherwise, it wasn't too bad." But we agreed about Maureen O'Hara in *How Green Was My Valley*.

We had fruit salad for afters – mainly bits of apple and pears – and then we sat down, me on the sofa, him on the armchair, for a pot of tea with real milk, which actually impressed me. Then Bob said for no reason I could think of: "This is a police house."

"Oh."

"I mean I don't own it. But it goes with the job. And it's nice, isn't it? I mean, a couple could live here."

I said: "I thought a couple had already tried that."

Bad mistake. He didn't laugh this time.

"Alright," I said, "where's this medal of yours?"

He went across to a big oak sideboard, opened it and took out what looked like a jewel case. He opened it and took out the medal. It was like a silver coin, the size of a penny, on the end of a white ribbon with thick blue stripes and thin red ones. The face of the silver penny had the face of the king; but it wasn't George VI. "I'm afraid," said Bob, "it's Edward the Eighth. The abdication took everybody by surprise and they hadn't made any George the Sixth medals when I did the bomb thing, so I just got what was going."

This time we both managed to laugh again.

*

Right. I'm not going through all the sitting on the sofa and the kissing and the touching because it's just like I said about my time with Denny: it's embarrassing to talk about and You know it all already, Father, and I don't think I should waste my time and Yours with smut.

What I will say is that I'd already decided to go for bust. Bob knew all about my time with Denny and he either wanted me or he didn't. So I didn't even do the thing I did with my so-called fiancé: pretending not to know what a rubber was for. The only thing I *didn't* do was bring my own. That would look a bit... What's the word? *Wanton*, that's it. Also, I assumed Bob would be bothered enough about me to go out and buy some if he didn't have them already.

So we did it. And it was a bit fumbly, if that's the right word. But I don't mind that, not if it's the first time anyway. I think a bit of fumbling helps you get to know the other person. Though, now I think about it, I didn't get much fumbling with Denny; but then I always felt I knew him well enough from the start.

And when it was over, I got dressed and used his lav and he drove me back to Leeds station.

*

And Ester was all over me when I got back, but I didn't rise to the bait. "Lips sealed," I said, "the way it should be."

"Well," she said, "I suppose you could have spent all this time dancing to the wireless."

"Yes, we could."

"But you didn't."

"Well, it's Sunday. It's only the Brains Trust and Elgar."

By the time we'd got to the Château Donny, I'd more or less said Bob and I had gone all the way.

"But it's more than all the way, Josie. It's like you've blossomed. You've got healthy red cheeks for once."

"I'm blushing, that's why."

"Well, I think it's love."

"Love? With a policeman who's got no taste in literature or art?"

"Sounds fine to me." Then: "There's a story in the *Yorkshire Post*."

"So?"

"So they've found Lonzo's body."

It was ten days since we'd gone out in Ester's Alfa and I'd had no idea how long it would take for them to find him. I knew Gerry had got himself pulled in for assaulting some bookie who'd subsequently dropped the charges. And I knew the bookie – and the copper involved – had done nicely out of the transaction. But I didn't know how things would have gone after that. First, Lonzo's own people would have

173

realised he'd gone missing fast enough. But what do you do when your boss is a crook? You don't go running to the law, talking about missing persons. So I guessed they would have done some general asking around and searching likely spots. And Gerry would have done his part, all furrowed brow and worry lines. But with Gerry involved, they'd not be quick to make a discovery. So it was most likely some outsider had stumbled on him.

"It was the surveyor found him," said Ester as though reading my thoughts. "Some fella who'd gone out to help with an estimate on whether to have it repaired or pulled down. And now they're talking about a tragic accident involving a local businessman."

She snorted and handed me the paper and it was exactly how she'd said. "And I can't imagine the boys in blue being too upset about Mr Mack's premature departure. More likely, they'll be looking out for whoever's coming up to take his place." She paused. "Like Gerry for instance."

That shook me. "You don't think…"

"I don't know. He spun us a line about getting out of the rackets but I wouldn't be surprised if he didn't fancy being the new Lonzo."

"You said he was a teddy bear."

"Yeh. But with a few grizzlies in the family."

"You never said this before."

"Why should I? It makes no difference. We did our bit to rid the world of an evil man. Imagine if somebody had taken the trouble to top Herr Hitler a few years back? OK, we'd have Stalin and Mussolini, but the world would still be a better place." She took a sip of the wine. "And anyway, I've done alright out of it. And so have you."

Yes, I had. I had the revenge I'd craved. Why then should it bother me that Gerry or any other crook was set to take Lonzo's place? An evil man always has plenty of other candidates ready to replace him. Was that proof that there were more evil men in this world than good ones? You tell me, Father.

Suppose Mr Churchill had been killed by a bomb in the

first days? Would we have found another leader to fight on? Or would we have given it up and flown the white flag? I didn't like white flags. I liked people who knew which side they were on. I liked Bob Peters.

"Ester," I said, "you're right about me and Bob. And I think it means I'd better move out of here. What with him being a policeman and all. And you being a whore."

Ester sighed. "You're right. It would be good for both of us. You've got your copper and I've got my flat, all signed and paid for. But I'll tell you something – I'll miss you."

"And I'll miss *you*. You're my friend."

We clunked glasses.

"But most of all, Josie, I'll miss you because you made my life so fucking interesting."

Stave V: Jelly Peters

He'll build a little home just meant for two, from which I'll never roam. Who would, would you?

> ......Ira Gershwin, *The Man I Love*,

1927

Revenge is a kind of wild justice.

> ......Francis Bacon, *Essays*, circa 1600

Chapter Thirty-four

BACK TO AUNT MAY. Loyal, brave, lovely May. Who nurtured me when I needed it and let me alone when I needed that too. I had a lot to make up to her. But also I felt I had a good chance of actually pleasing her this time round, setting her mind at rest. Because I'd set my *own* mind at rest.

I'd done the thing I promised myself. I'd killed Lonzo Mack. Oh, some people might argue the petty details the way Ester did. But I was responsible, Father, for ridding the world of him. OK, *Ester and I* were responsible. We knew the kind of thing Lonzo did would just go on with somebody else running the show – maybe Gerry, though I wasn't convinced – but it had never been my plan to change the world. I wasn't that arrogant. Just to change the breathing habits of Lonzo Mack from normal to nil. Now I could go back to my real life.

Gloria Mundy was dead. Long live Josie Cawthorne, miner's daughter, dutiful Catholic, barrage balloon operative and sooner or later policeman's wife. Because it was obvious Bob was the marrying kind. Maybe it hadn't worked out for him the first time. But it would work out with *me*. The one drawback (I realised when I bothered thinking about it) was: I would have to scratch *dutiful Catholic* off that short list because the Church wouldn't be too happy about his divorce. But that shouldn't be too much of a problem, not with the Father in the Sky.

I went back to May with my suitcase and my smart leather document case. The suitcase had all my new summer dresses, though I'd have to wait six months before wearing them again; and the leather case, zipped up and locked, had the gun and the bank books and the wallet folder full of Aaron Bassett's forgeries. Maybe I'd get rid of it all pretty soon. Maybe it was only habit that prevented me throwing the Ballsbuster in the Sheaf and burning the papers.

Ester had kept the second gun, Lonzo's gun. "Only for show," she said. "I don't aim to kill anybody else. Not for a

177

while. No, I'll put it on my wall next to my school-leaving picture. I know this carpenter lad that'll put me up a bracket for next to nothing if I give him a small treat."

"You *are* joking," I said.

"Yes," she said, "I'm joking. It's only *old* guns – like flintlock muskets and duelling pistols – that really look good on walls."

"You should throw it away," I said.

"No, I shouldn't. Not in *my* game. It's true I've never felt threatened up to now. But suddenly I can see why people keep guns. I can see how comforting a gun can be."

I thought she was crazy, but I couldn't talk her out of it.

"You're keeping yours," she said. And I couldn't argue with that.

*

"Your dad's getting married," said May when we were sipping the ceremonial homecoming cuppa.

"I'm not surprised."

"Making an honest woman of Dora."

"And making her his permanent unpaid housekeeper."

"Lets you off the hook."

"That's the good thing."

"We should go round and see them."

So we did. Dora was wearing the same pinafore and Dad was wearing the same vest and trousers and reading a newspaper.

Dora said: "Your dad's been telling me all about you, Josie."

"Only the good parts, I hope."

"Oh, I'm sure there aren't any bad parts."

"She's a good girl," said Dad. "She's int' Labour Party."

I thought: How long can I get away with May's little lie? Maybe I'd end up having to join.

"We'd like you to be our bridesmaid," said Dora.

Naturally, I said yes. Naturally, I did nothing to suggest that perhaps the term *maid* in its strictest sense was no longer applicable. I said: "I'd like to bring my young man."

Dad looked up from his paper for the first time. "Oo's this one, then? Is e in work? Ow come e's not at front?"

"He's called Bob and he's a policeman. He doesn't like being called Bobby."

Dad snorted. "I'm no friend of bobbies but I spose e's a damn sight better than t'last one." He looked across at Dora. "Er last one ad a big motor car but got isself killed in an accident." Then he went back to his paper.

Dora had the grace to look embarrassed. But I smiled to show things were OK between her and me.

May said: "Well, we've just had us tea so we won't stop for another." And everybody said *t'ra* and Dora even waved us off from the window.

"She'll be good for him," said May, buttoning her coat collar against the cold. "And your Bob will get chance to meet the family."

"Me dad's me dad and I've no reason to fall out with him. And I've nowt against this Dora. But *you're* my real family, May. Nobody else."

"Until you've got bairns of your own," said May in a voice that made me know I'd pleased her.

"Not till this bloody war is over."

"Language!" she said disapprovingly.

*

The war had a long way to go to be over. We all knew that. But the air raids had grown far fewer and there was a sense that, with the Americans coming in, the balance had been altered. Irrevocably. We were no longer alone, what with them and the Russians. People had started to talk about what they planned to do after the war rather than what they were going through now to survive it.

I said to May when we got back home: "I suppose you're pleased the Russians are on our side, you being a Socialist."

She said; "Nay, you know me better than that, lass. I'm no friend of Joe Stalin. To me, he's just another Hitler with a different moustache. No, there's a lot of rubbish talked in the Labour Party these days. But we've got a good leader in Clem Attlee. There's some say he should never have joined a National Government with Churchill, but it's a damn sight better than palling up with Hitler, which is what Stalin did before he got his bottom caned. Now all the Lefties are trying to make us forget that."

"I thought *you* were a Lefty, May."

"There's Lefties and there's Lefties."

"Like there's Catholics and there's Catholics?"

"Exactly, Thank God I've been able to teach you something. It means my life's not been in vain."

*

Then it was Christmas. I gave May *For Whom the Bell Tolls*. I feared she might have read it already, but I couldn't see it on her bookshelves, so I took a chance. I knew Hemingway had been a reporter covering the Spanish Civil War, so I thought she'd enjoy it. And she pretended to. But when I got to read it, it sounded like a tourist sort of book – somebody who'd taken a short break to have a bit of a war. Well, never mind.

She gave me *The Sun Is My Undoing*, about the slave trade, by a woman called Steen. It was brilliant. Funny, how somebody who's never been a slave can write about it and somebody who's been stuck in a war can't make it come alive. But there you go.

I gave Dad cigarettes and Dora some lavender water. They gave me a new rosary, since they'd obviously seen I wasn't using one very much these days.

Bob gave me a ring and asked me to marry him. I said yes and gave him a very good Saturday night.

Chapter Thirty-five

I'D MADE A POINT for some time of staying over with Bob on Saturday nights. In a way, it was much like my time with Ester – staying in, eating a meal, drinking beer and listening to the wireless. Except the meal was more likely to be egg and chips than chicken or beef. And occasionally we'd get out to the pictures: *Suspicion*, where Joan Fontaine was married to Cary Grant and thought he was trying to kill her – but I never thought it for a moment; and *Sergeant York* where Gary Cooper was fighting the Kaiser's Germans and doing OK. Bob and I never went to dance halls – he just wasn't the dancing type. And he wasn't the type for art galleries either. But it didn't bother me much.

In fact, I'd become such a different person lately I could hardly believe the things I'd gone through. Except when it came to death and destruction – everybody else was going through that stuff as well.

Sometimes I'd wonder what it would have been like if Hitler hadn't bothered to invade Poland. If May had given me Arthur's insurance money so I could go to University. If I hadn't broken up with Alan and gone home on my own and met Denny at the bus stop. But that was stupid. I was who I was. I was made up of all the things that I'd done and all the things that had been done *to* me. But I still had free will, didn't I, Father? I couldn't change the past but I could get on with my future.

And right now my future looked good. As long as we won the war.

*

Next thing I know, the banns had been read for Dad and Dora, and St Thomas's Church was hired, and it was a reception at the Kimberworth Arms, where I'd first met Alan. Bob got out his best navy blue suit.

I had to wear a frilly white bridesmaid's dress for the

ceremony. It was nice – somebody Dora knew in the WAAF had made it up out of parachute silk. But it was too cold for me to wear a dress all day, so I took a teeny little bit of what was left of Denny's £5,000 and a few more of Aaron's coupons to buy a costume. I changed in the Ladies for the reception. It was a plum-coloured utility suit. The idea was you could mix and match skirts and jackets for a new outfit every day. I ask you! You could even wear slacks with the jacket like Katherine Hepburn in her photos. But I didn't want to cause any stir so I wore a matching skirt and left it at that. Though I did allow myself a little bit of glamour with the blouse – mauve with a ruffle at the front.

And the weather held off – though there had been snow the night before – and the day went well. There were about 20 people there, most of them on my dad's side and a few strangers from Dora's. And May, of course. The Kimberworth was still standing and doing quite well for itself, having escaped much of the bombing. So this time we were in the function room for the buffet and speeches. Dad's brother, Uncle Derek, who was Best Man, made a long one full of smutty remarks. Then there was dancing to a jazz trio – saxophone and drums with the pub piano helping out.

I'd already introduced Bob to May in church, and she'd looked suitably impressed. When the dancing started, I went over to Dad, and went through the necessary. And Dad said: "I understand tha's a policeman and tha's courting my daughter."

And I said: "More than just courting. We're engaged." And I showed him the ring. And I said: "Two weddings in the same year. By God, we'll be a famous family round these parts." And Dad just stared at me, as I knew he would. But Dora kissed me on the cheek and kissed Bob too and said: "That's wonderful. I wondered why you didn't try to catch the bouquet, Josie, and now I see the reason. You've already caught what you wanted." And then she said: "I know your dad's keen to be a grandfather – he's already said so."

Bob and I looked at each other and I could see he was embarrassed so I didn't say anything. In fact, we'd had a false alarm only the previous week when my period was four days late.

*

Bob and I were sat at a table for two on the edge of the dance floor. And Bob looked awkward and he said: "There's something I should tell you. I lied about my ex-wife."

Little bells went off in my head. "Are you telling me she's *not* your ex-wife?"

"Oh, no, no!" He fiddled with the glass of lemonade he'd had to drink on account of driving home later. "No, I lied about why Clarice left me. That was her name. Clarice."

"Go on."

"We'd had arguments. I told you…"

"She didn't like the hours you worked."

"Yes. And other things."

"Are you telling me you were unfaithful?"

"No, no," he said again. He laughed as if such a possibility was beyond belief. "No. It's just…"

"Go on."

"Talking of babies…"

"You *want* babies, don't you?"

"Oh yes. Absolutely. And Clarice was expecting."

I thought: Oh no! There's a little Peters out in the world somewhere and Bob is paying Clarice half his wages! But I didn't say anything.

He said: "Then one day she wasn't expecting anymore."

For a moment, I couldn't understand what he meant. Not expecting any more than what?

"She said she'd had a miscarriage. She said how sad it was."

And then the penny dropped. "And you didn't believe her?"

"It was a miscarriage alright. But it was no accident. That was hard for me. That she so disliked me by that time, she couldn't stand the idea of having my child." He took a gulp of his lemonade like a drunk with a tumbler full of gin.

Just at that moment a man I didn't know came over to us. He was big and brawny and going bald and he wore a purple check suit that did nothing for him. He said: "I hear it's said you're a copper."

"You hear right," said Bob without lifting his head or turning round.

"You know what I think about coppers?"

"I imagine you're going to tell me."

"All coppers are fucking bastards." And he laughed at what he'd said. Like it was Oscar Wilde on a good day.

"Thanks for your opinion," said Bob.

"All of 'em," said the man. He laughed again.

"Why don't you," I said, "go and fuck yourself?" But I said it in a quiet voice.

"You what?" he said.

"You heard," I said.

I think he was a bit taken aback. He'd expected some backchat from Bob, not from me. Bob stayed silent. The man said: "I'm the sort of lad knows how to sort out fucking coppers." Then he snorted and walked away.

"You did the right thing," I said to Bob.

"You mean doing nothing?"

"Sometimes that *is* the right thing."

"Yes."

"You're a hero already. You don't have to prove anything to me."

"No."

"I don't know who he is but he must be one of Dora's people."

Bob said: "I didn't see him in church. But I noticed him when we got here and he got out of the car. Can't miss that suit anywhere. He's parked next to us in a grey Hillman Minx."

"So we'll be running into him again."

"Looks like it."

"He's gone back to the bar," I said. "Looks like he's getting tanked up."

"He was already sheets to the wind."

"Maybe we'd better leave early."

"No," said Bob, "not while we're enjoying ourselves."

*

When we did leave, I noticed Purple Check was ahead of us and he'd got a mate with him. When he reached the Hillman, he took out his keys and lurched towards the driver's door.

"Oi!" said Bob softly.

The man took no notice, but his mate turned round. He was a younger, smaller man with acne.

"Oi!" shouted Bob.

This time Purple Check also turned round. "You again?" he said.

"Me again," said Bob. "I'm a police officer, as you know..." He took out his warrant card and held it up. "And I think you're far too drunk to drive that car."

"You try and stop me," said Purple Check.

"And if you get in that car, I'll certainly arrest you."

"Drunk?" said Purple Check. "That's a matter of opinion. I'm not too drunk to look after *myssen*." I noticed he'd suddenly fallen into Yorkshire pronunciation.

"Is he drunk or not?" Bob said to Acne Man.

"Well, er..." said Acne Man. He turned to Purple Check. "You *ave* ad a few, Jed."

"Jed?" I asked. "Is that short for Jedediah?"

"What if it bloody is?" said Jed, shouting now.

"Only that it's a Biblical name," I said.

"Jed," said Acne Man, "you don't wanna to get into any *more* trouble."

"Oh," said Bob, "you've already been in trouble with the law, then? I didn't realise that. I'll have to look you up when we get to the station."

"Tha'll do no such fucking thing," said Jedediah. More Yorkshire in his speech. I thought: It has to be the drink talking.

"Now, hold on, Jed," said Acne Man.

"I'll mek up me own mind if I'm drunk or not," said

Jedediah.

Bob turned to me. "Do *you* think he's drunk, Miss?"

"Oh yes," I said, "he can hardly stand."

"Also," said Bob, "one of your front headlights is broken. And it's getting dark now. You'll have to get it fixed before you can drive this car."

Purple Check sneered. "Bullshit!" he said. "Light's OK."

Bob took a half step back and kicked out the left side headlight.

"Oh fuck," said Acne Man.

Bob turned to me again. "Miss, will you go back to the pub, please, and phone Sheffield police?"

"Yes," I said. I turned to go.

"Look," said Acne Man to Bob, "we'll take the bus."

"No, we won't," said Jedediah.

"They're pretty frequent," said Acne Man.

"Then you'll have to give me the keys," said Bob. He held out his hand.

Jedediah straightened up and started to say something. But Acne Man grabbed the keys out of his hand and gave them to Bob.

"Thanks," said Bob. "I can see the bus stop from here." And he pointed towards the road. Acne Man set off, dragging Jedediah behind him. "You can pick up your keys at the station," Bob shouted after them. "I'll tie a tag with your name on, Mr Jedediah."

We got in our car and Bob started it. "Well," I said.

"Well, what?"

"Well, I shouldn't be surprised, should I?"

"I don't like causing disturbances at weddings, Josie. I'm an affable man."

"Other people might have seen you kicking in the headlight."

"No. Like I said, it's getting dark. People make mistakes in the dark. You don't want to be witness against a police officer when you're liable to make mistakes."

Chapter Thirty-six

OK, FATHER. Remember how coy I was about Denny? About telling You all the things we did together? So You know what You're going to get with me and Bob. The same. And, like I said then, I know it's daft because You've seen it all anyway. It's just that I don't want to report on it, like it's a story in the *News of the World*.

OK. OK. It was 1942. It was a good year. Bob and I were engaged, but in the end we didn't bother setting a date because we kept thinking: Maybe the war will be over soon. Wouldn't it be great to get married in peace time? And we were very careful about me getting *with child* as it says in the Bible – especially after the scare I mentioned earlier. Because if you don't want to get married during a war, it stands to reason you don't want to have a baby during a war either.

By now, I was staying over with Bob at weekends and in the middle of the week as well and he'd give me a lift into work, which made some of the men smirk. We went to see some very good pictures: *Kings Row* with Ronald Reagan, who is bound to become a very big star; and *Random Harvest*, where Ronald Colman loses his memory twice but makes it up with Greer Garson in the end. Bob thought this was very silly, but I loved it. I thought: Well, it just goes to show that you can remake your life even after terrible things happen to you.

And then there was *Yankee Doodle Dandy*. It's the first time I've seen Jimmy Cagney in a singing part and it was really great – and it had the song that Corporal Hawkins sang to us in the Crown and Anchor, though Cagney did it better.

I never got Bob interested in dancing. But I did take him to art galleries once or twice. And he took me to concerts. There were orchestras from all over making tours again and he took me to Bradford to hear the Birmingham Symphony Orchestra do *The Planets* by Gustav Holst, which wasn't my usual thing at all. But it was OK.

We'd started knocking about with Bob's pals from the station – in particular there was a man called Rod Snapes that was close to Bob. He was the broad-shouldered man in the wide-brimmed trilby who'd called out "Ey up, Jell" when we were back in the street after our fish and chips. And he had a wife called Edna who was OK, a bit of a laugh but not too vulgar. All in all, I could see myself as a policeman's wife with other policemen's wives for neighbours. Settled with nice people. Oh yes, I could.

Since Bob and I were fixed to be married, we'd started saving up for our own house and all the stuff young marrieds would need. I'd still got the money Denny left me but I wasn't going to tell that to the policeman who was going to be my husband. Too many questions to be answered!

I never asked Bob about Lonzo Mack's body. And it took three months for Bob himself to mention it. I forget how he brought it up. But he managed to say: "I know you knew him through your fiancé. But that was a long time ago."

"A lifetime," I said.

"And I don't suppose you had much to do with him."

"Nothing, really," I said.

Then he told me it was actually a couple of kids playing in the bombed-out house that found Lonzo. The surveyor, apparently, didn't turn up until an hour later and was annoyed about the police refusing him entry.

"How did he die?" I asked, trying to put a bit of nonchalance into the question.

"Fell off a piece of scaffolding. Or might have been pushed. No way of knowing. One of our narks told us he used the house as a place for meeting drug dealers." Bob smiled. "You didn't kill him, did you?"

We both laughed.

"Well," he said, "I don't think there's any point dragging up ancient history. The man got what was coming."

So I still couldn't look at the stuff in the bank accounts. It wasn't that I thought Lonzo Mack could still come after me – not from the place he was in – and it wasn't even Catholic guilt, not entirely. No. It was because I was set to marry a copper, and that was the end of it. The end of mixing with crooks and gangsters and their rotten money. And that was also my punishment, I thought – all that money and terrified to do anything with it. And I'd always be that way, wouldn't I?

*

We were still working hard with the barrage balloons, but there were no more raids on Sheffield after about the middle of the year. Still, as Christine was always telling us, it didn't do to get complacent. So we kept the repairs going and we kept thinking about what we'd seen back in 1940 and how we had to make sure we didn't go through it again.

*

I was seeing Ester for a drink at least once a week, usually in the Knights of the Golden Sun because that was the only place two women could go without some spiv trying to pick us up. She was still on the game but she had got ideas about buying other properties and doing them up. "When you think," she said, "of all the people that's been made homeless, it stands to reason there's money to be made in repairing places and decorating them and selling them."

I said: "Owning your own flat has given you ideas above your station."

"Well," she said, "being in my line of work is like being a film star or a footballer. You know eventually you'll soon get too old for scoring, and you'll be on the scrap heap. So I'd like to develop a second string."

I asked if she still saw anything of Gerry but she didn't. She'd become a freelance, she said, finding her own pick-up spots and her own punters, smarming up to hotel people who didn't mind what their vacant rooms were used for if they could get a few quid in exchange. "That's the difference. I used to work for a percentage. Now I get the whole caboodle and give somebody else a piece of it. And I'm making more than enough to get by. But I don't do Badgers anymore. I needed a man for that." And then she said: "What about you?"

"What *about* me?"

"I suppose in a while it'll be all babies and doing the washing and making Bob's tea. But that doesn't seem like the sort of thing you would settle for."

"Yes, it is."

"No, it's not. Take my word for it. Not that you shouldn't do that sort of thing for a while. But not forever. You should remember there's other things in life."

Yes, I thought, like shooting people. But I'm thinking I'll soon get too old for that, just like you're thinking you'll soon get too old for what *you* do.

*

May was looking to the future as well. "I might stand for t'council one of these days," she said. "After all, why not? It's not like having to shovel heavy rocks. A woman can do it as well as a man. Better perhaps. And after that, I'll want to be an MP. Nothing less. I'll do all the things Arthur would have done."

"You really think so? You don't think Mr Churchill will run rings round you and the rest of the Labour Party when all this is over? He's the country's hero, May. I know you think a lot of Mr Attlee. But I don't think women will vote for a bald-headed man unless he's very old and fatherly."

She laughed. "Well, I'll tell you what I think. I think Mr Churchill has been doing the right thing for the past four years. But when you've got something like a war, or the Wall Street Crash, or whatever the crisis, when it's over, win or lose, people want a change. They won't want the man who won the war any more than they'd want the man who lost it. No, they'll want to start with a clean slate. Somebody who's never been in command, not completely. I think Mr Attlee could very well win, given half the chance."

"Daydreams, May."

"Maybe."
And we left it at that.

*

We passed two and a half years just being happy. It's difficult to think of now, but we did. We'd visit Dora and my dad on a Sunday. We went drinking with Rod and Edna on a Friday night. I went out for lunch now and again in Ester's Alfa. May finally got me to join the Labour Party. Oh, they were good days.

Then I got a phone call from Ester. I can actually remember the date: Wednesday 7 June, 1944. It was early evening. Bob and I were at home, with the papers strewn across the floor. We were reading about landings on beaches called Utah, Omaha, Gold, Juno and Sword. We were finding out where Caen and Carentan were. We were discovering that Bayeux wasn't just the name of an old tapestry. We were wondering what 24,000 people looked like in one place – because that was the official figure for the total of American, British and Canadian airborne troops.

I picked up the receiver. Ester's voice wasn't just scared; it was frantic.

"It's Gerry Tordoff," she said. "He's back. And I think he wants to kill me."

Chapter Thirty-seven

ESTER AND I FOUND A NEW PLACE. It was the Kings Head in Attercliffe, which was a proper pub with wooden benches and brasses and tankards and Punch cartoons on the wall and it had a nice snug with comfortable cushions and it was mostly empty if we went early evening. Well, empty of *men*, anyway.

"The Knights is too much for me now," she said. "Too many friends of Gerry hanging around. Or the *friends* of friends of Gerry's. One way or the other." And she told what had happened.

"It was last Sunday," she said "and, since you've been gone, you'll be glad to know I've started going to church again on a regular basis. And I never use the Alfa when I'm going to Mass because it stirs envy in the congregation and envy is a sin.

"So, I'm walking back, taking my time, thinking about pork and roast potatoes for dinner, and I get home, and I'm putting my key in the lock, and suddenly I know there's something wrong. And before I can turn the key, the door opens. All by itself. Well, *not* all by itself. All because of this man who's already in my flat, and who's opening it for me from the inside.

"He's a small man, wiry, with greasy hair, and I don't like the look of him. And he smiles at me and I see he's got razor scars on his face, and now I like the look of him even less. And he says: 'Hello, Ester. Come on in and make yourself at home.'

"So I do. After all, it *is* my home. And he knew my name right off, so let's assume he's not just your ordinary burglar. But he's not the law either – because the law doesn't normally do house-breaking, and anyway he's too short even for wartime recruitment. Let's assume he knows all about me and knows where to find me if I have a mind to take a sudden run down the street. And, anyway, where would I go? And, anyway, I want to know what the hell he thinks he's doing.

So I do as I'm told."

"That's a lot of anyways," I said.

"There's more to come. Well, I step into the living room and he invites me to sit down. On my own sofa! Anyway, I do. And I take a good look at him, head to toe, and I see his shoes are dirty and he's leaving mud on my Persian carpet. And his suit is a size too small. Anyway, I reckon that marks him down as small-time, no clout. Not there to do me any harm without consulting his superiors, whoever they might be.

"Then he says: 'I'm Nick.' So we're on first name terms.

"Then Nick tells me that, after all this time, Gerry's had a change of mind about the flat. And I say that's as maybe, but I've got a paper, signed by Gerry, that says Gerry gave me the flat. And Nick says: 'Let's see it then,' and I say it's with my solicitor for safe keeping. And then Nick comes up behind me, grabs my arm and shoulder, lifts me off the sofa, bends me over the coffee table and puts his hand up my skirt and does things.

"And it wasn't nice. I've done a lot of things with men for money, and some of those weren't so nice either. So I'm no shrinking violet. But suddenly I was frightened. I started to cry. And Nick lets me go and I stand up and straighten my skirt and Nick says: 'It doesn't have to be this way, Ester. Just give us the paper.' And we go upstairs and I pull this paper out of the drawer in my dressing table and Nick reads it and he says: 'There. That wasn't so hard, was it?'

"And I say: 'So you think you're a tough guy, do you? So you think you and Gerry run the world?' And he says: 'You'd be surprised how nice I can be, feeding the fishes and planting the fruit.'"

I'm stunned. I say to Ester: "He said what?"

"He said: 'You'd be surprised how nice…' "

I said: "Carp. And blackberries, raspberries, strawberries… I know where he lives." I said: "So it probably means that's where Gerry's living too. But it doesn't do us much good."

Ester went on: "Then this Nick comes up to me close and

grabs me by the shoulders and he says: 'You know things about Gerry. Lots of things that could do him damage.' And I say: 'I don't know what you mean.' And he slaps me across the face so I'm crying again. And I say: 'Gerry's my friend. I wouldn't snitch on him.' And he says: 'Gerry isn't your friend no more. But if you're a good girl and come back and work for him, he'll see you're all right. Meaning not having to use crutches the rest of your life.' And he laughs, very high like. It was like feeding time in the monkey house.

"And then Nick left. But he said: 'You'll be hearing from Gerry. When he gets round to it. Hearing through me. He'll line up some work for you.' And then Nick is off out. And I have a sit down and another good cry.

"And I'm thinking of all the things I know about Gerry — the pimping and the Badger Game and the way we got together to kill Lonzo Mack. And I'm thinking: Yes, there's plenty I know that could put him away for a long time. And maybe you and me as well, Josie; we could share a cell.

"But then I think: They're not going to kill me in my own home, which belongs to Gerry anyway. Oh no. They're going to do it far away from here. Far away from any connection with Gerry. And I think: They're going to make it so there's no obvious suspects — or maybe *too many* suspects. And I think: It'll be the next time Gerry sends me out. It'll be the next time he sends me out to a mark. And they'll make it look very nasty, like some perv looking for a bit of the rough who went too far. And then it'll be the sort of crime the police don't much care about. A tom getting topped by a mark. Serves the woman right. Because that's the way I'd do it if I were Gerry."

And she stopped and said: "I could do with another whisky and soda."

And I went to the bar and got it. And one for myself.

Chapter Thirty-eight

AND WHEN I SAT DOWN again, I gave her the glass and said: "You've got a gun. You've got a gun like mine. What have you done with it?"

"I've not done owt with it." She took a sip. "Why? D'you think I should shoot this bastard Nick?"

"No, I don't."

"Well, then?"

"Only I'm trying to put the pieces together. We got away with a lot, you and me, didn't we?"

Ester pressed a hand to her face. "Yes, we did."

"And we can get away with a lot again. Maybe. But I'm trying to tidy things up in my mind. I don't want guns being found, turning up, coming out of the blue to embarrass us. I'm worried Nick might come back to your place and do a search. I keep *my* gun at Aunt May's. In a document case in the top of my wardrobe. Maybe I should take yours as well."

"I don't know about that. Maybe shooting Nick isn't such a bad idea. I could say he was a burglar and I shot him in self-defence."

I snorted. I took a big gulp of whisky. "Let's be frank. We're neither of us going to shoot Nick. That would be a dangerous thing to do and probably a waste of bullets. Though we might shoot Gerry if we ever got hold of him again."

That made her laugh. At least the talk about us killing people was cheering her up. "OK," she said, "I'll give you the gun. And you can get Aunt May to keep it safe until we need to use it." She was silent for a second or two. "Of course, you've got more to protect, these days. Being married to a copper has made you more careful."

"Yes," I said, "it has."

But I was thinking about Gerry, about this sudden change of character. "I thought you said Gerry was a teddy bear."

"Well, he was. But it seems obvious now that getting rid of Lonzo was his big step up. And he's changed."

195

"Power corrupts," I quoted. Then: "How well did you know him anyway?"

"Are you asking if he fucked me?"

"You always did have a smutty way of talking."

"The answer is: yes. Why not? He was OK, pleasant to me…"

"I don't think *pleasant* is an adequate word for what we're talking about."

"I let him fuck me because he was nice to me and because it cemented our business relationship."

"And I've never heard it called *cemented* before."

So then we both laughed again. Maybe we were just getting drunk. Maybe we needed to get back to serious stuff. I said: "You'll have to get away from here, away from Gerry and everything."

"What? Leave my lovely flat?"

"It's not yours anymore, remember?"

She said: "Do you really think there's a bit of room left in Aunt May's wardrobe?"

"It's *my* wardrobe in May's house and I think we could find some."

"OK then. I'll bring you that bloody gun next time I see you."

Chapter Thirty-nine

MAY HAD GOT HER NAME on a short list for our council ward, though nobody really knew when the next elections might come up. She had to go for an audition ("It's not an audition," she said "it's a bloody interview. For a proper job.") and we were very excited.

She'd been talking to a lot of people round about ("Smarming up," I called it, and she slapped my wrist) and mugging up on stuff from the newspapers (what Mr Attlee had to say about the future – things like council housing and a public health service and full employment and bigger handouts on the dole). Though I couldn't see why you'd need more dole money when you'd got full employment.

But who cared about the little things? We were into our sixth year of war. The big difference was: everybody knew we were going to win.

"It's been six full years since we've had a council election," she said, "thanks to Adolf. Mind you, there's not much in the way of local issues. It's not as if there's too few jobs right now in a village like ours, where every young man is either down the pit or in uniform. And if you've got too few houses or bad roads with potholes, then that's Adolf's fault too, God damn him."

There were two seats up for grabs in our Sheffield ward and she spent a lot of time wondering how she'd get on with the other winner. Whoever it might be. "I don't want spending time with Walter Broome," she said, "or Digby Doom, as I call him. My God, that man's never got a smile on his face. If I spent any more time with him, I'd end up in a loonie bin." And she wasn't keen on the other likely favourite – Humphrey Ridout. "I won't say he's a drunk, but he's the only man I know who could catch pneumonia from having wet change in his pocket."

She was spending more time round the Labour Club, which was an old wooden building, ("rotting at the corners," as she put it) with a newly installed corrugated iron roof ("that's the only modern thing about it"), and it was badly lit and draughty. It had never been a favourite haunt of hers in the past, and not just for those reasons. "Too many stupid men," she said, "swearing and talking about the football and playing dominoes and spilling their beer. But I've got to show my face, else I'll look like a snob."

To me, this was a whole new May, actually worrying about what other people thought. "I've got to go there but I don't want to give the impression I'm too keen on drinking. The men won't like it and they'll go back to their women and tell em I've had three pints of milk stout and the women won't approve either."

It was mostly when she talked about other women that she became really serious. One evening, over the kitchen table, she looked straight at me and said: "Men aren't the biggest problem for women: it's women as is the problem. Women who think the kitchen is the only safe place for them. Women who won't stand up to men."

I laughed. "Look at you!" I said. "*You're* the one that's trying to impress the men now!"

"Aye," she said, "I am. And it's a bloody disgrace. But it's life. I'd change it if I could but I don't know how."

In the end, I'd go round with May to the Labour Club and we'd both have our stout; and, if I'm honest, the men weren't so bad at all. One of them even said how nice it was to see more women "using the facilities", as he put it.

"Patronising bugger," said May softly when he'd walked away.

*

One day, when I got back from work, May was sitting in the kitchen with a face like thunder. I said: "I'm not very late, am I?"

"No," she said, "you're not. But it looks as if *I* am. I had a visit from Douglas Pritchard this afternoon."

For a moment, I couldn't remember who he was. Then: "Oh, isn't he something in the Party?"

"Ward Party Chairman."

I sat down opposite her. I won't say she was crying. But her face was set in the mould of people trying hard *not* to cry.

"And he told you something bad." I didn't have to make it a question.

"He said he didn't want me to stand for the council."

"Why?"

"He said it was a pit area where men were the breadwinners and he had to have men. He said the war was nearly won – though I think that was a bit premature – and we had to get ready for the next war."

"The next war? You mean against the Russians?"

"No. He meant against the Tories. He said Mr Churchill was a class enemy. But he'd got a lot of working men on his side and the only way to win them back was to have men as candidates."

"And what did *you* say?"

"I told him it was a disgrace that the ward party didn't want women candidates. And then I told him to piss off. I think he was shocked."

"I'm sure he was. Well, that's it, then."

"That's what, then?"

"We'll get up a petition. Go round the houses. Talk to the women. Demanding a woman candidate."

"We'll never get that."

"Why not?"

"You know what miners' wives are like. If you go round to their house, they'll give you a cup of tea like a shot. But they won't give you an opinion until the man comes home."

"You know, May, I think you hate miners' wives as much as you hate miners."

"That I do."

"You've got the wrong attitude. You should think of it as being just like a game of rounders. Good exercise for us girls."

*

So May and I did lots of walking and talking. Evenings and weekends getting signatures. We talked to the miners' wives while the miners were in the pub. We stroked their dogs and made *oozy-goo* talk to their babies. We went to meetings of Young Socialists but there wasn't a woman in the place. We looked up the Women's Institute, though May thought they all voted Conservative. "Well," I said, "we'll have to change their minds." And the Catholic Mothers Union gave us cups of tea with surprising amounts of sugar, considering the rationing.

And I enjoyed it. It took my mind off Ester. And the months passed by without any more scary phone calls from her. And then it was Christmas and then the New Year.

And then we had a stroke of luck. A young man called Harry Holton turned up from the *Algrave Chronicle* and wanted to do a story about us. It came out the following Friday as "May's Petticoat Politics". And there was a picture of the two of us handing out leaflets in Algrave Market. (Aaron Bassett was glad to do some leaflets at cost because of the work I'd put his way.) And then the *Star* picked up the story and ran it as "Will Luck Smile on Lady of the Left?"

"Where in God's name do they get their headlines?" May demanded, throwing the paper on the kitchen table.

"It's nothing to do with God," I said. "Now just shut up and be glad of the publicity."

*

Rod and Edna saw the papers and thought it was, as Rod put it, "a reet good laugh".

We'd started going to the Kings Head, the pub I'd been to with Ester. Edna liked to stand up with her nose up against the walls and read the Punch cartoons. "But," she said, "it's all old jokes that I don't get. Napoleon and stuff."

"Just think Hitler for Napoleon," I said.

And Rod said: "It's funny how the British sense of humour never changes with time." Rod was what the Americans call *deadpan* – making the sort of remark that sounds as if it might be serious but then you realise it's only a joke. He often said things like that to annoy Edna, who always took him straight. Bob agreed with me there were hidden depths in Rod.

One night in the Kings Head we were talking about the latest war stuff – the allied advances in Italy and France. And the news that Mussolini had been shot dead by Communists.

"*And* his mistress," said Rod, "though what his piece-on-the-side has got to do with starting the Second World War escapes me." When he wanted to emphasise a point, he had a way of arching his eyebrows, which met in the middle.

I said: "People just get angry." But I could hear my voice fade a bit at the end of the sentence.

"Tarred with the same brush," said Edna, presumably meaning Clara Petacci. I remembered Ester saying she'd like to crucify Germans and how I'd agreed with her at the time. But when a young woman gets killed and strung up naked afterwards, it makes you think again. Edna said: "They wouldn't have killed his *wife* like that."

And I saw she was probably right. Clara hadn't been killed for the war; she'd been killed for sleeping with Benito without getting properly wed first. If she'd been the respectable married type, she'd have probably got away with it. The Commies would have sent Mrs Musso on her way with a "mi scusi, signora" before they shot Il Duce.

Edna, meantime, was thinking ahead. "I wonder if they'll get Adolf the same way."

"Shouldn't think so," said Rod, "he's got too many people round him. In his underground bunker. Cut off from reality. At least for a little bit longer."

"So what do you think will happen?" asked Bob.

Rod put down his pint. "He'll kill himself. Bullet through the head. That's Adolf's way out. Quick ride with the…" He paused. "What do they call them? Those women in chariots with blonde plaits and steel helmets and big tits?"

"Watch your language," said Edna.

"I meant," said Rod, "big bosoms."

"Valkyries," I said.

"Yes," said Rod, "Valkyries. That's it." He picked up his glass again, took a gulp, wiped his mouth. "That's Hitler's style, you mark my words. Thinks he's too good for anything less than grand opera."

"And what," I asked, "is going to happen to that woman of his? What's her name?"

"Eva," said Bob.

"He'll have *her* shot first," said Rod. "Because when I say he'll kill himself, I don't mean stick the gun up against his head and blow his own brains out. No. I mean he'll get somebody else to do it for him. A sergeant or somebody small beer whose name will never be known. That's *his* way. And then they'll burn the bodies or bury them under concrete like he's told them to. Keep a bit of mystery."

There was a short silence after that and Rod took another drink and so did Bob, and Edna and I had a sip of our G&Ts. And suddenly it struck me. "I'll tell you something else," I said. "This Eva, he'll marry her first."

"Why?" said Edna.

"To make it respectable."

And we all laughed. And a few days later we found out Rod had been pretty much right. And I'd been right too. And suddenly I thought I saw what May was about. It wasn't a game of rounders. It was a damn sight more than good exercise for the girls after all.

*

Father, You'll be sad to know (though You know it already and I've no idea if You ever feel sad in the way *I* mean the word) May didn't get a change of heart from Labour. They went ahead with their men after all. But we couldn't be bothered to cry over it. Other things to think about. Because the Germans surrendered! Somebody called Admiral Doenitz, whom I'd never heard of before, signed the treaty.

"There's still the Japs," said Rod next time we were in the pub.

"God, you're never happy, are you?" said Edna.

And Bob laughed. And Rod winked at me. Rather slyly, I thought.

Chapter Forty

EIGHTH OF MAY! V.E. DAY! People out on the streets! Bunting and banners and pennants! And dinner tables and pasting tables and chairs and piano stools and sofas! And singing and dancing and car horns and bells and screams and shouts! And getting drunk and falling over! And the girls kissing the men and their knickers turning up at lost property! We had a street party in our road. We had cakes and sausages and pigs' trotters – God knows where some of it came from! And gallons of beer – most of it home-made! We had a fancy dress parade for the kids and some of them came as Hitler with little moustaches painted on their lips. Oh, we could laugh at him now! There was a prize for the best fancy dress and I would like to tell you who won it, whether it was one of the little Hitlers or not. But I can't. I can't remember anything that isn't like a blur. Except...

May turned up. And she was with a man. "This is Mr Broome," she said, "or *Councillor* Broome, as I might be calling him soon." But she didn't say it with any sarcasm. None of that Digby Doom stuff for the Man Who Never Smiled. In fact, I swear she simpered.

And he was a personable chap for a man of his age. He was quite tall. He had wire spectacles and a bit of stubble on his jaw, whereas I knew it was May's general liking that a man should always have a smooth chin. "Please call me Walter," he said. I was rocked on my heels, as they say.

We talked for a bit about Mr Attlee's chances when the General Election came. "Clem won't stand for this National Government much longer," said Walter, as though he and the Deputy Prime Minister of the United Kingdom of Great Britain and Northern Ireland were blood brothers, boozing together every Saturday night. "Though Churchill wants him to stick it out until the Japs go down. But I'm thinking we might go to the country in a couple of months."

Rocked on my heels again!

*

At some point in late afternoon, Bob and I got away from it and we went home and switched on the wireless. Mr Churchill made a speech to the nation and the BBC said there were a hundred thousand people in Hyde Park alone and they all fell silent when the speech was relayed over loudspeakers.

Apparently, King George and the Queen appeared eight times on the balcony of Buckingham Palace. And it was said that the two Princesses – Margaret and Elizabeth – mingled with the crowds, though I don't know if this was true and I don't suppose there'll be any way of finding out. Though I bet there'll be lots of people saying: "Oh yes, they chatted away thirteen to the dozen. Very nice they were, too. I recognised them from their photographs."

Bob and I went to bed early. We sort of sank into each other, weary with the world, but full of our own energy. I'd warned him beforehand not to get too drunk because this was a special day for us. It was the first day after the war and there was no longer any reason to put off getting married and no longer any reason to delay trying for a baby.

"Those are two different things to be getting on with," he said, "and we should try to get the order right for a start. And there's still the Japanese. As Rod has pointed out. And your Mr Groome too."

"Broome," I corrected him, "and he's not *my* Mr Broome." And then: "Well, the Japanese are a long way off. And they'll not be getting any closer. Not now."

"Well," he said, "that puts a lot of responsibility on me."

"Well," I said: "Just make sure you're up to it!"

Afterwards we allowed ourselves a glass or two of Courvoisier brandy from a bottle that Bob had apparently been saving since Dunkirk. "Brought over by one of the rescuers," he said, "a mate of mine. He brought back 20 tommies and still found space for a crate of the stuff. I hope it's worth the wait."

I started to say something about the rest of our days, how we'd got to make sure *they* were worth the wait as well. But

Vera Lynn came on the wireless and we sang along to "We'll Meet Again". And I never got chance to finish my sentence.

Funny how we all of us miss so many chances to finish things the way we want to.

*

So our lives were a holiday. I'd turn up for work but we didn't have anything to do. We'd finally admitted we were redundant. No air raids meant no balloons.

The Japs were retreating, bit by bit, though I read this article in the *Sunday Despatch* which said they had a plan called *ketsu-go*, one last decisive battle to inflict so many casualties that the allies would relax their demands for unconditional surrender and negotiate a peace. This might safeguard the Emperor, and save the armed forces from prosecution for war crimes. And the Japs were also hoping Joe Stalin would turn against us. But all this would change if Stalin kept his promise to invade Japan. Which the *Despatch* thought he probably would.

And then something incredible happened. Well, *not* so incredible, considering. I missed my period again. And I looked at myself naked in the bathroom mirror. Did my breasts look bigger? Or my tum? No, they didn't. Not really. That sort of glowing ripeness that I'd so looked forward to hadn't materialised. Still, if I was pregnant, it was early days yet. What did I expect?

I gave myself a critical once-over. I'd said previously how Gloria Mundy was finally laid to rest and Josie Cawthorne was back. But now I had to acknowledge Gloria wasn't dead at all – the blonde hair was still her. And I wasn't planning to grow it out as long as men like Bob – and men like Rod, come to think of it – kept glancing at it. I was no longer the schoolgirl Josie, who drank whisky at Uncle Arthur's funeral and met a nice boy called Alan. I was twenty-three years old and it suddenly seemed like twenty-three going on thirty-eight.

When I gave Bob the news, he was suitably excited. In

fact, we had a high old time and we finished the Courvoisier. We looked at dates for the wedding, bearing in mind the amount of time it took for the banns and the fact that we didn't want it obvious on the day that I was expecting. We talked about which church we'd have; and Bob, who was an atheist, said any church was OK with him, even a Catholic one. Which was typical Bob. Got on with everybody, Rod always said.

And we discussed the usual stuff that I'm sure everybody does: Would it be a boy or a girl? Some women I knew said if a baby was conceived in the height of passion, when both the man and the woman were having a real go at it, then it would always be a boy; but if it was done at the end of a long day when you'd really rather go to sleep or were dying for a pee, it was bound to be a girl. "Right," said Bob, "it'll be a boy, then."

And what names would we choose? I'd already started two lists – boy or girl – with some of my favourites and I wasn't going to throw the girls' list away just because Bob thought he was Errol Flynn in bed. I wanted it Biblical but not too Catholic: Joseph and Mary were out but Daniel and Matthew and Ruth and Martha were still in. And, oh, it was fun!

Even better than the street party!

Chapter Forty-one

THIS TIME, ESTER'S CALL, when it came, was less frantic, as though she'd really made the effort. She said: "It's what I told you would happen. Gerry's finally going to have me killed. Now it's got a place and a time to it."

When I got to the Kings Head, I said: "This is like a second home to me now," and I got us the usual whiskies. I sat down. I said: "I didn't see the Alfa."

"I got rid of it." She sighed. "And yes, it was a bit of a heart-breaker. But I've got into a new life-style. I don't want to look conspicuous. In fact, I don't want to be noticed at all. Now I've got an old car – a 1938 Morris 14. It's a four-door. And yes, it's black. It'll never stand out in traffic. Or at a funeral."

"Don't be stupid. Nobody's going to kill you. Not if I've got anything to do with it. But you've got to get away from here. Out of Yorkshire. Out of England. The war will be over soon and you'll be able to do that." And I was suddenly reminded of the silly conversation I'd had with Denny about New York. Was I still being daft?

"No, Josie, I can't wait till the war's over. I need to get out now." She grimaced. "This is what's happened. Nick the Grease has been round again. I've got this date – that's *his* word – with a mark at a place called the Diamond Hotel in Bramley."

"And...?"

"It's a place I've never heard of and I've asked some of the other girls around and they don't know it either. If I had somebody like Gerry to look out for me – instead of threatening me – then I might go. But the way it stands, it's a no-no."

"So what happens next?"

"If I go, I reckon I'll get done in. If I *don't* go, Gerry will twig that *I've* twigged and he'll cut his losses and send somebody round. I lose either way."

"OK. You're right. You've got to get out right away. To

somewhere safe."

"How about with you and Bob?"

That took the wind out of my sails. I thought about it. I thought what might happen if we did it. So Bob's a copper and he's got a prostitute living in his house, a woman that's being hunted down by a known gangster. And he's got another woman there who used to share a flat with the prostitute and who's now pregnant out of wedlock by said police officer Bob. Not the best thing to put on your job application if you want to be Chief Inspector someday.

But I didn't know what else to do to save Ester. I said: "OK. I'll do that. *We'll* do that, Bob and me." I wondered what Bob would say. I couldn't imagine he would be very sympathetic. Then I remembered something else to say to Ester: "You've got the gun, have you? Like you promised?"

"Oh yes." She had a hessian bag next to her on the bench seat and she passed it over. There was the usual brown paper parcel inside. She said: "You can open it if you like."

I said: "No, I don't need to." But I was thinking: What if this is all a plot against Bob, against an honest copper, who always tries to do his job? What if I can't trust Ester any more than she says she can trust Gerry these days? Maybe she's been on Gerry's side all along. How would it look if Sheffield Police searched our house and they found a gun as well as a prostitute?

But then I thought: You have to trust *somebody* in this life. It was just a matter of deciding who. Or should that be *whom*? In any case, I didn't want to open the parcel in the pub.

"Alright," I said, "if that's what we've got to do, you can give me a lift back."

*

So we went home in Ester's Morris. All the way I was rehearsing what I'd say to Bob, but none of it was turning out right. It was quite dark by the time we parked in the street outside. Bob's Austin was there so he had to be in. I unlocked the front door.

"Bob," I shouted, "we've got visitors!" and he came downstairs in his shirt sleeves wiping his hands on a towel. I said: "Bob, this is Ester."

He put out one of his still wet hands to shake hers.

I said: "She's an old school friend of mine. She's also a prostitute. And somebody's trying to kill her."

"Well, I'll be blowed," he said and draped the towel over his shoulder. I was pleased he'd not actually used a rude word.

When we were sat down and I'd made some tea, I gave him a potted history of the situation. I was really pretty good, though I say so myself. I emphasised the school friend bit so he'd realise I'd first got friendly with Ester in a more respectable period of her life and it gave me credentials as a caring friend and a Christian person. I left out embarrassing details like how Ester and I had killed Lonzo Mack. I left out the fact that Gerry had given the flat to Ester, because that would have involved explaining what she'd done to deserve it, which would have brought Lonzo Mack back into the conversation. And I sort of played down the part where I lived with Ester, making it sound more like friendly visits with the occasional spare room when things got late, and I allowed him to assume I didn't know at the time what Ester did for a living.

And I made the threats to Ester sound like attempts by Gerry to keep her on the game against her will – so even if she hadn't been a good girl in the past, she was certainly trying to be one now. (I was glad she'd got rid of the Alfa because I didn't want Bob to be shocked when he saw it.)

But there was one part I couldn't hide, camouflage or avoid. So I didn't try. "This Gerry person," I said, "was a friend of Dennis Morrow, alias Dennis Morgan, who was once my fiancé, as you know. And I personally met this Gerry at the time."

"Well, I'll be blowed," he said again. But he'd recovered his cool by now and he helped himself to a second cup of tea. And I took the shopping bag with the gun up to our bedroom and put it in my knickers drawer.

Chapter Forty-two

WHEN I WAS AT ST ELFREDA'S, FATHER, we were doing *Much Ado About Nothing* with Sister Margaret Mary as was, and You know what a strange thing it is: first there's all the funny bits with Benedick's mates kidding him that Beatrice is in love with him; and her pals telling her *he's* in love with her. And, of course, they really *are* in love with each other, otherwise there wouldn't be a story. But the point is: the friends don't know that, they're just having a joke. And it's a silly joke, like a pantomime with "He's behind you!" It's just not very grown-up.

Then the mood changes. The play gets a bit dark, what with Hero having her problems with Claudio and all the stuff about whether she's a virgin or not. Then it gets *very* dark with Beatrice actually getting Benedick to agree to fight his best friend Claudio in a duel to the death.

Well, my life's like that. Light and dark, funny and sad, a bit of a joke and screaming horror every so often. But everybody's life *is* like that, isn't it?

You'll remember that Benedick doesn't have to fight Claudio in the end because it's one of Shakespeare's Comedies, not his Tragedies. But *Your* Comedies and Tragedies are all mixed up, Father, leaning into each other. I've just made a few jokes about Bob, wiping his wet hands and supping his tea. I've made fun of him, the man I love.

Now the mood changes, Father, now the play gets dark.

*

The three of us talked a long while longer but I could see Bob wasn't buying all of what we'd told him. He was just being his usual polite self. I smiled at him.

And I could see he was genuinely worried about Ester, her idea that Gerry Tordoff was out to murder her. Even if he didn't quite believe it yet. And we got to the point where she'd finished her story and I'd finished the little bits of detail I kept putting in to make it sound more likely. Then Bob clicked his tongue. He said: "Ester, I'm going to have to find out a lot more about what you've told me before I can do anything as a copper. But I won't let you leave here tonight as long as you're afraid like this. You can stay over and we'll change the sheets in the back bedroom. Have you brought some things you'll need for the night?"

She said her things were in the car and she got up and went out for them. Bob turned to me and I said to him: "Yes, I know. It's for me to make up the bed."

Bob laughed and said: "It's not just her I'm worried about. It's you. There's a lot of you I don't know about and probably never will. That's OK. But I want you to know that whatever you've done to get mixed up in this mess, it doesn't change anything between us. I want you to know I'll protect you whatever. If it's humanly possible."

"Even if it goes against everything you do as a policeman?"

He sighed. "Even if."

And then I knew what Beatrice felt like when she got Benedick to agree to the duel. Proud and terrified at the same time. And I hugged him and I burst into tears.

I could see the poor man was embarrassed by now. He hugged me back but then he pulled away. "I better help our guest with her suitcase," he said. And he followed her out while I went upstairs.

I was at the top of the stairs when I heard the car. I mean, not an ordinary car doing an ordinary run along our road. No. It was a screaming car. And I turned round at the top of the stairs and I ran all the way down. And I was screaming like the car.

And people tell me I didn't really see it. And I know they're right. I only heard it: the screaming car and the thud and the screaming woman afterwards. The screaming Ester. And me thinking: They knew she'd changed her car.

But I saw it all, Father. In my mind's eye, if You like, in the inner part of me that always looked out for Bob the same way he always looked out for me. I saw the car come round the corner. And I knew whoever they were, they'd clocked Ester's Austin and they'd followed Ester, and they'd seen their chance. I saw the terror in Ester's eyes as she realised what was happening. I saw the car head down on her. I saw Bob, my hero Bob, the man who could never stop being a bloody hero because that was just what he was. I could see him run across the road, grab Ester up in his arms and push her over onto the pavement and I could see the car hit him square.

Hit him like my mum. Hit him up in the air. Hit him to fall back on the paving stones. Hit him enough to be dead when I got there.

I said I screamed when I ran down the stairs. But not like I screamed then, holding his head in my arms. No, not like I screamed then. Not like I'm still screaming to this day, screaming inside. Where only You can still hear me, Father.

*

Sirens. Ambulances. Doctors. Nurses. Ester and me sitting on metal chairs with canvas seats in a hospital corridor. At some point I had to get up and go to the Ladies.

Funny. I can remember every detail of my mum's getting killed like I can remember whole scenes from *Gone With the Wind*. I can remember hugging the fireman and telling him it wasn't his fault. But I can only remember little bits of what happened after Bob died. Like sometimes when the film breaks at the pictures and the projectionist can't get it back together right and they have to miss a few frames.

But I came out of it. Suddenly. There was a uniformed policeman walking down the corridor towards us. There was something I had to say to Ester. I said: "It was an accident. Some hit-and-run bastard. Don't tell the police anything. We'll take care of it. You and me."

And she heard. And she didn't say anything. To me or to them. But she looked at me as though maybe I'd gone mad.

And maybe I had. When I went to the Ladies, there was blood in my knickers.

Chapter Forty-three

NOTHING LIKE A DEATH for comings and goings. Nothing like grief to renew acquaintance. So May came round (obviously, and thank God!) and Rod and Edna and my dad and Dora; though I learned from May that Dad had been against visiting because Bob and I weren't married and he didn't want to step into a house of sin – but Dora persuaded him otherwise. And Christine and Corporal Hawkins, who'd driven her.

And we told our story about the *accident* – to the police, to the friends who came to grieve with us, to everyone. Strange car. No, couldn't possibly identify it because it was already quite dark for June. Came over the hill and hit Bob and disappeared round the corner. Speeding, probably drunk.

Only Rod seemed not to buy it. I told you about his eyebrows meeting in the middle and I told you he'd got a nice line in arching them to show surprise. And he showed *big* surprise. Or maybe it was just his copper's way: accept nothing, query everything. Bob had been a bit like that.

And it turned out Walter Broome had been right about the General Election in July! And I turned out to canvass with May, though it wasn't going to make much difference in our neck of the woods. People round our way who said they didn't vote Labour were as rare as penguins in Venezuela – and they'd already had their windows smashed, so we didn't bother doorstepping them.

Some people who knew about Bob would say how terrible it must be for me and how brave I was to turn out for the Party when I was going through such a terrible time. But truth was – it was *good* for me. It kept me from falling into the temptation of going home at night and getting filthy drunk with Ester, and falling into bed in the early hours for a long sob.

And it gave me chance to sneak my document case out of the back bedroom in May's house and bring the Ballester-Molina round to mine. All my feelings now coincided with

Ester's. We needed to be alert. We needed to protect ourselves. We needed whatever weapons we could get hold of.

I say *round to mine* but it wasn't mine. It was a police house. And the senior officer who came round to offer his condolences and pledge that the drunken driver would be found and prosecuted to the limit of the law also made a point of saying it was a great pity that Bob and I had not completed the nuptial ceremony before his untimely death because it meant I had no right of tenure and would I please start making arrangements to find a new domicile? And I said: How long? And he said by the beginning of the New Year. And he smiled as if he was being extremely generous. And I said OK. What else could I say? It gave me a deadline to get my revenge on Gerry Tordoff. And it gave me enough time to think how to do it.

*

Funerals are never the best of days, whatever the season. But Bob's funeral was more terrible than most because we had all that sunshine and light nights of summer and it seemed the world was suddenly so full of life.

We held it at All Saints' church just outside Darnall. It was Anglican, the religion that Bob's dead parents had followed. Like I said, Father, Bob was an atheist – so please forgive him for that. But C of E was down on his birth certificate and work record and I didn't see any point in trying to correct it. Anyway, the elderly priest was very kind and polite and I was pleased by the ceremony, which featured a eulogy from Bob's uncle Everett who'd come up from Nottingham where most of the family still lived. Bob's family knew we'd been set to be married and they treated me well and made me the centre of things.

The pall bearers were all CID, friends of Bob. And there was a squad of uniformed police who saluted the lowering of the coffin. Then the same Deputy Chief Inspector who'd told me I would have to leave my house by January shook my hand and kissed me on the cheek.

My dad came with Dora, May with Walter, Rod with Edna. Even Christine brought along Corporal Hawkins, who'd apparently volunteered to drive her. Why do I remember it like that? Because most people go to funerals in couples, some as whole families. That day only Ester and I were on our own.

Best thing was, Bob's family made a point of talking to *my* family, getting to know them a bit. As if they were ever going to meet again! As if there was any reason why they should! But to me it was like they were imagining how things might have been, how they would have liked each other if they'd had the chance. Does that sound funny, Father? Yes, I suppose it does. But it touched me a little. Uncle Everett, a tall, well-built man with thick black hair, and his small blonde wife Irma invited me to come down to Nottingham sometime if I felt like it. They knew I wouldn't, but we talked about the trains and how there were more of them now the war was coming to a close.

We had ham and cheese sandwiches and sponge cake at the Crooked Billet, which was the nearest pub to St Thomas's. At one point, Rod and Edna came up to me and, after they'd repeated all the nice things they'd said about Bob when they first came round to the house, Rod said: "I'd like to have a chat about what happened, about the hit-and-run."

And Edna said: "She'll not be up to it, Rod. You've got to leave it a bit."

"It's just that I want to catch the bastard that did it. I want to catch him fast."

And I said: "I'll be glad to talk about Bob, about the accident, about whatever you want, at the station or at the house. You choose."

And Rod said: "I'll give you a ring."

*

Then Christine came up to me. She was wearing quite a smart costume – in black, of course, jacket and skirt, but that only made it more elegant, a far cry from the masculine uniform we normally wore at work. She held my hand and said the usual condolences, though I'm sure they were sincere. Then she said: "Well, what do you think of Edward?"

I said: "Who?"

She looked a trifle embarrassed. She pointed across the room and said: "Corporal Hawkins. We're going out together."

He saw me looking and waved from across the room.

Christine said: "In fact, we're engaged. I wasn't sure whether to tell you today because, well, it seems..." she hesitated, "it seems a bit unfeeling, what with all the horrible stuff you're going through right now."

Christine and Corporal Hawkins! Edward! Of course, it was obvious! I'd just not put two and two together, but why should I? Why should I have been interested when I had Bob to fill my thoughts? But there were other reasons why I'd been slow. Christine had been a nun when she taught me English Literature. Then she'd made a pass at me when we went to the pictures. Now...

I said: "Congratulations."

She said: "Thank you. But I shouldn't have..."

"No," I said, "no. Don't worry about it. I'm glad you're happy. We all have to be happy in this world as much as we can. One day *I'll* be happy again. I promise." And I wasn't just promising Christine, I was promising myself.

"Yes," she said, "you will." And she let go of my hand and walked back to Edward who looked like the cat with the cream. No. Like the cat with the cream and an open can of sardines for good measure.

*

Ester drove us home. She poured the Courvoisier and we sat down and switched on the wireless.

I gulped my drink. I said: "I'm being turfed out of here by the police in six months' time and I think May's set to flit to

Walter Broome's, so the coal bosses will want her house back for some poor sod of a miner."

"And I'm going away," she said.

I didn't say anything.

She said: "I have this friend. One of my clients, actually. But he's a nice chap. He's the one that gave me the Alfa. I told him I was in big trouble. Now he says I can come and stay with him. I'm not saying where it is. But it's far enough away that Gerry won't find me."

"Is that going to be forever, then?"

"No. Nothing is forever. It's going to be for however long it takes me to get my nerve back. I'll phone you when I'm ready to kill Gerry. So you be working on your plan, OK? You get the details sorted. And I'll drive."

"As usual."

"Of course as usual."

Then we went quiet and listened to the wireless. Alvar Lydell or one of those other plummy BBC announcers was saying something about the election, which I didn't quite catch. But I did say: "God! That Walter! He's not only Lover Boy of the Year – if you don't count Edward – but he's a bloody psychic as well."

"Who the hell is Edward?" she said.

Chapter Forty-four

ROD PHONED ME AT THE START OF JULY. I was still off work, and I invited him round the first evening he could make it. Ester had left by now. Left with that promise to come back when she was needed.

Rod arrived straight from work, wearing a smart brown suit and striped tie. He'd even combed his hair. I was all set to make him a cuppa but he asked didn't I have anything stronger? So I poured him a brandy and he settled down in an armchair and took out his notebook. I sat down opposite and waited.

"Josie," he said, putting on his deliberate take-it-slow policeman's voice, "I have to say right away I don't buy your story about Bob's death being a hit-and-run."

I said nothing.

"You know why I don't buy it? I don't buy it because I've been making connections. Because I've been checking up on you. You used to be engaged to a man called Dennis Morgan…"

"He was Denny Morrow when I knew him."

"Right." Rod wrote something down. "Your Mr Morrow had a criminal record. You lived with him in a house owned by a man called Alonzo McIntyre."

"That's right."

"Mr McIntyre also had a criminal record." He sighed. "Then Mr Morrow ended up dead."

I winced. I said: "Bob *told* me you were a good copper."

Rod grinned. "I'm glad you appreciate that. I'm glad you realise I'm not here to cause you trouble." He took a sip of the brandy. "I'm just here to get at the truth. For Bob's sake. For all our sakes. Now, does the name Gerry Tordoff mean anything to you?"

I made up my mind to it. "Yes," I said. I even nodded to emphasise I was being straight with Rod. I said: "I met Gerry Tordoff when he worked for Lonzo Mack."

"Right." Having got the initial result, Rod seemed to

relax. He took another sip of brandy. "Now, this man Tordoff was a pimp."

"I know."

"Yes, I thought you would. One of his women was called Ester Petheridge, though she had other *professional* names."

"Yes," I said. "Though I've no idea about any other names."

"Miss Petheridge lived in a house in Leeds owned by Mr Tordoff." He paused. "And so did you."

"Yes." I was about to explain that I knew all about Ester's life but I was never part of it. But I didn't get the chance. Rod said: "It doesn't bother me that you were on the game, Josie. Bob never worried about it, so why should I?" And he reached over and put his hand on my knee.

I nearly jumped out of my skin. But Rod didn't seem to notice anything. His hand stayed where it was. His fingers started to probe and rub against my skin. He said: "I also believe that Ester Petheridge is the woman you've got staying with you at the moment. Is she in the house right now?"

"No, no," I said, then thought it was safest to tell a small lie. "She's gone to the pictures. *Mildred Pierce* with Joan Crawford. She'll be back soon."

"Very good," he said. "I rather like Joan Crawford."

"Yes, men *tend* to like Joan Crawford."

"Well, I'm certainly a man, Josie, and I like you. I always have done since Bob showed you off to us. I'd always thought he was a lucky sod."

And I was thinking: This is good. I can make something of this. But what I said was: "What about Edna?"

"Edna's alright," he conceded, "but there's no reason why she should know about us. Let's understand that from the start."

"Yes. You're right, Rod. No reason at all." And then I said: "You're right to be suspicious about Bob's death. You and I both want to see the people who did it hang, don't we?"

"Of course."

"That's something we've got in common, right?

221

Something that brings us together?"

"Yes," he said and he moved his hand between my legs.

"I can't do anything for you tonight, Rod." I gave an embarrassed laugh. "Time of the month."

He took his hand away. Slowly. His face twisted into a schoolboyish look of regret.

"But," I said quickly, "we can get together next week maybe? It won't be *Mildred Pierce* after this weekend, will it? It'll be John Wayne or something. And Ester's a great film fan."

He smiled again, settled back in his chair and picked up his notebook and pen. "So," he said, "this has taken us a long way from Bob. Who killed him, Josie? And why?"

I stood up, got a second glass and filled it with brandy. "You mentioned Gerry Tordoff."

Rod said nothing.

"Well, I think Gerry Tordoff is involved in Bob's death. I think he's taken over Lonzo Mack's little business and he wanted rid of Bob because he knew Ester was talking to Bob. He was afraid of Ester spilling the beans." This was the best I could do, standing on my feet with half a glass of Courvoisier still in my hand. "Even though," I added, "Ester doesn't really know anything. And neither do I." This last bit rather deflated my great revelation. But I thought it would do for the moment.

"It's not Gerry Tordoff, Josie."

"Yes, it is. Him and Nick, his houseboy."

Rod looked puzzled. "Gerry Tordoff's got a lot of form with us. We've had a file on him since Sherlock Holmes was on the beat. And it's not him." He stood up. "Some time ago, we turned up a body. Elmwood, near the quarry. There's nothing in the papers because we wanted to keep it to ourselves for a while. It's a gang killing. A man. Stripped naked. And the hands and head cut off.

"Well, we've got a very good dog called Jimcrack. And he sniffed all over the woods and he sniffed down the quarry wall as far as the leash would let him. And he turned up the hands. Somebody had thrown them into the quarry, but they'd got caught on some little bush or other. I don't suppose we'll ever get the head because they'll have burned it.

"I can't reel off the actual date we found it, but I've got it fixed in my mind it was the day after Mussolini got killed and the day before Hitler died. Three big deaths in three days, you might say. We checked the prints against our records and there's no doubt the body was Gerry Tordoff."

I don't know what happened next. I didn't faint exactly but I sat down hard in the armchair and spilt my drink. Rod looked ill at ease for maybe the first time. He said: "Perhaps I'd best go now," and I told him: Yes, he should.

*

Next morning I got the bank books out of the wardrobe and I telephoned the bank in Barnsley and I asked to check the amount still in the account – I said I wanted to withdraw the whole lot. And the bank clerk took his time coming back. Then he passed me over to the manager. And the manager informed me that the account had been closed some months ago. He referred to the cheque book and that was the first time I'd even thought about it.

"Oh yes," I said, "I must have forgotten. How silly of me." And I hung up.

And then I telephoned the bank in Buxton and Barclays in Huddersfield, and the Westminster in York and the National Provincial in Manchester. And it was the same. I mean, *of course* it was the same. And £25,000 of my money – or Bill Netty's, or Lonzo Mack's or whomsoever – had gone.

*

And everybody knows what happened next. Mr Attlee became Prime Minister. The poll was started on the fifth of July but went on some time after that so the votes of the soldiers abroad could be counted. And parts of Lancashire didn't do it till the nineteenth of July on account of their

223

Wakes Weeks holding it back. So we didn't know what was happening until July twenty-sixth. It was a landslide for Labour. I read it in black and white in *The Star*: our Party had gained 145 seats.

People are always saying it was a shock to the Conservatives, given that Mr Churchill was so well spoken of all over, but it was a bloody bigger shock to me. And I think to May as well, though she pretended it wasn't. "Nobody wants to go back to the unemployment of the 1930s," she said knowingly as we got through a bottle of gin in her front room, "and it was unemployment that led to the rise of Hitler, don't forget. People blame capitalism for all of that. And rightly so."

But I thought she was maybe trying to convince *herself*. That's the thing with politicians: whatever happens, they don't like people to think they didn't expect it. And May, despite her tough style and don't-give-a-damn ideas, was always a politician at heart. Still, I didn't mind. She deserved her bit of happiness. Losing mine hadn't made me bitter about other people's.

"It'll be really different now," May went on. "We'll have Socialist planning so we don't let the economy go to ruin."

"Not ever?" I asked.

"Not ever!" she said. "We'll have nationalisation of industry, economic planning, full employment, a National Health Service, and social security."

I didn't ask my usual question about why you needed social security when everybody had a good job. Truth is, I was happy too. But I could see the paradox. I said: "It'll be like Heaven on Earth. But isn't that bad for the Church? I mean, why would people need religion after a change like that?"

"Now hold on. I know you're just trying to needle me, but you won't succeed. No. Because the answer is: they know they'll be dead someday soon." And then her face dropped. "Oh God, Josie, I'm sorry I said that. I'd forgotten. About Bob. For just one moment, I'd forgotten."

I said: "That's OK." And I meant it. It wasn't that *I'd* ever forget Bob, not for a moment. But the election had been great for me. It got me doing things: doorstepping, filling envelopes, riding shotgun in the campaign van and shouting out all the political spiel over the loudspeaker. And I was damned if I was going to live my life devoid of pleasures. Like teasing May. Or killing the people who killed Bob.

Now the election was over, I'd got no excuse to put off the thing that was most important to me.

But before I got round to it, there were Hiroshima and Nagasaki. There was that photo in all the papers that everybody said looked like a giant mushroom, though I thought it was more like an oversized cauliflower. *The Star* said more than 200,000 people were dead. And people threw up their hands and asked: *What is the human race coming to?* Except for Our Boys in Burma and their families. They just asked: *When will Our Boys be home?* And they had the right idea.

Chapter Forty-five

WHY DID I GO? I've no idea. I knew it would end in tears, as my mum used to say when I was throwing a tantrum or falling out with my friends. But I went all the same.

St Cuthbert's was a strange little church, a mix of red brick with plastic chairs – and old ideas about the order and arrangement of the Universe. But it was far enough away from where I lived to make it seem safe. No priest who might recognise my voice, though they'd need to have good memories to do even that.

The confession box was traditional, wooden, narrow, dark, smelly and uncomfortable to remind us sinners of the depths we'd already sunk to. So it suited me fine. I looked at the grille as soon as I got in. That was automatic. Even though you couldn't see anything except a vague shadow of confirmation that some human being would listen after all.

I remembered the drill. Of course I did. I knelt down. I said: "Bless me, Father, for I have sinned."

The priest on the Other Side said: "Tell me, my child, how you have sinned." And yes, I felt a strange sense of comfort. Though he had a funny accent which I couldn't place at all. Not Irish, which was a surprise.

"Firstly, Father, I have missed Mass." I tried to speak slowly and firmly. I suppose I was trying in my silly way to be a source of pride to the nuns for turning out a well-spoken pupil.

He said: "Ah, that's something new to me, then, because if you didn't come along, I'd never know about it, would I?"

I didn't know what to say to that. In the end I said: "This isn't *actually* my parish church." Then: "But I don't go along to the church that *is* my parish church, if you see what I mean."

He said: "Yes, I do." And: "How many times have you missed Mass?"

I said: "Approximately? Will approximately do?"

He said: "Approximately will *have* to do."

"I've not been now for five years. Five times 52 is…"

226

Then I thought: I don't want to be a show-off. I don't want to sound glib. In the end I said: "I've never been good at mental arithmetic."

"Two hundred and sixty," he said.

"Two hundred and sixty," I repeated, as though it was a revelation. I began to wonder how I should order my sins. I settled for small ones first. "And I have been guilty of Avarice."

The priest didn't say anything. OK. I better show willing. "And of Anger and of Pride. And…" I was embarrassed now. "also of Fornication."

Still nothing from the Other Side. So. Another deep breath. "And I've stolen money. But from people who deserved to lose it. *I* think so, anyway."

Then I thought: What the hell! And I gave him the Big Prize. "Also I have been responsible for someone's death. May the Father in the Sky forgive me." And then I thought: What a silly thing to say! I'm turning into Aunt May.

The priest didn't get as excited as I expected. He said: "God expects we obey His Commandments."

I thought: Yes, I know that. That's why I'm here.

There was a bit of a silence. My knees were getting sore and I eased my weight from left to right and back again.

Then he said: "Are you *sorry* for your sins?"

And that was the moment. Yes, I was sorry. Sorry my life hadn't worked out. Sorry I'd done things that were dishonest, cruel and cowardly. But not half as sorry –not a *millionth* as sorry – as I was that Bob was dead, killed by some thug of a driver who couldn't even hit the right target. Sorry I lost my baby because of it. Because those things were so much more cruel and wicked and damnable than anything I had done. And I would visit a just punishment on the people responsible.

"Sorry?" I shouted. I jumped up and burst into tears. "No, I'm not sorry. I'm the first murderer in our family, but I'm not sorry." I wiped my eyes and blew my nose. "I killed a man called Alonzo McIntyre and he deserved it. And I'm going to have to kill again."

There was a sound from behind the grille. It might have been a chair tipping over. Oh God! What had I done? "No, no," I said, "I don't mean *you*, Father. You have nothing to fear." And I put away my handkerchief and turned and opened the door and walked out into the church, into the light and airiness. And when I got out on the street, I went for a cup of tea and a Bath bun. To clear my head.

*

And then I went to the Cathedral. There! The second time I'd been to a Protestant church in three months. But I didn't go in. I knew they'd taken a hit during the Blitz and I didn't want to see any damage. Not today. All I did was stand outside. And I saw it all.

I saw Bob with the barber's towel round his neck. I saw – what had he called it? – *the suspicious package*. Oh, very formal, Bob, my love. Very policemanish. A brown paper parcel. Who'd think a brown paper parcel could rip a man to shreds? Wasn't brown paper good for you? Didn't Jack and Jill use vinegar and brown paper to heal their broken heads? And I saw the string and the black duct tape, just as Bob described. And I saw the bucket of water that Harry Dowd fetched for him. And I saw the penknife and the yellow sickly gelignite sticks which he took out one by one and put in a row along the pavement. And I remembered how he'd laughed when he'd told me about it. And how I fell in love with him.

And I remembered the night of the car with its screaming wheels and Ester's screams too, and my running out and cradling his head just like I'd cradled Mum's.

Oh yes, Father. I remembered. And I didn't want the absolution of the Father in the Box. I just wanted *You* to understand what I had to do. I dedicate to You my sacrifice, O my Father in the Sky.

Chapter Forty-six

IT WAS A BUSY DAY. First Ester phoned. So I had the chance to tell her the news about Gerry. And a few other things which I'd been working out.

Then I thought I'd better visit the ballooners. Just so they wouldn't forget who I was. And it was good. Christine was all over me and even Edward showed an interest.

I said: "I want to come back. Maybe next Monday."

"If you're sure," said Christine. She looked doubtful.

"Yes. I *am* sure. I want to stop being *bereaved*. Does that sound callous?"

"No, of course not." But the way she said it made me think: *Maybe it does.*

I said: "Can I use your phone?"

Christine took me to it and left me. I phoned Rod at the station. I said: "Let's meet at the Shakespeare."

"Why?" he asked.

"Because they do good mushy peas."

"I mean, why meet in a pub at all?"

"Because I don't want anybody in the station earwigging." And then: "Bob and I used to meet there when we started going out." And I was thinking: a wink is as good as a nod to a blind donkey. I told him when I'd be there.

I ordered the usual and I made him pay for it. I said: "I'm going to ask you a favour."

"Oh?" He looked more than interested.

"I want you to arrest somebody."

Now he looked worried, but still willing to swallow the hook if it was baited right.

"Only for a day, Rod." I thought it was a nice touch to call him by his Christian name at this point. It would show that we might be talking about arresting people, but our relationship was far more than just policeman-and-member-of-the-public. "This is what I want you to do, Rod. I want you to pick a Saturday when you're on duty. I want you to go round to a house in Dore. You know the house. It used to belong to Lonzo Mack. A long time ago."

"Not so long," he said.

"Length of time depends on how you live," I said. "And I've lived a lot since then."

"Who is this man?"

I took my time finishing the mushy peas. "His name is Nick. He's a sort of houseboy for the man who's living there now."

"Nick Levitt."

"I don't know Nick's second name."

"It'll be Nick Levitt alright. He's a general minder and petty thief. We call him *Levitt-alone* because if he'd taken that advice in the first place, he'd be a lot better off these days." He laughed.

I laughed too. It seemed the polite thing to do.

"And who else is it that's living there, Josie?"

"I don't know. I mean I don't know what name he's using right now. But that doesn't matter. I don't want *him* arrested. Got it?"

"I could find out what name he's using if you like."

"It doesn't matter to me."

"So." Rod drank the top off his tea. "What's this all about? I mean *really* all about?"

"I need Nick Levitt out of the way. Just for the morning. That's all. I want to have a talk with the man he works for."

"Talk about what?"

"Ah!" I put down my fork and wagged my finger. "You know all the right questions, Rod. Yes, when Bob said you were a good copper, he was right." He smiled the way he did when I'd first said it to him at the funeral. I sighed. "But that's between him and me. The man in the house and me. Let's say it's a bit of business I have to take care of. Before I can..." I hesitated, looked down at my plate and blinked so my eyelashes fluttered. I'd used mascara that morning, which was unusual for me. I raised my eyes to Rod's, clasped my hands under my chin and gazed dreamily into his face. "Before I can get on with the rest of my life, do the things I want to do. You understand?" And I reached out and put my hand on his.

He grinned. Then he said: "As long as I don't get into trouble."

I pulled my hand away quickly. I said: "I thought you liked to live dangerously." I could see from his expression he didn't know how to take this and I briefly wondered if I'd made a mistake. I said: "You and Bob were two of a kind, you know that? There was something about him, something exciting about the way he enjoyed life." I wondered if I was laying it on too thick, but Rod smiled again so I knew I'd got it right.

He grasped my hand. "I'm crazy about you," he said.

I said: "I know the feeling." And: "Anyway, I'm sure you can get something on this Nick person. I'm sure that's not beyond you. Show the Chief Constable you're not twiddling your thumbs on the Saturday shift."

"I'm sure I could."

"Kick out his headlights or something." Rod looked put out. He obviously thought I meant beat some sort of confession out of Nick the Grease. But You know what I meant, Father. You know Rod and Bob weren't the same at all, weren't even living in the same Universe. And You should know; You created them both.

*

I phoned Ester back. I said: "It's the same plan as before. Get the minder arrested on the day. Then go in and do the job. Last time Gerry set it up and it worked. This time *I've* set it up. And it'll work again."

"You're mad, Josie. What do you think Rod will do when he finds out we've killed somebody?"

"What can he do?"

"He can bring us in for the third degree."

"No, he can't. He can't do anything. Don't you see?" I wanted to take both her hands in mine, but instead I just held on tight to the receiver. "If he goes through with this, if he pulls Nick in, then we've got him. Got him forever. He becomes an accessory to murder. No, no, Rod will keep his mouth shut until the cows come home with bells on."

"I hope you're right," she said. Her voice was tense. But she didn't say anything about pulling out. And I thought: Yes. *I* hope I'm right too.

Chapter Forty-seven

I SAID TO ESTER: "We wait. There's a gym on the first floor. When this fella is all alone, what will he do? I bet he'll go up to the gym and have his workout. He'll put on the light and close the curtains to protect his modesty."

She said: "I hope I'm not going to be shocked, seeing a man in his underpants." Then she said: "What makes you think he'll do that? What makes you think he'll stick to the same timetable? What makes you think he won't twig what's happening and get a new bodyguard, double quick?"

I said: "Women's intuition."

She nodded. "That's alright, then."

We'd parked Ester's Austin on the main road and we could see the first floor back of the house over somebody else's fence. It was eleven o'clock on the Saturday morning and Nick the Grease had been in police custody for less than an hour. I'd had the call from Rod, from a phone box, once Nick had been lifted.

It was eleven minutes past eleven when the curtains were drawn and we could see the yellow light showing through. Nice little symbol then for our own special Remembrance Day.

We were both wearing black coats and shirts and trousers and sensible black shoes. I'd last worn those shoes at Bob's funeral. The coats had hoods. I'd not bothered with any make-up, Ester had just put on lipstick.

We put on our gloves and left the car carrying our shopping bags, walked round to the cul-de-sac, walked up to the front garden, opened the gate. The stained glass windows, with their red-and-yellow butterfly patterns, looked just as good as I'd remembered. There were autumn leaves scattered in the drive and the garage was locked. I looked through the garage window to see if the new resident had inherited Lonzo's Bentley along with his house and business, but the windows were too dirty for me to see in. The man of the house had not yet secured domestic help of the standard he'd grown used to.

I turned my key in the lock, pushed the front door open slowly, keeping a firm grip on it to avoid loud creaks or the moans of unoiled hinges.

"Have to be sure we're quiet," said Ester and winked. I gave her a hard look but kept schtum.

Nobody in the hall. Ester said: "No guard dogs, then."

"No," I said. But in a whisper, to provide a hint. I motioned her to leave her bag next to mine on the bristly mat.

I closed the door as quietly as I could and we took the guns out of the bags. We left the bags on the mat. We started to climb the stairs, me in front, both of us holding on to the bannister rail with our left hands, the guns held in our right.

We came to the landing. I tiptoed over to the door of the gym. I took a deep breath. I turned the handle. I pushed it open.

And there it was: the weights, the dumbbells, the barbells, the training bench and the mats. And the Charles Atlas advertisements still up on the walls: the skinny men getting their comeuppance on the beach but finding salvation in a new way of life. Almost religious then. And there *he* was. The broad shoulders, flat stomach and Stewart Granger cheekbones that had got a nice Catholic girl swooning all that time ago. The champ turned into a chump because he didn't think I'd ever come after him. And he smiled and his teeth were as good as ever. But his moustache was less Errol Flynn now, more thick and sprawly, more Clark Gable. That was the only difference to the Denny I'd known and loved. For a moment, it was as though nothing had happened to spoil that dream we'd had – today Manchester, tomorrow New York, next week the world.

Not unlike the dream of Mr Hitler then. Smaller, yes. With a different timetable and list of priorities. But just as evil, when you thought about it.

Ester followed me into the room and moved across to my left. Denny was sitting in a black wood-and-steel rowing machine, seat and oars and springs and joints. He had stopped rowing. Now he smiled.

I pushed back my hood. I said: "I like your tracksuit." It was navy blue with the initials DM woven in red over his heart. I said: "You've disappointed my friend. She was hoping to see a little more of you."

He said: "It's too cold in September for just the underpants." He let go of the oars, got up slowly, stretched his arms and legs, all the time smiling. He said: "This must be Ester." He stepped forward. I raised the gun and pointed it at his chest.

He said: "Nice to meet you, Ester" Then to me: "You've remembered what I told you. Always shoot them in the chest then..."

"Then in the head to make sure they're dead. Easy to remember because it rhymes."

"That's right." He sighed. "How *are* you, Josie?"

"Tell me it's been a long time, Denny."

"It's been a long time."

I thought: He's not surprised. It's as though he's been waiting for me. I remembered how I'd said to him so long ago: "You like to live dangerously." And he'd told me I did too. And I thought: Is that all it was for both of us? I said: "Lonzo Mack dead. Now Gerry Tordoff."

"I'm sorry about Gerry. I hoped I wouldn't have to do it. That's the trouble with this game. Somebody's got to be on top. And when you're on top, you've got to feel safe. But you can never feel safe. Not with people like Gerry, who know too much and are thinking of early retirement. And we've had this conversation before."

"About you and Lonzo."

"That's right. I wish I *could* stop it. Honest, Josie. But it's like the war, isn't it? You start with a few incendiaries and you hope it'll all be over by Christmas. But you end up with the atom bomb."

There was a silence then. Except for the breathing. I suddenly noticed that Denny was breathing quite heavily. Maybe it was down to his boating exertions. Maybe it was a little bit of fear creeping in.

He said: "So what do you intend to do, Josie?"

"I intend to kill you."

"For what? Gerry wasn't that close to you. Why are you so bothered? Is it the money?"

For a moment I couldn't work out what he meant. Then it dawned. "No, no. It's not about being cheated out of thirty thousand pounds, if that's what you mean. I wouldn't want you thinking that."

"*Twenty-five* thousand pounds." He waved a finger to underline the correction. "I let you have *five* thousand, didn't I? And I'd have given you more, but..." He rubbed his hands along the hem of his tracksuit trousers. "But I needed all that, Josie. Really I did. If I was going to win. If I was going to survive. It was me or Lonzo."

"Who was it whose body ended up in that car fire?"

"I don't know. Really. It was somebody in one of the gangs who got shot for some reason that's nothing to do with me. Honest. It was just that the body became available at the right time." Then: "Are you really going to shoot me, Josie?" And he stepped forward again. And I raised the gun again. And he smiled again. He said: "You don't want your friend to get involved in this, do you? Not in a murder. Not if she's really your friend." And he turned and walked across to her. "So hello, Ester. Look, I'm really sorry about Gerry, but you understand better than Josie what it's all about. You know Gerry would've done the same if he had to."

Ester raised the gun then lowered it again. I said: "It's not the money and it's not even Gerry. It's Bob Peters."

Denny turned to look at me again. I could see he couldn't place the name right away. But I was sure it would dawn. Then: "The copper," he said. "But it was an accident. He wasn't meant to..."

"Get killed? No, it was Ester who was meant for that."

"No, no. That was Nick. Always jumping the gun." He turned back to Ester. "I never meant you any harm, just wanted to make sure you were solid, OK? That you wouldn't go running to the law if you found out about Gerry. Now I know I can trust you..." He stepped nearer to her. "Nick's been arrested, did you know that? But I think the police are pushing their luck. The main thing is that we three can agree about things. Josie…" He spoke my name but his eyes were all the time on Ester. "Josie, you can have the twenty-five thousand, no problem. Ester, you can keep the flat; I'll give you another piece of paper."

And he laughed and reached across. And his finger touched the barrel of the gun and Ester was staring into his eyes like the proverbial rabbit.

And I said: "Denny." And I said it softly, but it made him turn round.

Kearrrrrrrraaaaaaaaaaaaaaaackkkk!!!!!!

I shot him in the chest. As he knew I would. And he stumbled back, but the rowing machine broke his fall. And he staggered forward a pace.

Kearrrrrrrraaaaaaaaaaaaaaaackkkk!!!!!! And I shot him in the head and his head exploded like a balloon spewing blood like red ink. And the rest of him fell – smack! – on the wooden floor and bounced a little before it settled.

And I walked across to the body and I shot him again, though I knew I didn't need to.

Kearrrrrrrraaaaaaaaaaaaaaaackkkk!!!!!!

And Ester screamed. I walked across and slapped her with my left hand. "David!" she shouted. "Oh my lovely David!" And she fell into sobbing. I was going to slap her a second time but I realised I'd made a mistake: the noise might bring out the neighbours. I should have used the silencer.

It was then I realised Ester was covered in Denny's blood. I took her gun away from her and guided her through the door and down the stairs. In the hall I dropped the guns into the bags. I picked the bags up. I said: "Turn your coat inside out."

She said: "What?" then realised about the blood. She did what I said.

I said: "You're OK, aren't you? You can drive, can't you?"

"Yes," she said.

"You're all done with the David bit?"

"Yes," she said. "Clever of you to think about the coat."

"When you're in barrage balloons," I said, "you learn about camouflage."

Stave VI: Wedding Bells

There'll be bluebirds over the white cliffs of Dover, tomorrow, just you wait and see. There'll be love and laughter and peace ever after tomorrow, when the world is free.

......Nat Burton, as sung by Vera Lynn (1942)

I want to ride to the ridge where the west commences and gaze at the moon till I lose my senses. I can't look at hovels and I can't stand fences. Don't fence me in.

......Cole Porter, Nat Fletcher, as sung by Bing Crosby (1945)

Chapter Forty-eight

SISTER MARGARET MARY, now known as Christine Daphne Eloise Cassidy, had her wedding at St Elfreda's two weeks before Christmas. It was a big church with bright stained windows and uncomfortable pews, but people tended to use their footstools as cushions so it was not really bad. There was a sung Mass, which added 45 minutes to the ceremony, but Josie Cawthorne didn't mind. She was pleased to say she thought Christine looked lovely in a long ivory damask dress with pleated skirt, a "V" neckline front and back, and a grey bird-and-floral design. It must have taken a lot of coupons, but at least it wasn't another parachute job.

Josie overheard somebody at the reception ask somebody else why Christine had chosen ivory. Josie herself had wondered whether the less-than-white decision revealed something about the current degree of intimacy between Christine and Corporal Edward Derek Thomas Hawkins. But she'd never know.

Ester came along too and they sat together at the third table in the function room at the British Oak, which was a pub well known for its receptions. They had beef for the main course and strawberry ice cream for afters. The relatives must have chipped in with their coupons as well as their cash. Close family took up all of the first table, most of the barrage ballooners the second, former pupils the third (though Josie didn't actually recognise the other three girls sitting with them). And May and Walter were relegated to table four, which was "people I hardly know but can't avoid inviting", as Ester put it. All this despite the fact that Walter was now *Councillor* Broome, having won a seat in the Sheffield elections in November when Labour got 59 seats against 39 for the Citizens Association, or whatever those sneaky Tories were calling themselves this year.

By now Josie had forgiven Ester for her failure to dispatch Denny, even though it had nearly caused the whole operation to abort, as they say in military circles. In fact,

Josie was properly prepared to forget the whole matter. But Ester wasn't.

*

On the car journey home from Denny's house, Ester had driven with her customary intelligence and care. But when they got back, she rushed up to the lav and was noisily sick. "Don't worry," she said, "I'll clean it all up." And she did. And then they put her coat in the bath and poured soap powder all over it to get the blood and vomit off. It was an expensive coat and Ester didn't want to have to replace it if it could be helped. But when she came down, she became sulky and aggressive in a way Josie hadn't known before.

"I can't understand how you could do it," Ester said.

"What do you mean, you *can't understand*?"

"I can't understand how you could just shoot him like that. You didn't give him a chance."

"What sort of chance did you want me to give him? The chance to let him take the gun away from *you*? The chance to let him shoot us both? Which was what you were about to let him do!" What really annoyed Josie was that she and Ester seemed to have changed positions. It was usually *Josie* complaining to Ester about *her* cynical ways. Now it seemed that... well, yes, Josie was prepared to use the word! Now it seemed the former (and possibly future) prostitute had experienced some sort of *epiphany*.

Ester had spent the night at Josie's house, the house that wouldn't be hers anymore after the first of January. "Well," Ester said, "everybody needs a change now and again. I'm giving up the flat. There's no virtue in basement flats when there's no bombing anymore. And if we have a war with Stalin, it won't be any good against atom bombs."

"Where are you going to live?"

"I don't know. Maybe a semi somewhere, not far from the countryside."

"You know nothing about the countryside."

"I can learn."

"And how do you plan to make a living? Most of those farmers would rather sleep with their cows."

"I thought I might take a course in shorthand typing."

Josie nearly laughed but stopped herself. Ester was serious. And Josie's notion of Ester – dangerously weird and probably beyond redemption – collapsed in ruins.

Whereas Josie's notion of herself – wild but essentially virtuous – had also suffered a setback.

*

The sweet was cleared away and the tables moved against the walls and the dancing began to Zoot Henshaw and His Louisiana Loafers, who came from the next village. Christine and Edward came out and danced to "Bewitched, Bothered and Bewildered":

I'm wild again,
Beguiled again,
A simpering, whimpering child again...

And then Edward kissed Christine, long and lingering. And all the other couples trooped out to join them, and Josie thought: How is this the same woman who took the veil, then joined the WAAF, then made a pass at me over a cup of tea, and now... ?

Josie was very much in favour of men but pretty unimpressed by Edward.

*

Before they had finished the Courvoisier, Josie had taken Ester's shopping bag with the second Ballester-Molina. And next morning they had driven to Elmwood Quarry.

"Right," said Josie, "we're getting rid of the evidence."

They stood on the edge of the quarry and looked down on the columns of dirty white rock, half-hidden by the dirty green water. Josie said: "It's not well sign-posted. But people round here know where it is and they know not to fall in. And they don't care about foreigners like us. An old friend told me all about it. When he was a kid, he used to swim in

242

quarries."

She took Ester's shopping bag and swung it high in the air and it dropped like the proverbial. Then she did the same with her own shopping bag,

"Gone forever," she said. "Nothing to tie us in with Denny Morrow's murder. Nothing to worry about now while you're doing your shorthand."

Oh, she thought, I'm such a little liar! Her own gun was still in the wardrobe in the bedroom. Her shopping bag had been filled with copies of *The Ragged Trousered Philanthropists*, *The Sun is My Undoing* and *Howards End*.

*

... Bewitched, bothered and bewildered am I.

May and Walter came over to them and May said: "I've got some news for you. Walter and I are set to be wed. He's been alone since his Alice died and we've decided to form our own union – affiliated to the Labour Party, of course." And she said to Josie: "I'm sorry to leave you in the lurch."

"That's OK," said Josie. What she meant was: *Don't worry, May. I'll always love you.*

Chapter Forty-nine

SO CHRISTINE AND EDWARD were married and Josie was happy for them. But when she got home, she had a big think about the future.

On the dark side, no home for much longer. She couldn't go back to Ester because Ester was now set on moving to the countryside and learning shorthand. She couldn't go back to May because the Coal Barons would take May's house away as soon as she moved in with Walter, and they'd put another poor sod of a miner in it. Just as the police wanted Josie's house back now that Bob was dead. And no job. No war, no barrage balloons – though she had been told she would get a small pension for her six years of service. That would be nice.

And no Bob, no baby. And she was twenty-three. She was *so old*! What was she going to do?

On the bright side, she'd been right about Rod. It had taken them three days to find Denny's body because Rod had found a minor charge to stick on Nick the Grease and it wasn't until Nick got released on bail and headed back to Dore on the Tuesday that the murder was discovered. And, as *The Star* pointed out, the deceased had underworld connections. Which meant in reality the police had many better things to do than look for his killer. There were, after all, still lots of black marketeers and deserters roaming around.

The only downside had been the phone call.

"I don't know what you think you're doing!" shouted Edna. And Josie was nonplussed.

Edna went on: "I don't know what games you think you're playing with my husband!" And Josie continued her silence.

And then: "Josie, you should be ashamed of yourself! You may think you're entitled to play your little games now that Bob's gone. Oh, Rod's been telling me all about it, don't you worry! Playing for sympathy, trying it on. Well, you've tried it on with the wrong man. And the wrong woman too. Rod doesn't want to see you again. He doesn't want you anywhere near him. And if you do try to see him, I'll come round and knock your teeth in."

And Josie laughed. She couldn't help herself. And Edna hung up. But that was on the bright side too, because now Josie had an excuse for never seeing either of them again.

Finally, if you could visualise even more bright sides than two, Mr Attlee was bringing in a new and wonderful world where everybody would manage to have everything they wanted and it would still be possible to have everything doled out equally to do away with injustice and see to it that everybody had a fair share. Or something like that. And she had campaigned for him, so that was one good thing she'd done with her life. Though she wasn't sure Mr Attlee's arithmetic added up.

What was it May had trumpeted on about? Nationalisation, full employment, and social security.

And what was it Josie had said? *It'll be like Heaven on Earth.* But wasn't that a heresy? Of course it was. And wasn't it always going to be a sham, a fix, somebody going on about how really good it was while it all fell apart into tyranny? She remembered before the war – people talking about Hitler and Mussolini and Stalin, how they really weren't so bad, how they had to do what they did to bring about a different world. And, God knows, it *was* different alright!

Funny about Stalin, how he'd ended up on the side of the Goodies, of Mr Churchill and President Roosevelt. And now he'd grabbed most of the countries that Hitler had grabbed and we might end up going to war with him too.

Josie had been lolling on the sofa thinking her sad thoughts for maybe half an hour when she decided to get up and walk round the room. Anything for a change! Then she went upstairs and did the one thing she knew would bring reassurance – she took out the Ballester-Molina. She'd started with one and inherited a second; now she was back to one again. But one was enough if you knew how to use it.

And now she did.

Ester these days was all done with shooting people and maybe all done with fucking them for money, but that was less certain. Josie stroked the handle of the gun. And she thought: Is this me? Is this the sum total? And then she thought: Nick the Grease is still alive.

And then the brown paper bag full of papers fell out of the wardrobe and spilled on the floor. And she saw Aaron Bassett's birth certificates and marriage certificates and the driving licences for a woman who hadn't even learned how to drive. She looked at the names: Margaret Matheson, Genevieve Brady, Clementine Weston, Joan Semple and Theresa Patchett. She wondered what sort of lives they could possibly make for themselves.

And she sat on the bed and thought:

Margaret might go to University as a mature student and get a degree in English Literature. (Wasn't Mr Attlee planning to give grants to ex-service people? Would that include women?)

Genevieve would marry a successful businessman – probably a man who owned a building firm, since half the homes in the country had to be rebuilt. (Though wasn't Mr Attlee going to nationalise the building trade to supply homes fit for heroes? She wasn't too sure.)

Clementine was more problematic. She might end up in the civil service or local government, making other people type things and file things and pinching the bums of the young male clerical assistants. After all, she had office experience.

What about Joan? People said she was good-looking as well as clever. She might become a model, pose for fashion pages in magazines. (Though she'd naturally refuse to do anything revealing, like underwear advertisements. People would say it was her strict Catholic upbringing.) She might even go to New York, a possibility she had once discussed with her boyfriend of the moment.

What about Theresa Patchett? With a name like that, she'd be best off getting married to the first man who rubbed her tits, just to get it changed.

And then there was Gloria Mundy. What a silly flibbertigibbet she turned out to be! With her blonde hair and her cupid bow mouth! Josie had already dismissed her as a tragic little nobody with ideas above her station who had died young because she hadn't got the sense to be normal like everybody else. But...

Josie fingered a strand of hair. The blonde was growing out. If she wanted to keep it, she'd have to get some more Light Top from the chemist. Well, she'd think about it.

There was one thing all these women had in common, one thing they would all have to do if they wanted to get on in life.

They'd have to learn to drive. Otherwise, they'd always have to rely on friends when they went out to kill people.

And friends can let you down. As experience had shown.

Also by Michael Yates

"Michael is a gifted writer with a wry take on life."
– **Emma Clayton,** *Bradford Telegraph & Argus*

20 Stories High
A dead author dictates his novel to a friend. A boy comes home early to discover his father's infidelity. A murderer's dad counts his blessings. And a drug addict is visited by his ghostly parents. Twenty quirky tales.
ISBN 978-0-9934811-8-5

The Gangers
In the violent 19th century world of navvies, railways and poverty, the embittered Sergeant Joseph rides his white horse into a Yorkshire town to avenge the murder of his army friend. **ISBN 978-0-9561513-9-1**

Homer's ODC
Raymond wants to go to Uni, but his dad wants him in the family business – and his dad is a gangster. Barry wants to be a poet but he is – in his own words – a user of the mental health services. A single bullet will soon change both their lives. **ISBN 978-0-9561513-7-7**

Branwell & Other Stories
The Bronte boy slips down the road of drink, drugs and despair. Disgraced architect John Poulson dreams of salvation in his prison cell. Plus four other spellbinding tales.
ISBN 978-0-9561513-4-6

Lightning Source UK Ltd.
Milton Keynes UK
UKHW011206010522
402319UK00001B/118

9 781916 016545